MUSICAL GAMES

EVIE ALEXANDER

EMLIN
PRESS

ISBN (eBook) 978-1-914473-06-7

ISBN (Print) 978-1-914473-07-4

ISBN (audio) 978-1-914473-54-8

A CIP catalogue record for this book is available from the British Library.

www.emlinpress.com

To
Erica Connors
&
Sarah Lin Turner

ALSO BY EVIE ALEXANDER

THE KINLOCH SERIES

Highland Games

Hollywood Games

Kissing Games

Musical Games

Wedding Games

Christmas Games

THE FOXBROOKE SERIES

One Night in Foxbrooke

Love ad Lib

An Unholy Affair

The Upper Crush

The Love Position

Christmas off Script

One Night Only

Righting Mr Wrong

Under the Influencer

Foxbrooke Extras

By Evie Alexander and Kelly Kay

EVIE & KELLY'S HOLIDAY DISASTERS SERIES

Cupid Calamity

Cookout Carnage

Christmas Chaos

**Get Evie's books in all formats as well as special offers, early
releases, and exclusive deals direct from her website:**

www.eviealexanderbooks.com

EMLIN
PRESS

'**O**i!' Sam stopped dead, her heart pounding. The shout was aimed at her.

'You slag!'

Striding towards her, heels click-clacking and fury crackling, was Lorraine.

Sam's feet stayed glued to the pavement. She clutched her handbag to her chest as if for protection. *She knew*.

Lorraine was a storm of anger and pain. 'You could've had anyone,' she screamed. 'But you had to steal my Wayne! How could you?'

Sam swallowed her panic. She tossed her hair and cocked her hip. 'Well, who would blame him when you won't give him what he needs?'

There was a beat, then Lorraine launched herself forward like a heat-seeking missile carrying a payload of rabid cats.

'You cow!' she screeched, her manicured nails locking onto Sam's face.

Sam dropped her bag and caught Lorraine's wrists just before impact. The women tumbled to the ground.

Lorraine straddled her on the dirty pavement, yanking a hand free and grabbing a fistful of hair. Sam tugged at her fingers, trying to break the grip. Lorraine was snarling, her bared teeth an inch away, spittle raining onto her cheeks.

Why isn't anyone helping?

One of Lorraine's dangly earrings caught in Sam's hair and a sharp pain tore across her scalp.

'Agh! Loz, stop!'

Lorraine went still. 'You okay?'

'Your bloody earring's just ripped half my hair out.'

'Fuck, love. Sorry, hang on.'

'Cut!' a voice rang out. 'Shelley, can you give them a hand?'

In Sam's peripheral vision another pair of hands reached into the bird's nest of her hair where Lorraine's earring was snagged.

'Hold still, ladies, while I sort out this wardrobe malfunction.'

'Cheers, Shelley,' said Sam. 'At least my boob didn't pop out.'

Lorraine giggled. 'If this show went out after the kiddies had gone to bed, I bet they'd write that scene in.'

Sam jiggled her breasts towards her friend. 'Too right. These puppies have power. You've seen them, haven't you, Shelley? They're mag-nif-i-cent.'

Shelley shook her head. 'Yes, darling, your boobs could awaken the dead. Now, hold still. Don't make me get my scissors out.'

An hour later, Sam had been surgically removed from Lorraine without lasting damage and was in a taxi heading into central London. The driver was a regular for the production and Sam was grateful. She wouldn't have to answer endless questions about Bethany—the character she played on the long-running soap—or deflect questions about future storylines.

Kicking off her vertiginous heels, she stuck in her earbuds and scrolled through the video library on her phone.

Three months ago, her best friend, Zoe, had moved from London to the wilds of Scotland. Sam missed her terribly and had hoped she'd come back. However, once Zoe fell in love with Rory, the Earl of Kinloch, it was clear her heart and soul were now in the Highlands.

Zoe had sent her a video of Jamie, her childhood friend from Kinloch, playing guitar and singing a love song he'd written. Sam refused to mark the videos, or any of the pictures of Jamie she'd saved, as favourites. That would be an admission of interest.

There was no way she was interested in someone three years younger than herself, who still lived with his mum, hundreds of miles away in the arse end of nowhere.

It was unfortunate, however, that Jamie possessed a certain level of physical attractiveness. He had deep brown eyes framed by long, dark lashes; thick, dark brown hair that looked as if it had just been ruffled out of place by an affectionate aunt, and a shy smile that pierced through the phone screen straight to her heart.

Even hunched over his guitar, she could tell he was tall. She stared at his thick, corded forearms, his long fingers plucking the strings. His big, gentle, *clever* hands...

Heat rose in her cheeks. *Forget about his hands!*

She'd watched the video hundreds of times, but each time her viewing followed the same script: stare at him as he chatted to Zoe and imagine he was talking to her. Look at his fingers as he started to play. Feel too hot. Close her eyes. Jump as he started to sing. Feel unwarranted emotions swirling inside her. Open her eyes and keep staring. Sing along with him in her mind.

'That's nice, love. What is it?'

Sam met the cab driver's gaze in the rear-view mirror with a start and fumbled to shut off her phone.

'What?'

'That song you were singing.'

She sucked in a breath. It was like he'd caught her watching porn. 'It's nothing.' This was ridiculous. Fuck, she'd be less embarrassed if it *had* been porn. 'Just a friend of a friend messing about.'

'Well, it gave me goosebumps.' He raised a tattooed arm from the steering wheel. 'See? And you've got a lovely voice, too. Beautiful.'

Sam huffed a laugh as she looked out the window, then checked her watch. She was early. 'Actually, Stan, can you drop me here?'

'No problem, darling.' He signalled and pulled over. Sam rammed her feet back into her heels and manoeuvred with practiced grace out of the car.

'Thanks, Stan. See you soon.'

He gave her a wave over his shoulder as he drove away.

SAM GAZED AT THE HUGE RED-BRICK VICTORIAN FACADE OF the Royal Marsden Hospital. Standing at the bottom of the stone steps leading up to the main doors, she felt small and inadequate. A familiar knot of tension coiled tighter in her stomach. She deliberately let out a long, slow breath, flexed her fingers, and took out her phone.

She couldn't remember the last time she'd reached out to

her oldest sister or spoken to her outside of family get-togethers.

The call connected.

'Esther Adamson.'

'It's me. Sam.'

She could hear her sister speaking hurriedly to other people in the background, then her attention was back. 'Is everything okay?'

'Yeah, yeah,' Sam replied. 'I had a minor head wound earlier from some cheap earrings, but—'

'Head wound? You've been checked over? Vision okay? Slurred speech? What happened?'

'Shit, no, I'm fine. I just got my hair caught in Loz's earring, that's all.'

'Jesus, Sam.' Her sister let out a loud breath. 'Don't do that to me.'

Fuck.

'So, you're okay?'

'Yep, all A-okay,' Sam replied brightly, squatting on the step and resting her forehead on her free hand. She chewed her bottom lip as she listened to her sister talking to others, the noises of feet running and doors slamming.

'Look,' Esther continued, 'I was meant to be finishing a twelve-hour shift, but there's been a serious traffic accident so I'm going back into surgery. Can I call you later? Where are you?'

'I'm still on set. You know, busy, busy.' Sam rolled her eyes at herself. 'Sure, call me—' The noises from her sister's end of the line stopped. Sam stared at her phone, then dropped it into her bag. *Way to go, Smulan...*

'Oi, oi, Bethany!'

Sam stood, the smile already fixed on her face. She saluted two men as they ambled past carrying takeout coffees.

'Fancy a quickie?'

Her smile froze. 'Not today, gentlemen. It's my day off.'

She strode briskly in the opposite direction, her arm raised to hail a taxi. Just because her character put out to half the street didn't mean she did.

HALF AN HOUR LATER, SAM WAS IN SOHO BEING SHOWN INTO her agent's office. Sandra Billings was in her sixties. She'd been there, done it, and had the photos and the gravelly voice to prove it. The walls were covered in black-and-white headshots of her clients and press shots of them holding awards. Each was signed with a gushing message thanking Sandra for their success.

Sam looked at her own, remembering how excited she'd been to land the part of Bethany on *Elm Tree Lane*. Yet now, less than a year after starting on the soap, she wanted more.

Sandra pulled Sam in for a kiss, then gestured for her to sit on the other side of her desk as she reached for a chrome and diamanté e-cigarette. She sucked deeply on it, accentuating the lines around her mouth, then exhaled a plume of sickly-sweet vapour.

Sam hated the smell of cigarettes, but this was worse. It was as if someone high on ecstasy and unicorns had staggered into a lab and instructed a minion to mix as many E numbers as they could until they came up with the smell of pink.

The stench from the real cigarettes Sandra used to smoke had seeped into every piece of furniture. It was now in a three-way fight for supremacy with the cloying vape and heavy punch of Cacharel's Lou Lou that Sandra had been marinating in since the eighties. No matter how many painkillers Sam popped in preparation before a meeting, she always left with a headache.

As they exchanged pleasantries, Sam tried to stay calm. Sandra's secretary had called her in for the meeting with the promise of 'something big', and her imagination had been running wild with possibilities.

Eventually Sandra put her vape to one side and leaned forward.

'Right, love, I've got you the biggie.'

'*Strictly*?'

Sandra shook her head. 'Not this year—it's Lorraine's turn. You're too new.' She paused for effect. 'I've got you another commercial.'

A few months ago, Sam had done an advert for a brand of instant coffee. The money and exposure had been good, but it wasn't as high-end as she wanted.

Doubt pricked at her stomach. 'It isn't the thrush medication again? I told you, there's no way I'm doing that.'

'No, love, I've got you the one every hot young thing wants.' Sandra sat back looking satisfied.

Sam's brain went into overdrive. *The Christmas advert for the John Lewis store? One for Coca Cola?*

'What is it?'

Sandra smiled enough to reveal yellowing teeth. '*Mopeoke*. I've gone and got you Mopeoke, love.'

What the fuck is that?

'Er, Mopeoke?'

'Yeah. Didn't you see the pitch on *The Bear Pit*? They literally got into a fight over who was going to invest. Come on. You must have seen it?'

Sam struggled to think. She was so exhausted with the long days on set she rarely watched TV. Sandra spun her laptop around and Sam stared at the screen.

'It's a mop.'

'And...'

She looked closer. 'Is that a microphone at the end of the handle?'

Sandra nodded. 'Syncs via Bluetooth to any device. Mop one end, karaoke microphone the other. Mopeoke. Fastest start-up since Trunkis and Loom bands.'

Fuck right off. She fought to buy time. 'Er, why me?'

'You're the target demographic: lower middle-class, in your thirties, young family, house to keep clean, dreaming of stardom. Plus, you're a household name now and I told them you could sing.'

'I only turned thirty last month,' Sam spluttered. 'I'm single, childless, and my entire family are doctors.'

Sandra sat back, her smile gone. 'Yeah, but *you're* not a doctor, are you? And millions of people every week don't hear your Home Counties accent. They hear Bethany, who's rough as a badger's arse.'

Sam stared at the edge of the desk and rubbed her forehead. The headache had arrived and was dancing the cancan inside her skull.

'Look, are you interested or not?'

No, no, no, no, no. 'Can I think about it?'

'You've got till the end of the day.'

Sam nodded, and Sandra sighed.

'What do you want, Sam?'

She glanced up. 'You know what I want. I want bigger. I want films. I want *more*.'

Sandra dragged on her vape and engulfed Sam in a fog of overripe fruit.

'You need a stronger platform before we make that move. You've got to start small. Your contract with *Elm Tree Lane* is up for renewal in a couple of months. Don't rock the boat. Take the Mopeoke gig. Trust me, it's the best thing in your life right now.'

. . .

SAM PUSHED OPEN THE DOOR TO THE BASEMENT STUDIO WITH her backside, holding coffees for her co-stars, Lorraine and Ian. They were filming a love triangle storyline on *Elm Tree Lane* and were doing a photoshoot for the cover of *Soap First* magazine that would go out when the plot aired the following month.

The shoot wasn't complicated—just portraits of the three of them looking sufficiently angry or aroused, so they only needed a green screen backdrop and a few lights. The studio was small, old, and damp. Sam repressed a shudder as the soles of her shoes stuck to the tacky floor.

A door at the end of the corridor opened and Lorraine rushed out.

'How's your hair? I'm so sorry about earlier. How did it go with Sandra? What's the big job she's got for you?'

Sam pushed the coffees towards her friend. 'I'm fine, sweetie. Can you take these?'

'Are they for us? You're a diamond.' Lorraine read the sides of the cups. 'Bethany.' She rolled her eyes. 'Loz, yep, like it. And... *Dickhead*?' She giggled. 'He's not here yet, so we can drink these while we wait.'

They entered a small room and perched on a cheap and uncomfortable sofa that had once been red but was now a muddy brown.

'So tell me,' asked Lorraine, 'what was the job?'

Sam tapped the side of her nose. 'It might not happen, so I've got to keep schtum about this one. But I did hear a rumour that a certain someone is going to be on *Strictly* this year?'

Lorraine squealed and tapped her feet on the floor. 'I'm so excited! I've been watching that show since I was a baby. I can't believe I'm going to be on it!'

Sam squeezed her arm. 'You deserve it, Loz. You're going to

be amazing. I'll be glued to my telly every Saturday night and have your voting number on speed dial.'

Lorraine teared up. 'You're the best, Sam. The older sister I never had.'

Sam smiled back, her throat tightening.

The door opened and Shelley bustled in, followed by a photographer, an assistant, and two of the wardrobe and make-up team from *Elm Tree Lane*.

'Sorry we're late, ladies. There was a snarl-up on the drive in.'

'No worries, Shelley,' replied Sam. 'Can we give you a hand?'

Shelley dismissed her with a wave. 'You two stay put. I'm going to sort your outfits, then you can get changed. Ian here yet?'

They shook their heads.

Shelley glanced at the word 'Dickhead' written on the third coffee cup and grinned. 'Any later and that'll be cold.' She gave them both a wink and turned away.

'Sam,' Lorraine whispered. 'Can I tell you something else?'

She leaned in. 'Of course, sweetie. I presume it's something good?'

Lorraine was jiggling again, her eyes darting about to make sure they weren't overheard. 'Yes! It's almost as exciting as *Strictly* and I want you to be the first to know.'

Sam hadn't seen such excitement outside of a child on Christmas morning. 'Come on then, out with it, or you might have an accident and improve the colour of this sofa.'

Lorraine snorted and moved closer. 'I'm second on the shortlist to do the ad for Mopeoke!' She held her finger and thumb a millimetre apart. 'I'm *this* close to promoting the product of my dreams!'

Sam swallowed. 'That's amazing, Loz.'

Lorraine sighed. 'I love cleaning. I know it sounds sad, but I do. I get so excited when the Lakeland catalogue arrives in the post. Do you know what I mean?'

Sam grinned. 'I'm afraid the only way I'd get excited about a mop would be if it had a ten-speed vibrator attached.'

Lorraine laughed as the door to the studio was flung open with a bang.

'Speaking of giant dildos,' Sam murmured.

Lorraine's laugh turned into a snort as a man strode in. The last point of their love triangle had arrived.

Ian Berresford had gone from stage school to a moderately successful boy band to being cast as the 'bad boy' on *Elm Tree Lane*. It was a role he was born to play and the only difference between his onscreen and offscreen persona was that 'market trader Wayne' wasn't sponsored by a condom company.

'Ladies!' he announced to the room. He shucked his leather jacket, ran his hands through his slicked-back hair, and stood in front of Sam and Lorraine with his legs too far apart. 'The king has arrived.'

'Have you disinterred Elvis?' Sam asked.

'The king is dead; long live the king,' he replied with a wink at Lorraine.

Sam passed him his coffee cup.

He screwed up his nose as he read 'Dickhead' on the side. 'Have you spat in this?'

'No, but if you put your tongue in my mouth again during a scene, I will. If you're that desperate to taste my saliva I can spit in all your drinks for you.' She stood. 'I'm just going to make a quick call.'

Pushing past Ian, she left the studio.

When she returned a couple of minutes later, Ian was next to Lorraine on the sofa, showing her his phone. He glanced at Sam.

'I've got one hundred and sixty-four thousand Instagram followers. You'll never catch up now, Adams.'

'I wasn't aware we were in a race, Berresford.'

He grinned. 'Yeah, yeah, keep telling yourself that when you're watching me accept "best bad boy" at the soap awards for the third year in a row. Remind me, you've yet to be nominated for anything, right?'

Sam willed her hands not to clench into fists.

Lorraine slapped Ian on the arm. 'Don't be such a twat.'

He flexed his muscles in response. 'Do that again, Loz... you almost gave me a semi.'

Lorraine rolled her eyes and moved to Sam's side.

Ian leapt up, fiddling with his phone. 'This is your best mate, right?' he asked, shoving the screen under Sam's nose.

She glanced down and adrenaline drenched her like an icy bucket of water.

Ian had Brad Bauer's account open, showing a photo of him sitting next to Zoe on wooden thrones in Kinloch castle.

Brad was the biggest star in Hollywood, a polymath who'd put his foot down on the accelerator of life and never once raised it. He was an actor, writer, producer, director, and serial shagger. Whatever he touched usually turned to gold, including the careers of his exes.

He'd recently discovered Zoe's Instagram account and Kinloch castle. Now he was preparing to shoot *Braveheart 2* there and had decided Zoe was his muse.

'If we weren't shooting so much, I'd be up there like a shot,' said Ian. 'Look. He's following me. Game recognises game. Has he followed you back yet?'

Sam gritted her teeth. 'I don't follow him,' she lied.

Ian laughed. 'Yeah, right. You're too small to register on his radar.'

'Ian, can we have you first?' Shelley called over.

He ripped off his T-shirt and flexed his pecs. 'Sure, Shelley, you can have me anytime.' He winked at Lorraine and strode off across the studio.

Sam felt her friend's hand on hers, squeezing. 'Ignore him. He's being a royal prick today. Come sit down. Don't let him get to you.'

Sam sat with a thump and let out a breath. 'It's like he knows every single fucking button to push.'

Lorraine curled up next to her and rubbed her arm. 'I should warn you. He told me yesterday he's also been offered *Strictly*.'

Her head dropped. 'Fuck's sake.'

'Shh... you can't trust what comes out of his mouth, but I wanted you to have the heads-up. In case it's true.'

Sam gazed at her friend. 'Loz. I need to get up to Scotland. Brad's single, I'm single, and Zoe can get me in front of him.'

'But we're filming without a break until the summer. There's no time.'

'What if my grandmother suddenly got ill? And wanted me at her deathbed?'

Lorraine gasped. 'But that's not true! You can't lie.'

'Loz, I'll never have a chance like this again. I can't miss it.'

'Sam, you can't take that risk. We're so lucky to be on this show. Promise me you won't do anything stupid. Please?'

❧ 2 ❧

ONE MONTH LATER

Sam's hands were on her thighs, fingers splayed as she sat in the hire car waiting for Zoe to arrive. She concentrated on her manicured nails and her breathing.

Breathe in, two, three, four, and hold, two, three, four. Breathe out, two, three, four, and hold, two, three, four.

She'd been taught 'battlement breathing' at drama school as a way to calm her nerves before a performance. Was meeting Brad going to be the performance of her life? The wind buffeted the side of the car and her heart rate increased. What the fuck was she doing? Could she really expect Brad Bauer to fall in instalove with her?

Her fingers itched to move. The manicure was done solely to prevent herself chewing her nails to the quick. She bit her bottom lip, then forced herself to stop. She closed her eyes. *Breathe in, two, three, four, and hold—*

'Sam!'

Her eyes snapped open. Her best friend was waving at her

from across the car park, her crazy red curls bouncing in the breeze.

Zoe.

Suddenly everything was brighter and better. Sam leapt out of the car and into Zoe's arms. They hugged as they jumped up and down, screaming with excitement.

Zoe held her at arm's length. 'I can't believe you're actually here! I'll have to make friends with Hollywood megastars more often.'

Sam giggled nervously. 'Fuck, Zo, am I completely mad?'

'Yes, but that's why I love you so much. Next to you, I look normal. Let's grab your bags and get you to Morag's before it starts to rain.'

She grimaced at the low grey clouds. 'Does it rain a lot here?'

Her friend fixed her with a look. 'Let me guess, your preparation for this trip involved a manicure, pedicure, eyelash tint and sourcing boots with a six-inch heel rather than checking the weather forecast?'

Sam shrugged. 'I'm never going outside. I don't want to be abducted by a haggis.' She opened the car's boot and lifted out the first suitcase.

Zoe's jaw dropped. 'Have you brought the contents of your entire flat?'

'I packed for all eventualities.'

'How many pairs of shoes?'

'Do slippers, boots and sandals count as shoes?'

'Sandals? Seriously? Have you packed bikinis and a sarong as well?'

'I could be in LA in a couple of weeks,' she blustered.

Zoe howled with laughter. 'I'm definitely taking you to the leisure centre pool in Inverness. Apparently they've got a slide. Or maybe you fancy a dip in the loch?'

Sam shuddered. 'Just because you decided to go feral and eschew the trappings of civilisation doesn't mean I have to. I still can't believe you live in a shed with a rat.'

'And Rory. Don't forget him,' Zoe replied with a devilish glint in her eyes.

'Yes, that is a consolation. Your boyfriend's the hottest earl Asgard's ever produced.'

'Promise me you won't call him Thor when you meet him?'

'Only if you make sure I've got a box to stand on. I don't want to break my neck trying to make eye contact with the brother of Ben Nevis.'

They emptied the boot and trundled the suitcases down the high street. Kinloch was a small village, dominated by the castle. With the arrival of the cast and crew to shoot *Braveheart 2*, the population had swelled by over two hundred per cent.

Sam was going to be staying with Morag, who lived behind and above the post office she ran. When Zoe was a child and had visited Kinloch, she'd been best friends with Fiona and Jamie, Morag's children. Their father had died in an accident on an oil rig when Morag was pregnant with Jamie. Fiona was now married with a baby and Jamie still lived at home. Sam was staying in Fiona's childhood room that she used whenever her husband, Duncan, was working away offshore.

'Are you sure Morag is okay with me staying?' Sam asked.

'Are you kidding? Given half the chance she'd *pay* you to stay. You're my best friend and you're starring in her favourite soap. I wouldn't be surprised if she laid an egg with excitement.'

'And Fiona? She doesn't mind me using her room?'

'Don't be daft. She's at her house these two weeks with Duncan anyway. She's already put a bar of chocolate on your pillow and a vase of flowers on the bedside table.'

Sam's throat was full. She was being treated so well by people she'd never even met. She swallowed. 'And Jamie?'

'Jamie what?' Zoe asked with a sly grin.

'Does he mind that I'm staying?' she mumbled.

'Jamie's an absolute sweetheart, but he's currently acting like a grumpy teenager living in a house made of sticks and straw awaiting the arrival of Hurricane Sam.'

She groaned. 'I'll have to dial myself down to zero.'

'Bollocks. Don't you dare. Morag and Fiona are a riot. He's just scared, that's all.'

'Of me? I'm like half his height.'

'And four times the volume. Look, he's lived in that house since birth with his mum and sister. He's never had anyone else in his personal space. And certainly not anyone quite like you.' Zoe paused. 'You know there's only one bathroom upstairs?'

Sam's tummy flipped. *Do not think of Jamie in the shower.* 'Yeah. You said he works long hours? I'll just stay in bed until he leaves in the morning. I'll be on my best behaviour, I promise. I won't wind him up.' Zoe gave her another look and Sam giggled. 'Okay, I won't wind him up *too* much.'

They went to the back entrance of Morag's house and knocked. The door was flung open by a small, slightly plump older woman with short, curly grey hair and a beaming smile of welcome.

'Ah, there you are. Come in, come in. I'm Morag and this is Fiona and Liam.' Morag ushered them into the kitchen as Fiona came to meet them, carrying a baby.

'Hello, I'm Fiona, but you can call me Fi if you like, and this is Liam. Say hello, Liam. Do you want a cup of tea or the loo? How was the drive? Here, Zo, take Liam and I'll get Sam's bags.'

'I'll put the kettle on,' continued Morag. 'Are you hungry, love? I've made a gluten-free cake for you. If it's no good, I also got one from the shop as a backup. You can put your boots down there. Let me take your coat.'

Sam glanced at Zoe, who grinned. Sam's family always thought she talked too much, but she was a monk undertaking a vow of silence in comparison to Fiona and Morag.

Fiona took her arm. 'Come upstairs and I'll show you your room.'

'Ta da!' Fiona put one of Sam's suitcases by the window and flung her arms wide.

The room was small and pink with a single bed, bedside table, chest of drawers, wardrobe, and long bookshelf running along one wall.

'I know it's not big, but Liam's travel cot is in Mum's room, and I've cleared out the clothes I keep here so there should be enough room for you. The bathroom's next door, then Jamie's room, then Mum's at the end of the corridor. Help yourself to anything you need and if we don't have something, just ask.'

Sam's gaze was drawn to the shelf running along the entire side wall above the bed.

Fiona laughed. 'That's my satellite collection of romance novels. If you think that's a lot, you should see how many I've got at home.'

Zoe entered with another suitcase and a big bag over her shoulder.

'Ah yes, Fi's lending library for lovers. Don't be fooled by the ones with sappy names and women in ball gowns on the front. They're hot as fuck. I borrowed *Ensnaring the Earl* to wind Rory up. I bookmarked one of the sex scenes and left it where I knew he'd find it.'

'What happened?' Sam asked.

Zoe raised her eyebrows. 'He saw it as some kind of challenge. I didn't sleep for a week.'

Sam snorted with laughter. She hadn't yet met Rory, but it was clear he was a force of nature.

'We'll leave you to settle in,' said Fiona. 'Just come down when you're ready.'

She left with Zoe, and Sam sat on the edge of the bed. Had she ever been with anyone as insatiable as Rory seemed to be? Had she ever been the entirety of someone else's world? Their sun, their moon and all their stars?

She blew out her cheeks and squared her shoulders. *Eyes on the prize*. She was here to be the whole bloody universe for Brad Bauer. Nothing else mattered. She unzipped one of the suitcases and pulled out a pair of high-heeled pink fluffy slippers and her washbag.

In the bathroom, she glanced at the selection of toiletries. It was clear the majority belonged to Morag and Fiona. Her hand drifted towards a black bottle of shower gel she guessed belonged to Jamie.

Don't touch it!

Her body refused to obey. She flipped the lid and brought it to her nostrils, breathing in the scent of citrus, sandalwood, warmth, and spices. Her mouth watered. Was this what Jamie smelled like?

Get a grip!

She snapped it closed and went downstairs.

Morag, Fiona, and Zoe were sitting around the kitchen table with big mugs of tea and an uncut cake in front of them. Liam gurgled away happily.

'Got everything you need, love?' asked Morag, getting up and steering her into a chair. 'I have to say it's nice to be around people of a similar height. When our Jamie, Duncan, Zoe, and Rory are around, Fiona and I feel undersized.'

'Yeah, no offence, Zo,' continued Fiona, 'but when you're here I can't decide whether I'm an Oompa Loompa or from Lilliput. Can we swap you out for Sam?'

Morag gave her daughter a gentle shove. 'Swap? We want both of them. Cut the cake and we can see if it's worked or not.'

She reached into a cupboard, retrieved a jar and presented it to Sam.

'I've even got your coffee in. I loved you in that advert—so posh and sophistimacated. Can you do it for us?' she asked hopefully.

'Of course,' Sam replied with a grin. She took the jar from Morag and dropped her voice. 'If you're looking for a deeper experience, there's only one choice, one taste... Look for the Connoisseur label and drink richly.'

Morag and Fiona whooped, and everyone clapped.

'That's wonderful,' said Morag. 'I don't think it would sound the same coming from the likes of me.'

'Oh, I don't know,' replied Sam.

Mimicry was a skill she'd had since childhood and honed over the course of her career. She put on a lilting Highland voice and repeated the advert. Morag and Fiona's mouths dropped open.

'Oh. My. God,' said Fiona. 'That's uncanny. 'What else can you do? Can you do Glaswegian?'

Sam obliged.

'Edinburgh?'

She rattled off the advert again.

'Aberdeen?' asked Morag. 'That one's bloody impossible.'

Sam did the accent so perfectly that Morag nearly fell off her chair.

'You're so clever!'

Fiona nodded and passed out slices of cake. 'That's a gift.

Whenever I try to do an accent, it sounds like someone Welsh trying to be Indian.'

'I've always been able to,' Sam replied. 'I'm like a parrot. That's all acting is, really.'

She felt a lump in her stomach remembering her father's words: *You're like a parrot, Smulan*. They never hid their opinions of her life choices and job.

Taking a big bite of cake for distraction, she rolled her eyes with pleasure at the taste. 'This is amazing.'

Morag's cheeks turned pink. 'Well, that's a relief. I've never baked with gluten-free flour before.'

'Thank you, I really appreciate it.'

Morag squeezed her arm. 'Not at all, love. It's been very interesting and keeps me on my toes.' She stood. 'Speaking of which, I must get dinner on.'

'Can we help?'

'Och no, you're a guest.' Morag glanced at the clock on the wall. 'Tell you what though, you can be in charge of making sure the chef remains fully lubricated.'

Sam glanced at Fiona who grinned and opened the fridge door. It was filled with Prosecco.

'Zoe said you were a fan, so we're using you as an excuse to get pissed.'

TWO HOURS LATER SAM HAD COMPLETELY FORGOTTEN THE reason she'd come to Scotland. She was happily drunk and revelling in being back with her best friend. She'd also fallen in love with Morag and Fiona and wanted nothing more than to be part of this family forever.

The only thing needling at the edge of her happiness was unease about the imminent arrival of Jamie. It was one thing to watch him incessantly on her phone, quite another to be physically in the same space as him.

Eventually she couldn't hold the question in any longer.

'What time does Jamie come back?' she asked as casually as she could.

'He's on a very important mission,' Morag replied, tapping the side of her nose.

Fiona rolled her eyes. 'Kirsten Bjorkstrom can't function without fresh guava, so Jamie's gone two hours out of his way to track it down for her.'

Unwanted jealousy stabbed in the pit of Sam's stomach. Kirsten was a thinner, blonder, prettier, more talented version of herself. She was also starring in a multi-million-pound Hollywood blockbuster and had already won an Oscar, whereas Sam was a bit player in a TV soap.

Did Jamie *like* Kirsten? Why else would he go so far out of his way for her? She caught Zoe staring at her and glanced away.

'Jamie's doing the favour for Rory,' said Zoe. 'Kirsten's the worst kind of princess. She keeps looking at Rory like she wants to eat him.'

'You're not like that, are you?' slurred Fiona. 'You seem waaaaaay too nice for any of that bollocks.'

'Oh, I don't know,' Sam replied. 'All my contracts stipulate I can't perform without water made from angel tears and gluten-free toilet roll.'

The laughter was broken by Zoe yelling, 'Jamie!'

A tall figure was standing behind the glass back door. He didn't seem to want to come in. Fiona banged her fists on the table and they all joined in.

'Jamie! Jamie!' everyone chanted, as butterflies took off inside Sam's tummy.

He pushed open the door and stepped inside as Fiona,

Morag, and Zoe cheered. He gazed at the table, frowning. There were a few crumbs left from the cake, three empty bottles of Prosecco, and a fourth halfway gone.

Sam took him in, her heart hammering. *Fuck, fuck, fuck.* Why was she having this reaction? He was so tall, his hair so dark, his jaw dusted with stubble.

Eyes on the prize.

She tried to remember she was here to bag a completely different dark and handsome stranger, not this one.

'All hail the guava king!' yelled Fiona, toasting him and spilling Prosecco over her hand.

'Ma wee boy!' cried Morag. 'Meet Sam! She's my new celebrity friend!'

Zoe staggered unsteadily to her feet. 'Sit down. Take my seat. You need to meet Sam.'

Jamie seemed to be doing everything in his power to avoid acknowledging her presence. He stared at his feet and shuffled around the table towards the stairs.

'I just need to jump in the shower,' he mumbled.

Sam swallowed. His voice was so deep. Why wouldn't he look at her?

Morag grabbed his arm and pulled him into her vacant chair. 'Son! Sit down and have a drink. Whaddya want?'

'I'll have a coffee, thanks,' he said quietly, his voice stilted.

Sam could read body language. He *really* didn't want her here. Hurt flared inside her. Morag and Fiona had accepted her with open arms. Couldn't he at least try to make an effort?

'Ooh!' yelled Fiona, grabbing the jar of coffee and pushing it into Sam's hands. 'Do it! Do your advert!'

All the years of feeling small, inferior, and overlooked scorched through her like a comet.

She would make Jamie notice her.

Leaning across the table, she squeezed her upper arms into

the sides of her breasts, accentuating her cleavage. She gave him no choice but to either stare at her boobs or raise his head. He glanced up and for a second her heart stopped. Then it hardened at his blank expression. She stroked the jar of coffee.

'Hey, Jamie,' she purred. 'I'm Sam.' She paused. His eyes were so dark, she couldn't tell where the pupils ended and the irises began. 'If you're looking for a deeper experience, there's only one choice, one taste.' She licked her lips and lowered her voice. 'Look for the Connoisseur label and drink richly.'

Morag, Fiona, and Zoe whooped with delight, and she stood, bowing for them.

Jamie pushed back his chair with a screech, his face flushed. 'Forget the coffee. I'm going for a shower.'

❧　3　❧

Jamie stomped up the narrow staircase, his head too hot and his clothes too tight. He pushed open the door of his room, threw off his jacket, then paused holding the bottom of his T-shirt. He was used to getting naked, then walking to the bathroom. Now he couldn't.

He rubbed his jaw, teeth grinding together. This was a nightmare. He had his routine, and the familiarity and safety of the only home he'd ever known. The walls of this house were more impregnable to him than Rory's castle, but were now under siege from a small, pretty blonde woman.

In the corridor he yanked open the stiff door of the airing cupboard with a bang and grabbed his towel. Slamming the bathroom door shut behind him, he pushed a small chrome bin against it, then shook his head. It wouldn't even keep Liam out.

He sighed, exhausted. He worked long hours in a physical job. All he wanted at the end of the day was to come home, wash off the dirt from the building site, have a hot dinner, then crash out in front of the telly with a beer.

But after nine hours of dust and dickheads, he'd gone hours out of his way to pick up tropical fruit for a small blonde actress with the smile of a siren and the eyes of a velociraptor.

He shuddered. Kirsten Bjorkstrom scared the shit out of him. He'd escaped her clutches only to find his home had been invaded by another small blonde actress... this one with the bright eyes of a summer's day and a voice that caressed his skin like velvet.

He stared at the bathroom windowsill, an unfamiliar washbag sitting on it. Sam was already everywhere. Angrily tugging off his T-shirt, he knocked a cup of toothbrushes off the side of the sink to the floor with a clatter. *Fuck's sake!* He put them back, then pulled his work trousers and boxers down over his thickening cock. *Seriously?*

Stalking into the shower, he turned it on and let the cold water shock some of the stupidity out of his body.

This is why you need a girlfriend, idiot.

He reached for his shower gel, rubbing it over himself aggressively, trying to ignore his burning need for release. There was no way in hell he was going to give in to that temptation.

This had nothing to do with Sam. Any woman could have this effect on him right now.

So, Zoe? Does she get you going like this? the devil on his shoulder piped up smugly.

Fuck off, his pissed off inner angel replied.

He was just confused, that was all. Sam was objectively pretty, and he liked watching her on the telly. But whenever she opened her mouth on screen it sounded like a lower-class cat had been gargling with drain cleaner. Jamie had seen her in the coffee commercial, but had assumed her voice had been dubbed.

Now she was here. And the reality was nothing like he'd

imagined. She was so alive, like a shorting wire he couldn't control. And her voice...

With an audible groan, he rested his forehead on the back wall of the shower. It was so rich. So smooth and warm. It had run into him like the drugging heat of the finest whisky.

He turned the shower to ice cold. He could hold it together until she buggered off back to London. He *would* hold it together.

'JAMIE! COME ON, SON. DUNCAN'S HERE AND DINNER'S ON the table!'

Jamie was sitting on the edge of his bed reading a book when his mother bellowed up the stairs. Despite how knotted his stomach was, he couldn't put off going down any longer.

He wished he'd taken the half-finished bottle of Prosecco into the shower. He needed something to soften the edges of his irritation. He didn't want to be rude to Sam, but he didn't want her there and felt stretched to the point of snapping.

Following everyone into the dining room, he waited until his mum sat Sam next to herself, then he moved to the other end of the table between his sister and Zoe. They would be his buffer; he knew where he stood with them.

His mum had gone to town as per usual, cooking a pork roast and extra crackling, apple sauce, goose fat roast potatoes, and vegetables drowning in butter. Zoe nudged him and he glanced up to see his mother holding Sam's hand on her left and Duncan's on her right. He took Zoe and Fiona's and closed his eyes.

'Dear You Upstairs,' began Morag. 'Bless this family and bless this meal. Thank you for bringing Sam into our lives and keep safe in your love the ones who are no longer with us. Amen.'

A squeeze rippled through everyone's hands and Jamie opened his eyes to see Sam wiping the corners of hers. He stared at her as his mother gave her shoulder a rub.

Is that real emotion?

'Come on, tuck in,' his mum urged. 'If you're shy, you'll go hungry.'

Sam loaded up her plate.

'I thought actresses weren't supposed to eat?' he muttered under his breath.

'Oh, I do the 5:2 diet,' she replied.

He felt a flash of adrenaline. He needed to keep his mouth shut.

'I know that,' said Fiona. 'You pretty much starve yourself for two days, then eat normally for five, right?'

'Almost. Except I starve myself for five days, then stuff myself for two!'

Jamie's eyes rolled before he could stop them as the women around him laughed. Was everything a joke to her? Were *they* a joke? Was his family a convenient means to an end? Zoe was Sam's best friend, but this was the first time she'd made the effort to visit.

'So, are you up here to see Zoe or just to try and meet Brad?' he asked before his brain caught up to what his mouth was saying.

'Oh, Brad one hundred per cent. Zoe's a bonus,' Sam replied as his sister and Zoe laughed on either side of him.

Jamie couldn't believe she'd throw herself at a stranger just for what she hoped she could get out of him.

'But what are you going to do when you finally meet him?'

'Seduce and marry him of course! What else would I be doing with him?'

Jamie's irritation flared. How could either of them be happy if they were only using each other?

'But you don't know him. What if he's unfaithful?'

'That's exactly what I want him to be!' replied Sam, her eyes dancing. 'The whole point of marrying Brad Bauer is for the divorce. And all his Hollywood contacts...'

The table erupted with laughter and even Liam chuckled as he banged his spoon. Jamie stared at his plate and shook his head. How could they find this funny?

His sister kicked him under the table.

'Undo the belt on your judgy pants,' she whispered out of the corner of her mouth. 'They're so tight they've given you a wedgie.'

He glanced at her and couldn't help a smile. 'Judgy pants?'

'Yeah, the ones you bought two sizes too small 'cause you won't admit you're a lard arse.'

'Fuck off.'

'Jamie!' said Morag, jerking her head towards Liam. 'The baby! I'll never live it down if that's his first word.'

'It's Fi's fault.'

His sister put down her cutlery and opened her palms wide. 'Did I just throw my voice and take it down an octave?'

'Yes, you did,' came a deep voice from Sam in a perfect copy of Jamie's.

Everyone's heads swivelled in her direction. Her eyes were wide and innocent.

'You're always landing me in it,' Sam continued with a closed mouth, throwing her voice and imitating Jamie. 'It's so unfair. Muuuuuum. Muuuuuum. Make Fiona go sit on the naughty step...'

There was a brief silence, then she collapsed into giggles.

Duncan clapped and Morag, Fiona, and Zoe laughed until they cried. Jamie stared at Sam and couldn't help his smile growing to match hers. She winked at him and his tummy flipped.

'Oh my god,' Morag wheezed. 'You're a genius.' She turned to Duncan and Jamie. 'You know, boys, she can even do Aberdeen.'

'Not possible,' replied Duncan. 'It's easier to speak Klingon.'

'Heghlu'meH QaQ jajvam!' replied Sam in a perfect Aberdeen accent. 'Today is a good day to die!'

Duncan reached across the table to high-five her. 'TlhIngan maH!' he roared. 'We are Klingon!'

Jamie laughed as Fiona sank her head into her hands.

'Not another fucking Trekkie,' she groaned.

'Fiona! The baby!' replied Sam, sounding exactly like Morag.

AFTER NEARLY TWO HOURS OF EATING AND LAUGHING, Morag pushed everyone through into the living room. Jamie waited until Sam and Zoe sat together on one of the sofas before sitting on a chair next to his sister.

He'd drunk more alcohol than usual in an attempt to temper his annoyance at having Sam in the house, but it had given him the biggest beer goggles he'd ever worn. By the end of the meal, he couldn't look at her without feeling a powerful tug of attraction that made little sense to his logical mind.

The only solution was to close his eyes and let the white noise of female chatter send him to sleep.

His attempt at a nap was broken by his sister kicking him on the shin and brandishing his guitar like an offensive weapon.

He shook his head. 'Not tonight, Fi.'

'Ah, come on now, son,' chided Morag. 'You have to. Sam's come all this way. It's the very least you could do.'

'Please, Jamie,' said Zoe. 'You haven't made me cry in ages.'

He looked at her, seeing Sam in his peripheral vision. Familiar dread and panic rose at the thought of playing in front of anyone new, but it was mixed with a strange thrill.

He realised he *wanted* to play. He wanted to impress her.

Before he could question himself, he started tuning the strings. *What am I doing?* Liam was asleep in Duncan's arms and the room was completely silent.

Sam sat forward on the sofa, hands clasped on her lap.

Jamie closed his eyes and dropped his head. As long as he imagined he was alone, he could do this. He tried to remember the song Zoe had filmed last year and put on her Instagram. Had Sam seen it? He decided to start with a simple love song, one of the first he'd ever written.

Plucking out the intro, he sang the first verse as almost a whisper. After the first chorus he began the second verse with more confidence, but a couple of words in, a gentle humming started. He glanced up in shock to see Sam smiling at him, adding her own harmony to his song.

It was only the fact he knew the song almost as well as his own name that enabled him to continue on autopilot as the front of his brain froze and the rest of his body caught light.

In a breath, there was no one there except the two of them. He held her gaze as he sang the last verse. It was like they'd suddenly entered another world where all communication was non-verbal. He'd never experienced anything like it and didn't want it to stop.

At the end of the song, he continued straight into another, giving Sam a tiny nod, willing her to join him. Her smile was tentative, but it sent a surge of joy through him. Whatever was happening, she could feel it too.

He sang the first chorus twice, and by the second time she had the words as well as the tune. Her voice was so pure it thrilled him. Woven with threads of light, it lifted his music to a place he never thought possible.

Had she heard him play before?

At the end of the second song, he took a gamble and played the one Zoe had filmed. From the first word he had his answer. Sam knew every word, every tiny change to the phrasing, every intonation. She knew how the song should be sung. How *he* wanted it to be sung.

His heart stuck in his throat, stopping his voice as his fingers played on. It was as if she knew the secret part of him. He swallowed to push down the lump in his throat as her voice soared. He blinked, his eyes hot and stinging.

She leaned forward even further, smiling in a way that bolstered his confidence. He took a deep breath and joined his voice to hers, holding back as she rose above him, then rising in volume to meet her on the way down.

It was his first ever transcendental experience—something so blissful and otherworldly he never wanted it to end. They sang the final chorus three times. When the last notes echoed away, he felt as if his soul had left his body to dance with hers in the silence.

Then it crash-landed into a world of noise. His mother, sister and friend couldn't decide whether they were crying or screaming, and even Duncan gave a whoop before rushing Liam out of the room to stop him waking.

Jamie held Sam's gaze for as long as he could, trying to hold onto the magic before his mother grabbed the two of them and crushed them to her, blubbering hot tears onto their foreheads.

'Oh my, that was the most beautiful thing I've ever heard!'

Jamie looked across his mother's heaving chest at Sam. Her eyes swam into focus just a few centimetres away. She smiled at him, and he felt his heart would burst.

'Please can I film it, *please*?' cried Zoe.

'Yes! Film it!' yelled his sister.

Morag released them from her embrace and grabbed a handful of tissues from a box. 'You must film it, Zoe love. We might never get to hear that again.'

Jamie glanced at Sam, suddenly shy again. He raised an eyebrow and she nodded.

'Okay,' he began. 'Please ensure all noses are blown before the performance commences.'

Everyone laughed. Fiona got out of her seat next to Jamie and Sam sat in it, angling her body towards his. He could feel the heat from her knee almost touching his. Had he ever felt this good?

'Okay, I'm filming in three, two, one, go!' Zoe cried.

Jamie paused, asking with his mind if Sam was ready. She nodded and he started playing.

The first time around, their singing had been a discovery, the meeting of strangers for the first time. Now it was the song of soulmates. Jamie had never been so confident, so sure what he was doing was right and that he was singing with the right person.

The rest of the world faded away once more as their voices wrapped around each other, tighter and tighter. On the second chorus, her knee touched his and a zing shot through him, completing the circuit between them.

Part of him drifted out of his body, watching them together, watching her as their music filled the room. He saw his smile, the happiness shining from him. It was like seeing himself for the first time.

As they sang the final words his heart overflowed.

I love you. I love you.

The words came from his heart, unbidden as the final notes faded away. He stared at Sam as the room filled with a cacophony of screams and cheers. She looked at him uncertainly.

No, no, no, no.

He stood abruptly, putting his guitar away as Sam was engulfed by all the other women in his life. Panic kicked and bit inside him. He had to get out. Now.

'I've got work in the morning. I've got to go to bed.' He left the room and strode through the kitchen, giving Duncan a terse 'goodnight' before jogging up the stairs.

He made it into his room, slammed the door, and slumped to the floor, his back against the side of the bed. *What the fuck?* His breath was ragged, hands clasped in front of himself so tightly the knuckles were white.

He tried to control his breathing, but each time he exhaled, panic throttled him, forcing him to suck in another breath. His head was spinning, lights flashing behind his eyes.

Come on, Jamie!

His chest tightened and he lost control, falling to the floor on his side, his muscles spasming. Rolling, blinding fear ran roughshod through him, so painful it felt like death.

He forced his eyes open, trying to focus on the wall as the edges of his vision turned black. His breath was laboured as he fought to stay conscious.

The light narrowed to one tiny point, then vanished. The only things left were the pain in his body and the sounds of him gasping to stay afloat.

Then there was nothing left at all.

THE LAST SENSE TO GO WAS ALWAYS HIS HEARING, AND IT WAS the first to return. Everything sounded fuzzy as if he were underwater. Jamie heard murmurs of voices and laughter from downstairs, doors opening and closing as people moved into the kitchen.

His own heartbeat and breathing were now almost imperceptible. He listened to Zoe leave, then Fiona and Duncan with Liam. His mother moved around the kitchen, laughing with Sam. Then he heard their footsteps on the stairs, whispers outside the bathroom, the taps going, the toilet flushing.

Eventually there was a brief silence before the low rumble of snoring started from his mother's room. He let out a sigh, feeling the movement of air past his lips, the carpet against his cheek.

He unclasped his hands and stretched his fingers. Everything was stiff and uncomfortable. Pushing himself up, he sat on the edge of the bed, staring into space.

You don't love her. You can't love her.

He dropped his head and pinched the bridge of his nose. He was exhausted. Whatever had happened this evening, he'd been completely unprepared for it. It couldn't happen again. He shucked off his clothes and crawled into bed, facing the wall and the direction where Sam was lying, just a few feet away.

You can't do this.

He rolled over, turning his back on her, and forced his eyes to shut.

❧ 4 ❧

Jamie woke to the distant sound of his mother yelling his name. He'd been convinced he was already awake, reliving the previous evening in jagged and disjointed moments, but his mother's urgent voice cut through and dragged him into reality.

His sheets were twisted around his limbs, and he flailed about to pull himself free.

'I'm coming!' he yelled as he chucked the bedclothes to one side, ran out of the room, and down the stairs.

'Son, get dressed. One of the trucks for the film has crashed into Mrs McCreedie's house. Zoe's called the police and the fire brigade, but you have to get up there and help Rory get her to ours.'

He nodded and ran back up the stairs, colliding at the top with Sam as she came out of her room. In the panic, for a brief moment, he'd forgotten she was in the house. Now he stood in front of her wearing only his boxers.

Her hair was loose around her shoulders, and she was dressed in a tight vest and shorts with a Disney cartoon of

Stitch and the words 'cute but crazy' on the front. He leapt back as if scorched and slammed his bedroom door behind him.

Fuck, fuck, fuck!

Tugging his jeans on, he dashed back into the corridor. She was still there, her cheeks pink. He ignored her and rushed down the stairs, pulling on his boots and running out the back door.

The early morning air was a cooling balm for his fevered skin. He sprinted up the high street towards the castle, trying to push all thoughts of Sam out of his head. She'd been in his life less than twenty-four hours and he'd totally lost the plot. The sight of her in that pyjama set had been more powerful than snorting Viagra.

Why couldn't she be like her character, Bethany? Or Kirsten Bjorkstrom? Why did she have to be so... *her*?

Striding down the hill towards him was Rory, the six-foot-five Earl of Kinloch. Half mountain, half warrior, and all Zoe's. He was holding a bundle of bedclothes topped with a grey-haired head, and met Jamie with a nod.

'Good morning, Mrs McCreedie,' he bellowed.

She frowned at him. 'Jamie, ma boy, I'm slightly deaf, not dead.'

'Sorry,' he replied, his cheeks heating.

'You okay to take it from here?' Rory asked him.

'*It?*' interjected Mrs McCreedie. 'I'm not a piece of baggage, young man.'

Now it was Rory's turn to blush. 'Sorry, Mrs McCreedie.'

She patted the side of his face. 'You're a good lad.'

Rory carefully transferred her into Jamie's arms. 'Jamie's going to take you to Morag's. Are you okay?'

'Yes, yes, just go and make sure my house doesn't fall down.'

Rory nodded and ran off.

'I'm perfectly capable of walking, you know,' Mrs McCreedie said as Jamie strode down the hill towards the post office. She looped her tiny arms around his neck. 'But it's far more exciting to be carried by a half-naked man. I feel like I'm in *An Officer and a Gentleman*, just with less clothes.'

Jamie had never once considered the most embarrassing moment of his life would involve carrying a little old lady down the high street wearing only his jeans and work boots.

The population of Kinloch appeared to have invented 5G telepathy as every door and window had someone hanging out of it, staring, clapping, or filming on their mobile phones. It didn't help that Mrs McCreedie was singing 'Love Lift Us Up Where We Belong' very loudly and tunelessly.

By the time they turned off the high street to reach the back of the post office, he was praying Sam was still upstairs.

Unfortunately, she was standing next to his mother outside the back door and trying not to laugh.

Morag ushered them into the kitchen and fussed as Jamie helped Mrs McCreedie into a chair. She was staring at Sam. 'Bethany?'

Sam lifted her chin. 'Yeah, who wants to know?' she said in her character's brittle cockney voice.

Mrs McCreedie clapped her hands and Sam curtsied. 'It *is* you! You're off the telly!'

'Cup of tea, Mrs McCreedie?' asked Morag. 'And would you like some breakfast?'

Jamie sidled around the table towards the bottom of the stairs, suddenly hyper-aware he was almost naked, and that Sam was staring at him.

'Are you an officer or a gentleman?' she asked out of the corner of her mouth.

'Neither,' he muttered. 'I'm an electrician.'

. . .

Fifteen minutes later Jamie was driving to work. His phone rang and the words 'Boss-man' appeared on the screen. Accepting the call, his boss's voice echoed around the inside of the car.

'Jamie, you alright, son?'

'Yeah, sorry, Gregor, I had a family emergency. It's all sorted now and I'm on my way. I'll be there in about half an hour.'

'Nothing wrong with the wee boy, Liam?'

'No, I just had to help rescue an old lady after a lorry crashed into her house.'

'Good god, is she okay?'

'Yeah, she's with Mum now and seems fine.'

'Well, thank goodness for that.' Gregor paused. 'Jamie, could you drop by the office around eleven?'

'Yeah, sure. Sorry about this morning, Gregor. It won't happen again.'

'Don't be daft, son. Drive safe now. I'll see you later.'

Jamie had been working for Gregor since he finished his apprenticeship with Duncan. When his brother-in-law left to work offshore on the oil rigs, Jamie hadn't felt ready or confident enough to strike out on his own, so had started as a jobbing electrician for Gregor's construction company and never left.

The jobs were a blank slate, usually straightforward, and he was glad to have regular work with none of the hassles of running his own business. However, the work was monotonous and most of his co-workers were dickheads.

Jamie hadn't fully appreciated how happy he'd been working with Duncan until he'd arrived for his first day on site and witnessed a fight between two brickies who were off their heads on drugs.

Gregor had sent them packing, but couldn't be everywhere at once and had ended up relying on Jamie to make sure jobs were done properly. Most of the people he worked alongside were lazy and stupid. Jamie knew they took advantage of his work ethic, but he wasn't going to sink to their level and let Gregor, or himself, down.

The current job was a small development of ten houses on a former playing field. Jamie was working with Callum and Hamish, who were in their early twenties. When they'd first arrived on site, he'd tried to mentor them as Duncan had done for him. It had been a total waste of time.

As he entered the open door of house number two, it wasn't the noises of work he heard coming towards him, but the sound of sex.

Standing with their backs to him in the unfinished shell of the living room, Callum and Hamish huddled over a phone. Jamie caught a flash of a naked woman before he looked away, dropping his bag to the floor with a thud.

'Classy. Being paid for watching porn.'

Callum glanced over his shoulder. 'Where the fuck have you been anyways?'

'None of your business. How do you think Caitlin would feel if she knew you were watching that?'

Callum grinned. 'This *is* Caitlin.'

'Aye,' added Hamish, eyes still glued to his friend's screen. 'She's got incredible tits, man.'

Jamie lunged towards the pair, pushing Hamish away and rounding on Callum. 'You fucking Ned. Put that away and have some respect for the woman who's having your baby.'

Callum shrugged. 'Don't get your knickers in a twist just because you're not getting any, nancy boy.'

Hamish laughed. 'Bender.'

Jamie paused, ice running in his veins. 'Tony on site today?'

Hamish frowned. 'Chippie Tony? The massive fucker with all the tats?'

Jamie nodded. 'That's him.'

'Yeah. Why?'

He looked between them, smiling. They had no idea.

'Well, lads, Tony's gay and he just loves the opportunity to address homophobia with his fist.'

As the penny dropped, their faces turned white.

'I think it's time to invite him round for some impromptu equality awareness training,' Jamie continued. 'What do you think?'

The threat of having the shit kicked out of them by a man who always carried a hammer and outweighed both of them combined was enough to make Callum and Hamish shut up and apply themselves that morning.

Ordinarily, Jamie would have welcomed the silence, but without the steady stream of mindless drivel that usually emanated from them, his mind was dragged back to Sam.

He couldn't keep up with all the feelings and emotions fighting for his attention. It was like he'd lived his life at a four out of ten and she'd come along and cranked everything up to eleven. He was sick, dizzy, confused, lost and utterly over-whelmed.

The only thing he knew with certainty was that he'd never be in any form of relationship with her. Even if their lives weren't at either end of the UK, she clearly had no interest in him.

His stomach rolled and he swallowed to suppress the rising tide of nausea. Right about now Sam would be heading to the castle in her mission to seduce the man every woman wanted: the multimillionaire and Hollywood superstar, Brad Bauer.

He checked his watch. Five to eleven. Time to see what his boss wanted.

. . .

THE SITE OFFICE WAS A PORTAKABIN FILLED WITH LARGE desks covered with plans for the site. It was messy but efficient. Gregor was in his late fifties with short grey hair and a lined face that was alternately frowning or laughing depending on who he was with.

He glanced up from his desk with a big smile as Jamie entered.

'Take a seat and try this.'

Jamie sat and gazed at the gleaming coffee machine on the desk.

'It's a present from Meg, but so far I've only managed to burn the back of my hand and create a sludge-a-chino. Can you get it to work?'

So this was why Gregor wanted to see him. 'Have you got the instructions?'

Gregor opened a drawer and pulled out a thick book still encased in Cellophane. Jamie raised his eyebrows.

His boss shrugged. 'It's just the manufacturer's *opinion* of how it should work. How hard can it be?'

Jamie stared at the red burn mark across the back of his boss's hand until Gregor laughed.

'Okay, point made. Now, are you going to help me or not?'

Since meeting Sam, Jamie hadn't believed his heart could beat any faster. However, fifteen minutes into playing with the coffee machine he had enough caffeine in his system to jump-start a tractor.

'Right, that's enough of that,' said Gregor, pushing it to one side with shaking hands. 'I'm either having a heart attack or you've been moonlighting as a backstreet barista.'

'Don't die on me, Boss-man. I need this job.'

Gregor sat and rubbed a calloused hand across his cropped

grey hair. He let out a huff, then reached for a pen on the desk and started fiddling with it.

'Jamie, you know how much I appreciate you? How much you bring to the business?'

'Are you letting me go?'

He glanced up in surprise. 'Jesus, Jamie, no.' He sighed and tapped the pen on the table. 'Are you happy?'

Jamie stared at him blankly. 'Happy?'

'Yeah. Happy. Do you wake up every morning excited about the day? Do you come to work with a spring in your step?'

'I dunno.' He shrugged. 'I've not really thought about it.'

'You're twenty-seven now? Nearly twenty-eight?'

Jamie nodded. *Where is this going?*

His boss sighed again. 'Don't you want more out of life?'

Jamie's heart was now racing double time. 'Don't you want me here?'

'Jesus, Jamie. If I had four of you, I wouldn't have to employ twenty useless Neds. If you could clone yourself, I'd retire within five years. But that's not it. I want more for you. Think about the money you could make if you worked offshore.'

Jamie shook his head violently and Gregor held up his hands.

'Sorry, son, I forgot.' He rubbed his head again. 'You can do this work with your eyes shut. Don't you want more of a chal-lenge? Be your own boss?'

Jamie shrugged again. He *had* thought about it. But with each passing month and year it seemed harder to make that change.

There was a knock at the door. Gregor stood and checked his watch, his expression suddenly bland.

'Ah, that'll be Lois.'

'Lois?'

'Yeah, yeah, my niece. First year civil engineering at Edinburgh. I've told you all about her, remember?' He didn't wait for a response. 'Anyway, you're perfect... to give her a site visit. I can't do it. I've got a meeting. Somewhere else.'

He pushed past Jamie and opened the door for a small brunette wearing a yellow hard hat.

'There you are, lass,' he said, pulling her in for a hug. 'This is Jamie, the one I told you about.'

Jamie stood and held out his hand. 'Nice to meet you,' he said woodenly.

She took it and smiled at him, blushing furiously. *Fuck*. She looked like a teenager straight out of school.

'So I'll leave you to it then? Take the whole day if you need it,' said Gregor.

He rushed back to his desk and pulled the coffee machine forward.

'Jamie, why don't you start by making Lois a coffee and you can get to know each other a bit before you give her the tour?' He opened a drawer and brought out a box of fresh pastries and two china plates with roses on them. 'Help yourselves, kids, I've already eaten.' He grabbed his phone and briefcase. 'Okay, have fun.'

He gave Lois another hug and gazed over her shoulder intently at Jamie before dashing out the door. Lois glanced at him, her cheeks still bright red, a nervous smile on her face.

Fuck's sake. Jamie repressed a sigh.

'Okay, Lois, what's it to be? Espresso, flat white, mochaccino, or your uncle's specialty, sludge-a-chino?'

❧ 5 ❧

S am had spent her life wanting what she couldn't have. Growing up in a family of Vikings, she wanted to be taller. At drama school she wanted better parts. Now she was working, she wanted bigger jobs. But never, in all her thirty years making the planet quite a bit noisier, did she expect to be jealous of a tiny woman in her eighties.

That morning, coming out of her room at the sound of Morag screaming for Jamie, she'd run into a wall of hard muscle and heat.

Where the fuck had he been hiding all of that?

There was no joke to be made, no witticism to be plucked from the air. She'd simply frozen whilst her hormones ran off for an emergency meeting, returning a millisecond later with the unanimous decision she should have sex with him immediately.

Who even *had* a body like that? He was a bloody electrician, not an underwear model. And he'd just woken up, so hadn't had time to do a hundred and fifty press ups to get his pump on.

She thought back to one of the bedroom scenes she'd done with Ian for *Elm Tree Lane*. He'd come straight from the gym to the studio and had a set of weights behind the camera. Between each take he'd leapt out of the bed and started furiously lifting, determined to look his best. Sam had deliberately annoyed him by slowly eating a bar of chocolate whilst moaning more effectively than when he'd been grunting above her five minutes earlier.

She'd been so shocked at the sight of Jamie's nearly naked body she hadn't been able to move once he'd disappeared into his room. Then he'd returned, buttoning up his jeans, and that had been even worse.

Her eyes had been drawn to the line of black hair running down from his navel as his fingers fastened the top of his trousers. She could feel her nipples hard and aching underneath her pyjama top, her skin hot, her head pounding.

He'd run straight past her down the stairs and she'd staggered back, pressing her palms against the cool lines of the vinyl wallpaper, her chest heaving as she let out the breath she'd been holding. With every gasp, her body cried *YES!* whilst her mind ran around like an out-of-control schoolteacher, screaming *no, no, no, no, no!*

She'd dressed shakily, forcing herself to focus on Brad while her body chanted Jamie's name. Shortly after, standing outside the back door, she'd watched as he strode towards her, Mrs McCreedie singing in his arms.

He'd seemed absolutely mortified, which made the situation even funnier, but her body had been raging with jealousy. It had taken all her years of acting training to hide what she was feeling and focus on entertaining an eighty-year-old woman who wouldn't stop banging on about being carried by 'such a braw young man'.

And now she was preparing to go to the castle so Zoe could

introduce her to Brad. She'd been thinking about this moment ever since she'd seen her best friend sitting next to the world's most famous movie star on his Instagram feed. Chances like this came about once in a lifetime and she was going to seize hers with both hands and hold on for dear life.

She knew all too well the fickleness and vagaries of her business. Success had little to do with talent. It was about your appearance, who you knew, how old you were, and your sex.

Sam knew she wasn't ugly, and she was short enough to make even the smallest male actor feel tall. But she didn't come from an acting family, was now thirty, and being a woman, the number of available roles were tiny compared to what was on offer for men.

So she networked, she schmoozed, she smiled, and she went for every opportunity without hesitation. She hardly saw her family and apart from Zoe, all her friends outside the acting world had fallen by the wayside. She couldn't begrudge Zoe her happiness with Rory, but her departure from London had left a far bigger hole in Sam's life than she'd expected.

Staring at her reflection in the bathroom mirror, she carefully applied make-up. Her gaze drifted to the shower cubicle behind her and the bottle of Jamie's shower gel. She blinked, brushing feathers of mascara on the skin under her eyes.

'Fuck it!'

She dropped the wand and reached for a tissue to remove the mess. She couldn't remember the last time she'd been this nervous.

Breathe in, two, three, four, and hold, two, three, four. Breathe out, two, three, four, and hold, two, three, four.

She steadied herself. If she didn't make another mistake, she could have a reward.

Ten minutes later, feeling like a shame-filled addict, she pushed the small chrome bin against the bathroom door and reached for Jamie's shower gel. She flipped the lid, put it to her nose, closed her eyes, and breathed in.

SAM LEFT MORAG'S LATE MORNING, WEARING A CONFIDENT smile and four-inch heels. She knew that whatever height a male actor claimed to be, knocking at least two inches off from the get-go was more accurate.

Extrapolating from Brad's stated height and Zoe's up close and personal description, she'd chosen footwear that would elongate her legs without being off-putting to the man she was trying to impress.

She'd got Zoe to leave copies of *Soap First* magazine in Brad's trailer and around the castle so he'd already know who she was. The only issue was that in the photos she was playing Bethany, who dressed like a bargain-basement stripper at her first court appearance.

With each step up the hill Sam's confidence waned to be replaced by self-doubt and blind panic. What *was* she hoping to achieve? As if within ten seconds in her company, Brad would fall in love, kick Kirsten Bjorkstrom to the kerb, and give Sam the leading role in *Braveheart 2*?

She slowed her pace. She thought back to singing with Jamie and her heart fluttered. On stage she'd sometimes been so lost in a role she'd forgotten where she was. But last night with Jamie, she'd not only forgotten where she was, she'd forgotten *who* she was as well. There was only the music and him.

She'd fantasised about singing with him every time she'd watched the video Zoe had taken. But then, sitting so close to him, she couldn't help herself. Something deep inside her soul had cried out to be free and she'd let it fly.

Being there live, his voice and the sounds of the guitar

vibrating through her had felt so right. She ran her mind back over the biggest events of her life, the best of times, trying to find a comparison.

Her feet stopped moving. Standing on the grey pavement, halfway to the castle, she realised that singing with Jamie was the first time in her life she'd felt complete. The first time she'd been truly and authentically herself, rather than who she, or others, thought she should be.

A smile spread across her face. *So, this is what contentment feels like.*

But singing with an electrician from the Highlands wasn't a job. It wasn't home. She could never make anything with Jamie work on any level. She closed her eyes and remembered his knee touching hers, the sound of their voices entwined.

What was she doing? Could she turn around and go back to Morag's? Give up on her ludicrous idea of seducing Brad Bauer? Try and make something, *anything*, work with Jamie?

'Hey, Bethany!' The voice shocked her out of her dream. 'Want a quickie?' An overweight man was leaning out of a white van with a pasty in his hand, crumbs stuck to the bristles around his chapped lips. 'Fancy a bit of Scottish sausage, eh?'

Rage rushed through her like wildfire. She broke into a run, her eyes on the castle ahead. The man's comment was why she was doing this. She didn't want her life and career defined by playing a tart in a soap.

Anything to do with Jamie was a fantasy; it wasn't real. Meeting Brad had more certainty than daydreaming about singing love songs with a man who didn't want her in his house and spent most of his time avoiding her. Who the fuck was she kidding that he felt what she did? The moment they'd finished singing, he couldn't wait to get away.

A lump formed in her throat remembering his horrified expression. He'd seemed appalled by her. She gritted her teeth.

It was just another rejection to add to her long list. He was no different from all the casting directors, producers, directors, and exes who'd told her she wasn't what they were looking for.

She slowed to a walk, took out her phone and rang the only person she knew she could count on.

Zoe answered after one ring. 'Hey, babe, you nearly here?'

'Yeah, I'm almost at the main entrance now.'

'Okay, I'm coming down. I think it's Fraser on the door this morning. Just to warn you, he doesn't seem to give a shit about Brad, Kirsten or Valentina, but when I told him I was expecting you, he nearly wet himself.'

'Okay. Anything else I should know?'

'Hmm, I personally think he could be bribed with jelly babies. He always keeps a packet inside his uniform and thinks no one has noticed. You don't have any on you, do you?'

'I'm afraid I had to make a hard choice between jelly babies and a family-size box of condoms when I was packing, and the jelly babies lost out.'

'Family-size box of condoms? Isn't that an oxymoron?' Zoe snorted.

'Well, "family size" sounds better than "fun size", surely?'

'How about bumper pack? Or value pack?'

Sam shuddered. 'Can you imagine the quality? Might as well use cling film. See you in a sec, sweetheart. I think I've just spotted Fraser.'

Sitting outside the big front doors to the castle was a young man in a black polyester suit a size too small. He stood as Sam approached, his cheeks brighter than his hair, and tugged down the cuffs of his jacket.

Sam smiled and held out her hand. 'Fraser?'

His mouth opened and his Adam's apple yo-yoed up and down as if rehearsing the mechanics needed for speech before he gave up and nodded, thrusting his hand out to shake hers.

'I'm Sam Adamson, although you might know me as Sam Adams?'

Fraser nodded again. Sam was used to this reaction.

'Would you like a selfie with me?'

His mouth dropped open and a strangled 'aye' wheezed out.

She gave him a reassuring smile. 'Do you have a phone?'

He wiggled to pull it out of his back pocket.

'I cannae believe it's you. Wait till I tell me mam.'

Holding the phone out, he hesitantly leaned in towards Sam as if afraid he was getting too close. She put her arm around him as they smiled together. After a few shots, he straightened, then checked them.

'Thank you, Miss Adams-son.'

Sam adopted a serious look. 'You need to make payment now.'

Fraser's eyes widened and he frantically patted his pockets. 'Do you take cards?'

She shook her head. 'I'm afraid I only take payment in jelly babies. Are you carrying any?'

He giggled, then pulled a packet from his inside pocket and passed it to her.

'How did you know?'

Sam tapped the side of her nose. 'I have my sources. I see you still have lemon ones left, so your secret is safe with me.'

She popped one in her mouth and handed over the bag. He put it hurriedly back inside his jacket as Zoe exited the castle.

'Hey, Fraser,' Zoe said. 'You taking good care of my BFFF?'

Sam stage-whispered to him, '"Best Fucking Friend Forever". I tell you, this one's got a right potty mouth.'

'Bollocks!' cried Zoe. 'That was *your* idea.'

Sam glanced at Fraser. 'See what I mean?'

Zoe rolled her eyes and grabbed her arm. 'Alright, Saint Samantha, let's get you inside so you can meet the Almighty.'

Sam let herself be dragged away. 'See you later, Fraser,' she called over her shoulder.

INSIDE THE FRONT DOORS, SAM STOPPED. EVERYTHING WAS huge. The entrance hall was bigger than a small house, with a grand staircase you could have driven a car up. And there were people everywhere.

She thought the set of *Elm Tree Lane* was busy, but this was another level. *Yes, it's called Hollywood. Now up your game.*

'You sure you want to do this?' Zoe asked.

Sam's heart was ping-ponging around inside her chest and her palms were sweating. She rubbed them down the outside of her pencil skirt and lifted her chin, tossing her hair back.

'Yeah, yeah, I'm ready. Let's do this.'

She followed Zoe through the ground floor of the castle until they reached a door. Zoe pushed it open and they entered. Sam swallowed.

There he was. Brad Bauer: megastar, man-whore and maker of dreams. He smiled at Zoe, the unveiling of his teeth brightening the room by a hundred watts.

'Hey, babe, everything okay?'

'Yeah, great, it's been such a fun morning. I wanted to introduce you to my best friend, Sam.'

Brad stood and strolled over, lifting Sam's hand and holding it in both of his. 'A real pleasure to meet you, Sam. I'm Brad.'

She stared. Brad Bauer was in front of her. He was touching her. Her synapses froze with overload and her brain crashed. She could feel a distant part of her consciousness screaming at her across the void.

Say something!

Her mouth opened, but there was nothing inside to come out.

Brad put his head to the side and a tiny bit of his ultra-smooth forehead moved. 'Hey, do I know you?'

Her brain fired back up. *Yes!* The magazines had worked. He knew she was Bethany, one of the stars of *Elm Tree Lane*.

'Yes, I'm—'

Brad dropped her hand and slapped his thigh with a crack that made her jump.

'Yeah, baby! I knew it! You sang the song with Jamie! I saw it on Instagram. Man, that was sick. The two of you...'

He thumped his fists together, then splayed them apart, mimicking an explosion.

'Boom!' He whacked himself in the centre of his chest and she jumped again. 'It got me here. Sucker punch to the heart, baby. Have you been together long?'

Sam's brain went from barely functioning to hyperdrive in a nanosecond. She saw herself and Jamie high up on the glen under a summer sky. Jamie was shirtless, playing his guitar, and she was wearing a dress with a white pinafore over the top, singing as she spun in circles. They were accompanied by an orchestra of grouse, goshawks, songbirds and sea eagles, all perching on the ground or the bushes of purple heather around them.

Her dream was disturbed by an internal klaxon informing her she was now speaking.

'Yes, we have. We've been writing for a couple of years now.'

What the fuck?

'We've been really inspired by your work, especially what you're doing with *Braveheart 2*. In fact, we've written an entire album dedicated to you. The title track is called "The Heart of Scotland".'

Brad's mouth fell open. 'Hot damn! Sing it for me now! I have to hear it!'

By now, Sam's fantasy had collapsed. Jamie had disappeared, lightning tore the sky to shreds, and the birds were killing and eating each other.

She kicked her terror under a rock. 'I can't without Jamie. Maybe later?'

Brad turned to a beautiful blonde hovering beside him. 'Speak to the dude at the pub, set something up the night before we wrap.' He stared back at Sam. 'This is intense, baby. I wanna hear it all!'

She plastered on her red-carpet smile. 'Absolutely. We can't wait to share our music with you.'

The door opened and a head popped around. 'Mr Bauer, they're ready for you now.'

Brad squeezed her hands. 'Crystal will be in touch to arrange it.' He strode out of the room, his assistant following, leaving Zoe and Sam alone.

The moment the door shut, Sam collapsed into a chair, her head in her hands.

'Oh fuck, oh fuck, oh fuck, oh fuck! What have I *done*?'

Zoe pissed herself laughing. '"The Heart of Scotland"? You're priceless!'

A new realisation burned through Sam, and she glanced up in horror.

'Shit, you've got to remove all those magazines you stashed about the place. He's got to think I'm a musician, not a bloody soap star.'

'That's the least of your problems. What are you going to tell Jamie? That he's got to come up with a load of new songs dedicated to Brad Bauer overnight?'

Sam groaned and sunk her head again. *Jamie*. 'Ugh. He doesn't even like me.'

Zoe rubbed her shoulder. 'That's not true. He's just never met anyone like you before. You're pretty intimidating.'

She gazed at her friend. *Please make this better for me.* 'Promise you'll come with me when I talk to him? There's less chance of him saying no if you're there.'

Zoe rolled her eyes. 'Of course, but then you're on your own.'

She let out a sigh. 'Thanks, sweetheart. You're the best.' She sat up straighter. 'I need a piece of paper.' There was a pile of call sheets on one of the tables and a pen. Turning the papers over to the blank side, she scribbled a title.

'What are you doing?' Zoe asked.

'Writing the lyrics for "The Heart of *bloody* Scotland". Now bugger off and leave me in peace, but keep your phone on. As soon as I'm done, you're coming with me to Morag's.'

Zoe grinned and left the room, quietly shutting the door behind her.

❦ 6 ❧

Sam stared at the piece of paper with the words 'The Heart of Scotland' at the top. *What now?* She closed her eyes and took a deep breath, resisting the temptation to bang her head against the table, then crawl underneath it and hide.

What had she been thinking? She'd spent her life acting out other people's words. She'd never written any of her own before. She gazed out the window. It was at the side of the castle and slightly elevated from the ground. Across the tightly parked trailers and the castle wall the mountains rose up to meet the clouds.

What did Scotland mean to the people who lived within its borders? Could millions of people's experiences be bottled and distilled down to a universal truth? What did Scotland mean to *her*?

Images of Jamie flashed through her mind like a slide show from the seventies. Jamie smiling, Jamie playing his guitar, Jamie in his boxers, Jamie half naked in a kilt, Jamie carrying her in his arms whilst half naked in a kilt, Jamie—

'Fuck's sake!' she yelled, shaking her head as if she could cast off the fantasies.

Her heart rate was rising, panicked pressure building. She stared out the window, focusing on the mountains.

Breathe in, two, three, four, and hold, two, three, four…

When she felt more in control, she wrote the word 'Scotland' in the middle of the piece of paper and drew a heart around it. Then she created a mind map, lines coming out of the heart with words she associated with Scotland and the Scottish people she knew.

She thought about Morag and Fiona. The way they'd opened their hearts and home to her. And Jamie and Duncan, who might have been considered taciturn had you not seen how they were with their families.

Loyalty, warmth, openness, fairness, power, pride, freedom, untamed, raw, wild, resolute. Words tumbled onto the paper. Suddenly she wasn't Sam anymore, she was a conduit. Ideas, phrases, feelings rushed through her and onto the paper. It was an outpouring she didn't stop to question.

Part of her knew that to stop for even a minute would cause the flood to slow to a trickle, then dry up. So she kept writing page after page of lyrics, for one song, then another, then another, mixing her memories, her dreams, her soul's deepest wishes into the stream of consciousness flowing through her.

At the end of writing the fifth song, she paused and looked at the table. It was strewn with paper, her handwriting a dynamic and almost unintelligible scrawl as if a spider had snorted speed, then gone to a breakbeat rave.

Whilst every part of her was still buzzing, she went back over each song, editing, tidying, then wrote them out again onto blank pieces of paper. She glanced out the window at the lowering sun. How long had she been writing?

Checking the time, her excitement tripped and fell into a pit of anxiety. *Shitsticks.* Jamie would be home from work soon. How could she tell him what she'd done? And how the fuck could she convince him to say yes?

AN HOUR AND A HALF LATER, SAM'S MOOD HAD BEEN rescued by Zoe, Fiona, and Morag, and given a fuel injection of nitrous oxide. The three women hadn't even needed Prosecco to hype themselves up. They'd decided Sam and Jamie were going to be the greatest song writing duo of all time. Morag was already planning which pictures in the living room she was going to take down so she could put up the Grammys they were going to win.

Sam's excitement had been genuine when she'd got back with Zoe, but now it was forced as she counted down the minutes till Jamie returned. There was too much chatter for her to practice her breathing technique. She pinched her thumbs and fingertips in turn under the table, counting up to four over and over again whilst her heart rate outran the second hand on the kitchen clock.

She was the first to notice Jamie's shadow behind the glass of the back door and wished she'd drunk something stronger than tea to prepare herself.

As he stepped through, all conversation around the table stopped. His body was still, but his eyes flicked from his mother to his sister to Zoe. He avoided looking at Sam altogether.

'What's going on?' he asked.

All heads around the table swivelled to look at her. Jamie's eyes were cold. She dug her nails into her palms and opened her mouth.

'No,' he said abruptly. 'Whatever it is, it's a no.' He turned his back, shucking his tool bag to the floor and his boots off as the room erupted.

'But you haven't heard what she's going to say, son!'

'Why don't you take your head out of your arse and listen!'

'Jamie, just give her one minute!'

Sam sat back. This was a disaster. He'd said no before he even knew what he was saying no to.

Liam began to cry, and Fiona bounced him up and down. 'Now look what you've done, you big lump.'

'It's not me that's done that, it's you lot!'

Morag grabbed him by the arm, steering him into a chair. He sat with a thump. 'Just open your ears and keep your mouth shut for five minutes. This is your big chance with Brad Bauer! He wants you to play for him again like you did a few months ago!'

Jamie shook his head vigorously. 'No way. Once was enough. Sitting up there on my own? Playing for *him*? Never again.'

'But you won't be on your own. Sam will be with you,' said Morag.

His cheeks were red. 'What?'

Sam felt her face heating under the intensity of his glare.

'She's arranged for the two of you to perform for him the night before the shoot ends,' said Zoe.

Confusion crossed his face as he did the maths.

'But that's the end of next week! Even if I agreed, *which I haven't*, she'd never have time to learn all the songs. It would be a mess.' There was another silence. 'What? What aren't you telling me?'

Sam cleared her throat. It was now or never. Meeting his gaze, she felt like a buttercup facing off against a flamethrower.

'Erm. We aren't going to be singing your songs. We're, er, going to be singing some new ones.'

There was a beat.

'*New* ones?' Jamie asked, his tone ominously low.

Her heart was galloping headlong towards the edge of a cliff. 'Yes. I, er, told Brad he'd inspired us to write an album.'

'Us?' yelled Jamie. Everyone jumped. '*An album?*'

Sam dug her heels in and reined her anxiety back.

'Yes,' she replied, sitting up straighter. 'And the title track is called "The Heart of Scotland".'

Jamie stared at her as if she'd completely lost her mind, then dropped his head to the table, thumping it up and down. Liam started crying again and Morag grabbed the back of Jamie's collar and pulled him up.

'Don't be a ninny. This is an incredible opportunity! You two are amazing together!'

'Mum, I can't dash off songs that quickly. It takes time. I need inspiration. "The Heart of Scotland"? I wouldn't even know where to start!'

Sam took the papers from the bag at her feet and placed them in front of him.

'I've already written the lyrics. And for at least four other songs.'

He looked away.

'Jamie!' said Morag sternly.

He sighed, picked up the sheets and slouched in his chair. No one moved. The room was silent, save for the sound of Liam snuffling in Fiona's arms. Sam watched the movements of Jamie's eyes, trying to read his expression as he turned the pages.

When he got to the end, he started again, and his face seemed to soften. The tips of his fingers were moving ever so slightly as if he were imagining what it might sound like on the guitar.

Sam's head felt so light she didn't know if she was about to pass out. She dug her nails into her thighs.

Eventually he put the sheaf of papers on the table. He didn't look up. 'They're actually quite good,' he said grumpily.

The room breathed.

'See! I told you—this is going to be amazing!' cried Morag. 'Let me get your guitar and you can start immediately.'

She bustled away and Jamie slumped a little lower.

'Do I get a choice in this?'

'Not really,' Fiona replied.

Zoe was looking uneasily at Jamie's bowed head. She gave Sam an encouraging smile, but it didn't reach her eyes.

Morag returned with his guitar, brandishing it as if she were the Lady of the Lake presenting King Arthur with his sword.

'Now why don't the two of you go upstairs to your room and get started? I'm going to put tea on.'

Jamie stared up at his mother as if she'd just suggested he take off all his clothes and start belly dancing.

'Why can't we do it in the living room?'

'Because I'm in there with Liam,' snapped Fiona. 'It's quieter upstairs. Anyway, you've got the biggest bloody room, you might as well use it.'

He took the guitar from his mother and stalked out. Sam pushed her chair back and grabbed her notes. Morag handed her a pen. She grinned at them all and mouthed a *thank you* before running out of the room after him.

Maybe, just *maybe*, this could work.

❧ 7 ❧

Jamie ran up the stairs, his body so hot he was sure his brain was melting. First Sam was in his house, and now she would be in his bedroom. It was too much.

He flung the door open and cast his eyes around. What would she see? A king-sized bed was on the left, up against the wall shared with the bathroom. He put the guitar on top of the duvet, grabbed the book he was currently reading and kicked it under the bed.

There was a desk he once used for schoolwork with clothes draped over the back of the chair in front. He bundled them up and threw them into the wardrobe. For the first time ever as an adult male, he was grateful for the fact his mum still tidied his room.

He spun in a circle, trying to see the room through the eyes of a woman. A confident, clever, beautiful, famous, self-assured woman. She was literally everything he wasn't. He wanted her with every part of his body and soul, but he also wanted her permanently beyond the borders of the known universe.

There was a tentative knock on the door.

He sat on the edge of the bed, legs together, hands folded in his lap.

'Come in.'

Sam poked her head around the door, then entered. She put the papers on his desk.

'Do you want to take a shower?' she asked.

'What?'

'A shower. You normally have one when you come back from work?'

Sweat was trickling down the back of his neck. *She doesn't mean a shower with you, idiot!* He exhaled a ragged breath and stared at her pink fluffy mules.

'I'll have one later.' There was no fucking way he was going to stand up right now.

An excruciating silence filled the room.

'Are you okay?' she asked.

He met her gaze again. She looked concerned, chewing on her lower lip. He swallowed and gripped his hands together tighter to stop them shaking.

She sighed. 'I know this wasn't what you were expecting to come home to today.'

He shook his head.

'Thank you for at least giving it a go.'

He nodded, unable to find any words.

She clapped her hands. 'Okay! Shall we get started?'

He stared at her, his mind a screen of white noise. He'd never done this before. His songs were personal, private. They'd been created in secret over months and years. And now she was expecting him to write new ones with her? A stranger? Just like that?

'I know what we need to do.' She toed off her slippers.

'Let's start with some warm-ups.' She ran her hands through her hair. 'Okay, just follow me.'

She rolled her head in circles, breathing in deeply through her nose as it went back, then exhaling loudly through her mouth as it came forward. She interlocked her hands in front of her, pressed the palms away, and raised her arms over her head.

'Follow my lead,' she instructed as she windmilled her arms.

Jamie stared. The only thing he was following was the fabric of her top as it framed and caressed her breasts with every movement she made.

Fuck's sake!

Now she was jumping up and down and exhaling 'ha, ha, ha,' each time her feet landed on the carpet. His heart was hammering in his chest. He couldn't do this. His breathing started to change.

She flung her arms up, gazed at the ceiling, and started ululating. He dropped his head, focusing on the whiteness of the tendons stretching across the back of his knuckles as his mouth fell open to draw in more air.

'Jamie?'

He struggled to calm his breathing in the sudden quiet. Small hands covered his and he flinched.

She withdrew. 'I'm so sorry.'

Sam pulled the chair away from the desk and sat, far enough away from him that he knew she couldn't touch him.

You can do this. As long as she stayed out of reach, he could stay in control. He deliberately released his hands, stretched them out and ran them through his hair, nails raking across his scalp.

'We can do your warm-up instead,' she suggested. 'What do you normally do?'

He huffed out a short laugh. 'I just start singing.' He felt like he'd been run over by a truck. 'That was your warm-up?'

'That was only the beginning.'

'The beginning? What's coming next? The alarm for a nuclear attack? Warning sirens for the zombie apocalypse?'

She giggled. 'Do you want to see?'

'Only if I don't have to join in.'

'You don't want to participate?'

Jamie crossed his arms in front of him.

'I could give you a sticker?'

He raised his eyebrows and she held up her hands.

'Okay, okay. So, I'll make this quick. I won't do the full half-hour.'

'Half an *hour*?'

She was already shrugging her shoulders up and down. 'Uh-huh.' She raised her arms over her head again and Jamie glanced away. In his peripheral vision he saw her bend at the waist, her hands grazing the floor, bottom wiggling from side to side. He closed his eyes.

'Raaaaaaaaahhhhhh!'

He leapt back on the bed. *What the fuck?* Sam was in front of the mirror on the door of the wardrobe with her mouth open wide, roaring like a lioness. She then scrunched her face up tightly as if she was biting into a lemon. After a few of these, she stuck her tongue out and tugged on it, pulling it out, down, then from side to side. He looked on in horror and she caught his eye in the reflection.

'Ih ohay, ih ugun hur,' she reassured him. She let go of her tongue and flexed her lips. 'The tip of the tongue and the teeth and the lips,' she repeated over and over again so fast, her mouth was a blur.

When she finally drew breath, she started saying 'onion' at a really high pitch, stretching out the 'ny' sound as she brought her voice down low. 'Red lorry, yellow lorry, red lorry, yellow lorry,' she repeated, getting quicker and quicker until she ended with another roar and folded her body forward again.

'Am I meant to clap?'

Sam straightened with a laugh, put her high-heeled mules back on, and sat in the chair facing the bed. 'Not at all.'

'Does everyone on *Elm Tree Lane* do that?'

'Most people do something. Me and Loz do the exercises together. Ian warms up by practising his orgasm face in the mirror.'

She picked up the pile of papers she'd written her lyrics on and flicked through them.

Jamie felt his face flood with heat. He'd seen Sam kissing Ian on screen and attending red-carpet events on his arm. Now he knew they were even closer in real life. Did Ian mind that she was here trying to catch Brad Bauer's eye? Did he even care?

He reached for his guitar and tuned it.

'I don't know how to do this,' he said quietly.

He heard her exhale and glanced at her. She was so beautiful it made his chest hurt. She seemed unsure.

'If it makes you feel any better, neither do I,' she said.

'But you've written music before?'

She shook her head.

He indicated the paper in her hand. 'What's all that then?'

Sam shrugged. 'Desperation and divine intervention? I have no idea how I came up with this. How do you write your music?'

'It takes a long time. Months sometimes before a song comes together. A lot of trial and error and playing to the harshest critic ever.'

'Your mum?'

'God, no. I could have come up with "Baby Shark" and

she'd still think I was Mozart. No, it's Fi. She's the first to tell me what I've written is a crock of shite. But if she's bad, then there's someone even worse than her.'

'Duncan?'

'No, he's my best mate, so he's usually got my back. The Simon Cowell of this family is Liam.'

She snorted. 'Liam, as in *baby* Liam?'

He nodded. 'When he was about three months old, Duncan was away on the rigs and Fi and Liam were staying here. It was late at night and he was going mental. There was nothing they could do to soothe the wee man. Mum was about to bring out the whisky, so I played my music as a last resort, and it did the trick. Fi now calls me the baby whisperer. If they can't get him to sleep, they call me in. But if he doesn't like what I'm playing he kicks off.' He smiled at her. 'There's no politeness filter on a baby.'

Sam grinned. 'A lot of shit, but no bullshit?'

'Exactly.'

The smile hung in the air between them and his heart filled. He could never have Sam, but he could have this.

Making music was something he had over all the Ian Berresfords and Brad Bauers of the world. They may have been rich, good-looking, and charismatic, but they weren't sitting here with her now, about to create something unique that might outlast them all. Despite the gnawing anxiety inside, he was determined to try and make this work.

'Okay, why don't we start with "The Heart of Scotland"?' he asked, taking his phone out of his back pocket. 'I thought we could record bits as we go along and see how we get on. Sound okay to you?'

. . .

AT NINE O'CLOCK, AFTER AN HOUR OF ASSURING MORAG they were about to come down to dinner, his mother entered the room, took Jamie's guitar off him, and ordered him and Sam downstairs to eat.

Jamie was relieved for the break. Being with Sam was like being perpetually tasered by Eros and Aphrodite. It was the first time he'd ever fallen truly in love, and he was exhausted by the experience.

Everything about her was more than he could handle.

Her energy and creativity were explosive. While he was cautious, she threw ideas around like rice at a wedding, happy to immediately discard them if they didn't seem to work. She was encouraging, listening with rapt attention to every chord progression he played, then asking what he thought of it before she gave her opinion.

It was as if he'd just learned to walk and now she was expecting them to enter a ballroom dancing competition and win first place.

'So, how's it going up there?' his mother asked.

He shrugged and Sam rolled her eyes. 'Grumpy guts here doesn't realise how good it's sounding. I think we've already nailed the chorus for "The Heart of Scotland".'

He took a swig of beer. 'I think it's more stuck to the wall like a Post-it note at the moment.'

Sam inhaled the last bits of food on her plate and sat back with a sigh. 'Thank you, Morag—that'll give us our second wind. Can I wash up?'

His mother took the plate from her. 'Don't be daft.' She turned to him. 'Come on, son. Don't keep the lady waiting.'

They were staring at him like he was an exhibit at the zoo. He pushed his plate away, his appetite gone.

'I'm done.'

Sam clapped her hands and bounced on the balls of her feet, then skipped out of the room.

Jamie glanced at his mum. 'Did she just *skip*?'

Morag grinned and winked at him. 'Aye, son, yes she did.'

BACK UPSTAIRS, SAM WAS SITTING ON THE CHAIR AT THE desk, far enough from the bed that accidental contact was impossible. She was singing quietly to herself, the pages of notes in her hand.

The pen was twisted in her hair to form a bun, revealing the line of her neck. Jamie wanted to kiss it, feel her soft skin against his lips, then pull the pen out to have her hair fall over his cheek.

She smiled at him. 'There you are. I thought we could go through the chorus again and try and nail the verse. Or Post-it, if you'd prefer?'

He nodded and turned away, picking up the guitar as if it were a shield.

They worked into the night and Jamie didn't think to look at the clock until there was a lull in their talking and the unmistakable sounds of his mother's snores filtered through the wall.

Sam giggled. 'Oh my god, last night I heard that and thought it was you.'

His neck prickled. 'I don't snore.'

'Are you sure now, Jamie MacDougall? How many women have confirmed that fact?'

He looked away, his face on fire.

'Oh, I'm only teasing. Your sex life is your own business.' She yawned. 'Well, I'm going to bed before I turn into a pumpkin. Do you want to use the bathroom first?'

He shook his head.

'Okay, I won't be long. Thank you, Jamie.'

He shrugged.

'Sleep well,' she continued.

He nodded.

There was a pause, then she shut the bedroom door.

He exhaled the tension away. How the fuck could he sleep after all of that? He put the guitar down carefully and sat in the chair by the desk. It was still warm. He picked up the pieces of paper, running his fingertips over the chaos of her handwriting.

Sam was unlike anyone he'd ever met—a beautiful little party popper that didn't stop popping. Or a hand grenade he longed to go off in his arms. She had the power to bend time and everyone to her will and he was completely defenceless against her.

'Jamie?'

He jumped. She was standing in the doorway, dressed in her 'cute but crazy' Stitch pyjama set, her make-up off and her cheeks pink. She was breathtaking.

'I knocked but you didn't answer.'

How long had he been sitting there, staring into space like a muppet for?

'I just wanted to say it's all yours.'

Huh?

'It's available.'

'Er...'

'The bathroom?'

'Yeah, thanks,' he mumbled, turning to hide his face. 'Good night.'

'Sleep well, Jamie.'

. . .

Jamie lay in bed, staring at the swirls of Artex on the ceiling, running the past couple of days over and over in his head.

A cold shower had done nothing to turn down the heat of his desire and even the hypnotic sound of his mother's snores couldn't lull him to sleep. He faced away from the wall closest to Sam as if by turning his back he could stop her running roughshod through his mind and body.

Still awake at 2.00 a.m., he calculated how many hours of sleep he'd already lost to her. Eventually, in desperation, he turned over, touching the wall. He rested his forehead against it and closed his eyes. Sleep finally took him.

&8&

Jamie slept fitfully, back and forth across the border of dreams, chasing Sam like a fugitive. But she was always one step out of reach. He called out to her, again and again, but she just laughed over her shoulder and skipped on in her 'crazy but cute' pyjama set.

Finally she stopped and faced him. They were in the desert, a line in the sand between them. She held out her hand as if in invitation. Could he take it? As he reached across the invisible divide, a shrill siren sounded. He glanced down. The ground between them was moving, the line growing into a wall.

It was now as high as his knees.

'Jamie! Jamie!' she shouted. 'Come on!'

Everything was dust, noise and confusion. He wanted to climb over, but the more he thought about it, the higher it grew. Sam was now wearing a yellow hard hat, yelling his name, trying to make herself heard over the sound of the alarm. He tried to move but his legs didn't work. A snake was twisting around them, tighter and tighter.

'Sam!' he cried desperately. 'Sam!'

'Jamie!'

He opened his eyes and crashed into reality. The first thing he saw was Sam, fully dressed, standing above him. The second thing he saw was his phone in her hand. She was holding it out to face him and the words 'Boss-man' were flashing on the screen. The room was filled with the sound of the siren he'd given Gregor for a ringtone.

He glanced at his bedside clock. *Half past ten?*

'What do you want me to do?' she asked. 'He's been ringing all morning, but you wouldn't wake up.'

He stared blankly at her. He needed to move. But he was naked. *Very* naked.

'I can't,' he began, trying to drag his mind to the same level of alertness as his cock. He squeezed his eyes shut. He needed her out of his room. 'I can't. Please, can you...' He drew in a terse breath. 'Can you just—'

'Mr Andrews? This is Dr Esther Adamson speaking,' Sam said into the phone. 'I'm one of the registrars at Raigmore hospital. I need to inform you that Mr MacDougall won't be back to work until a week on Monday at the earliest.'

Jamie's mouth hung open as a perfectly posh and melodious Edinburgh accent filled the room.

Sam caught his eye and winked. 'What's wrong with him?' Her confidence seemed to falter, and her eyes widened. 'Um...'

Her cheeks were pink and the tip of her tongue ran out to wet her lips.

'I'm afraid I'm not at liberty to say,' she replied. She gave Jamie another wink as if she had the situation completely under control. She frowned. 'Yes, it is serious. They're currently prepping him for surgery.'

What?

There was a pause, then Sam put her free hand on her hip. Her posture changed as she stood straighter.

'Are you trying to tell me how to do my job, Mr Andrews?' she asked, pacing up and down. 'The foreign body is clearly visible on the X-ray just above the iliac crest. And despite the acute cramping peristalsis waves, it's gone past the rectum and ascended into the sigmoid colon.'

What the fuck?

Sam was now facing away, gesticulating as if auditioning for a medical drama. 'There's a perforation risk if we attempt to remove the object via endoscopy. That's why we're prepping Mr MacDougall and the colorectal surgery team for a laparotomy.'

No, no, no, no!

He could still fix this. He just needed to get to his phone. He thrashed to free himself from the sheets, but his legs were still caught. He was already near the edge of the bed and before he could stop himself, he rolled off and landed on the floor with an almighty thump.

'Yes, of course, I'll make sure he gets the message. The object? Well, I'm not at liberty to divulge any details, but let's just say Mr MacDougall now knows the correct purpose for a deodorant stick. Okay, bye now, Mr Andrews.'

Sam finished the call and turned to face him, a huge smile on her face that dropped off when she saw the look on his.

He was shaking with rage and shame. 'What the fuck have you done?' he growled.

Sam chewed her bottom lip. 'I, I got you time off work.'

'By telling my boss I shoved a deodorant stick so far up my arse it got stuck?'

She laughed nervously and blushed. 'I, er, um, I—'

'Get out!' he yelled. 'Go!'

She scurried out and he pushed himself to his feet, untangling the bedclothes and throwing them angrily to the floor.

He stared down at his cock, still wanting Sam despite everything she'd done.

'Fuck off!' he roared at it.

It responded by bobbing as if to remind him it wasn't going anywhere.

'I said, FUCK! OFF!'

He sat on the edge of his bed and sank his head into his hands. How could he ever fix this?

TWENTY MINUTES LATER JAMIE WAS STANDING OUTSIDE HIS sister's house, his heart racing.

Fiona opened the door and her face fell.

'Jesus Christ, Jamie. What's happened? Why aren't you at work? Is it Mum? Is Mum okay?'

'She's fine. Everything's fine.'

Fiona slapped him on the arm. 'Don't you *ever* do that to me again, you big lump,' she yelled, her chin wobbling.

'Fuck's sake, Fi, I haven't done anything!'

She hit him again and swiped at her eyes. 'Then why are you here with that look on your face? Jesus, Jamie. You can't do that to me.'

Duncan appeared behind her, holding Liam. He stroked Fiona's shoulder and kissed the top of her head. 'Hey, Jamie, what's up? Wanna come in?'

He shook his head, trying to communicate he needed help that didn't involve his sister.

Duncan nodded at him, then turned to his wife. 'Fi, love, why don't Jamie and I take Liam for a walk? There's a cup of tea and a biscuit with your name on them inside. Go enjoy a bit of peace and quiet for half an hour.'

Fiona nodded, gave him and Liam a kiss, shot a dirty look at Jamie, and went back inside.

Duncan grabbed the pushchair, strapped Liam in, and they set off.

'Have you had any breakfast?' Duncan asked.

Jamie shook his head.

'Let's head into town.'

He stopped and shook his head more violently.

'To the café. I'm not taking you back to your mum's.'

'We can't. If people see me eating there they'll know something's up and tell Mum.'

Duncan sighed. 'You'd rather go hungry than risk your mum finding out you've eaten at the café?'

Jamie nodded.

He shrugged. 'Okay, mate. Let's go to the park.'

They walked in silence until they reached an expanse of green with a few swings and a modern adventure playground. Liam had fallen asleep, so they sat on a park bench and watched the toddlers playing.

'So, are you going to tell me what's happened?' Duncan asked.

Jamie sunk his head into his hands.

'Did she walk into the bathroom when you were in the shower?'

He shook his head.

'Did you walk into the bathroom when *she* was in the shower?'

Jamie shook his head again and sighed.

'Did you piss her off?'

'No.'

'Jeez, this is like twenty fucking questions. Did she piss *you* off?'

He nodded. 'I'm not talking about Mum, you know.'

'You're not talking at all, mate. And I don't have to be

brains of fucking Britain to know this is about Sam. Just tell me what's happened. You'll feel better once you let it out.'

JAMIE DID NOT FEEL BETTER ONCE HE'D TOLD DUNCAN. HIS brother-in-law—and now ex-best friend—laughed so hard he cried, making high-pitched 'he, he, he' sounds that woke Liam up.

'It's not fucking funny,' Jamie hissed.

Duncan wiped his eyes as he pushed Liam back and forth. 'I'm sorry, mate, but it's fucking hilarious. She's even wilder than your sister. No wonder they get on so well.'

'I can't do this, Dunc. I can't write music with her. I can't be anywhere near her.'

'So, what are you going to do then? Ring Boss-man and tell him it's a joke? Go back to the site this afternoon? Live with us and bunk in with Liam until she goes?'

Jamie hung his head. Even if he fessed up to Gregor, he couldn't sleep on the floor of Liam's room. It wasn't just the logistics of sharing a small room with a baby, but the fact his mum would throw a fit if he did.

'Jamie. Listen to me. Sam is the best thing that's ever happened to you.'

His head jerked up. 'Are you having a fucking laugh?'

Duncan shook his head, his face serious. 'I mean it.'

He stood, his body wired. 'How the *hell* do you come to that conclusion? I've had a good life for the last twenty-seven years and now she shows up and it's a fucking train wreck.'

Duncan ran his hand over his face. 'Jamie, you're my best mate. Even if I wasn't married to your sister, I'd do anything for you. You know that, right?'

Jamie shrugged, suddenly afraid of what was coming next.

'But you're hiding from life. You have nothing to challenge

you, and fuck all responsibility. No property, no business, no girlfriend. Mate, you're twenty-seven and you still live at home with your mum. Your comfort zone is about an inch away from your body and each year it shrinks. Sam is *exactly* what you need because she's shaking you up. She's forcing you to do things you don't want to but need to. What would have happened if she'd never showed up, eh? Would you still be living at home when you're thirty-seven? Forty-seven? The longer you stay, the harder it is to leave.'

'But Mum needs me.'

'Does she? Really? She was pregnant when she lost your dad, and she raised you and Fi on her own. If she could do that, then she can cope without you under her feet. Look, I know she doesn't let you do stuff around the house, but she worries about you, and I know for a fact she wants more for your life. And maybe having you moping about cramps *her* style.'

Jamie looked at Duncan as if he'd suggested his mum wanted to start pole dancing in the village hall.

He shook his head. 'You're cracked.'

'Am I? Have you asked her what she really wants for the rest of her life? Because from where I sit, the two of you are living half lives. And in this case, they don't make a whole.'

Jamie stared at the mums playing with their kids in the park. Some of them were from his year at school. He felt tired and empty. He knew in his bones what Duncan had said was true. But it was too tight a knot to unpick. There were too many strands to unravel.

'So, what am I meant to do now?' he asked.

'Go back home and apologise to Sam.'

'What?'

'Yes. Apologise. Be the fucking man, Jamie. She didn't mean any harm. She just got flustered and carried away. What she did is a gift. You've finally got the opportunity to make something of your music and hang out with someone who's got enough spark to power the whole of Kinloch. Look, Sam's a long way from home and living in a stranger's house. You're twice her size and you yelled at her, then stormed off. Zoe can't be there for her as she's too busy with the shoot and she'll be too embarrassed to speak to your mum. Go home, Jamie. Go home and take a chance on life.'

﹡ 9 ﹡

Sam sat cross-legged on her bed, hugging a pillow, replaying what she'd said on the phone to Jamie's boss and the look on Jamie's face as he yelled at her to get out.

She'd scuttled back to her room but couldn't escape the vehemence in his voice as the words 'just fuck off' had reverberated through the walls. The thundering of his feet down the stairs and the slamming of the back door had shaken her further.

You fucking, fucking idiot.

When would she learn? She snapped back into her childhood memories as easily as a brand-new rubber band. Her father incredulous, her mother confused, her two elder sisters amused or exasperated whenever she did something out of left-field.

'*Smulan,*' her father would say, his patience wearing thin. '*This is not the time or the place for your theatrics.*'

Her stomach tightened and she pursed her lips to exhale a long, slow breath.

She'd never fitted in. The Adamsons had been the perfect nuclear family until she'd shown up and turned them thermonuclear. Her mother had easy pregnancies with her sisters and they'd slept through the night from birth.

Sam shook her head. *Of course they had.* Esther and Anna were incapable of putting a foot wrong: beautiful, studious, well behaved.

'You weren't an accident, darling, you were the best possible surprise,' her mother would reassure her. However, Sam soon understood that when her father referred to her as 'a gift from Loki', it wasn't a good thing.

Sam been born premature, with gut issues that caused her to scream for hours. Her sisters, then aged five and seven, found themselves living with a banshee they couldn't return to sender, whose capacity to annoy them only increased as Sam became mobile. She was a cuckoo crossed with a gremlin and had never fitted in.

She took out her phone, feeling awful about what she'd done. She knew how busy Zoe was and she was also Jamie's friend, so she couldn't speak to her. Could she ring one of her sisters?

Esther didn't answer, neither did Anna or her mum. She didn't have Jamie's number and didn't want to disturb Morag, who was working in the post office, and tell her what she'd done.

What now? She picked up the song lyrics she'd been working on. At least this was something she could do.

AN HOUR LATER THE BACK DOOR OPENED. SAM RAN DOWN the stairs, stopping at the threshold to the kitchen as Jamie entered. His eyes met hers, then flicked away. He took a big breath.

'I'm sorry,' she interrupted. 'I didn't think and then it was too late. If you let me have your boss's number, I'll ring him now to explain and apologise.'

Jamie shook his head and her heart rate increased.

Fuck! How could she make this right?

He gazed at her with his deep, soulful brown eyes. '*I'm* sorry.'

Oh god, this was it. He was stopping their song writing just as it was getting started. A surge of emotion pushed against the tightness of her throat.

Don't cry! You've created this reality. Deal with it.

'I shouldn't have shouted at you like that,' he continued. 'It was just, erm, I hadn't, er.' He shut his mouth and swallowed. 'There's no excuse.'

Sam stared at him in shock. Before she was even aware, his face had blurred and fat tears spilled down her cheeks.

'Jesus, Sam... don't cry.'

She gasped in a strangled breath, shocked at how much emotion was pouring out.

He rushed to her, his hands wavering as if uncertain what he was meant to do with them.

'Are you okay?' he asked, looking so unsure and lost it made her giggle.

She nodded. 'You look like you don't know what to do with me.'

'I don't.'

'What do you do when your mum or sister cry?'

'Mum only cries when I play my guitar, so I just roll my eyes. If Fiona cries, she's usually hitting me at the same time, so I don't have to do anything except get out of the way.'

Sam wiped her eyes. 'We could always have a hug?'

He backed away and collided with the kitchen table.

'Or not?' She couldn't work out whether he was petrified or

horrified by the prospect.

He sat down on the other side of the table.

Well, if you were in any doubt about if he likes you or not, there's your answer. She leaned back against the worktop.

'Have you had any breakfast this morning?' she asked.

He shook his head.

'Would you like me to cook you brunch?'

'You can cook?'

'Er. I'm thirty and left home at eighteen. It's a pretty basic life-skill to have.'

He blushed.

Shit! Had she put her foot in it again? She went to the fridge and rummaged around. 'Bacon, eggs, black pudding?' She glanced over her shoulder at him. 'Any good? If you want vegetables, I could squirt some tomato ketchup on the side?'

He smiled and rubbed his hand into his hair. Sam itched to touch it.

Why does he have to be so fucking hot?

'It sounds amazing and I am hungry. But...'

She continued taking food out of the fridge. 'But what?'

'Mum doesn't trust me in the kitchen.'

Sam made a show of inspecting herself. 'Yep, all confirmed. I'm definitely not you.' He grinned and her stomach flipped. *Oh my god, his smile...*

'She doesn't really trust *anyone*.'

Sam waved a spatula in the air. 'Well, I'm not just anyone. I'm *special*. I'm Sam Adams, star of *Elm Tree Lane* and bessie mate to the future Countess of Kinloch.'

'Zoe and Rory are getting married?'

She shrugged. 'I predict they'll be married and pregnant by the end of the year. Have you seen the way he looks at her? Jesus. The intensity practically melts her clothes off. No one's ever looked at me like that. Ever.'

He blushed even deeper and stared at his lap.

Was she being too much again? She repressed a sigh. She was *always* too much. Donning one of Morag's pinnies, she turned the stove on.

'How do you like your eggs and bacon? And *unfertilised* is not an acceptable answer from a man.' She heard a snort of laughter behind her and smiled.

'I don't mind. However they come.'

'Unfertilised it is then.'

'Are you eating?'

She shook her head. 'I ate earlier with your mum. I think she's trying to fatten me up. I'm a bit worried I'm going to wake up one morning with an apple in my mouth.'

She glanced over her shoulder to drink in his laughter again. It was like mulled cider, making her warm and drowsy inside. She needed to stop staring at him.

She turned back to the stove. All-day cooked breakfasts were her specialty. She was quick and efficient, having worked in a greasy spoon café during her drama degree.

Everything was smelling delicious when the door flung open with a crash and Morag ran in, wielding a fire extinguisher. Jamie leapt to his feet to grab it from her. She was wide-eyed, looking around the room as if to check it was still in one piece.

'Is everything okay?' Sam asked.

Morag was eyeing the stove top as if Sam were cooking crystal meth and it was about to go critical. 'I, er, if you need any food, I'm here, love. I, er, you, erm...'

'I was just cooking brunch for Jamie. Is that okay?'

She turned to Jamie as if discovering the kingpin behind the meth operation. He put the extinguisher down and held up his hands.

'I told her you don't trust anyone to use your kitchen.'

His mother smoothed down the outside of her skirt, her cheeks pink. She let out a nervous laugh.

'I never said that, son.' She turned to Sam. 'It's just he tried to cook his tea and it went wrong. I had to use the fire extinguisher. And he hurt himself very badly.'

'Mum, I was ten! I burned some toast and baked beans, that's all. And there isn't even a scar.'

Morag put her hand to her heart as if the memory was the deepest scar of all.

Jamie tugged up the sleeve of his T-shirt. 'Go on then, show me. Where is it?'

Sam followed Morag over, feigning interest in a scar she could already see no longer existed. His arms were mouth-watering. Maybe if she got a little closer, she could see if he smelled like his shower gel?

Morag patted her head. 'Hang on, I need my glasses.'

Jamie lowered his arm and moved away. 'See? There's no reason why you can't let us cook.'

His mother glanced back at the stove. 'Well, Sam seems to know what she's doing. There's no point in you doing it, son. It's quicker for me to cook than show you how.'

Jamie rolled his eyes and went to a cupboard for a plate.

Morag dithered, appearing reluctant to leave the room and get back to the post office.

Sam turned the burners off, which seemed to reassure her.

Morag nodded. 'Okay, then.'

Jamie lifted the fire extinguisher. 'Do you want this? We've already got one in here.'

But his mother was backing out of the room. 'No, you keep it. Just in case, okay?' She didn't wait for a reply, but exited and closed the door behind her.

Sam caught Jamie's eye and giggled as he raised his eyebrows. 'Okay, I get it now.'

She dished up his food, thrilled as she watched him tucking in. She took off her pinny, feeling like she'd just been transported back to the fifties, and sat opposite him.

'This is fantastic, thank you,' he said. 'No one has ever cooked for me, apart from my mum and my sister, and this is...' He glanced at the closed door as if his mother might be listening. 'Merely passable,' he said loudly before lowering his voice to a whisper. 'It's the best, but if you tell anyone I said that, I'll deny it to the grave.'

Sam preened.

'Can I ask you something?'

She shrugged, suddenly nervous.

'How did you know all that medical stuff you told my boss? You've never played a doctor or a nurse in anything.'

How did he know?

'My family are doctors,' she replied. 'My dad is an orthopaedic surgeon, and my mum is a GP. My eldest sister, Esther, is a neurosurgeon and Anna is a GP.'

'They're all doctors?'

She nodded.

'And your eldest sister is an *actual* brain surgeon?'

She nodded again.

'So, no pressure on you growing up then,' he said with a smile.

Did he understand?

'Yeah, being a doctor is a piece of piss,' she replied. 'It's basically a hobby. My parents were so relieved someone in the family finally got a *proper* job. Acting is where career stability, longevity and pensions really lie.'

EMOTIONS COMPETED FOR ATTENTION INSIDE JAMIE. RELIEF the apology had worked, pain that he'd made Sam cry, joy that he'd made her laugh, nerves about being in her company, excitement about what might happen next, and warmth that she'd cooked for him.

So, this is what love feels like.

The emotions were a kaleidoscope of storms and sunshine, all making up a blinding rainbow. He was glad he'd avoided falling in love before now. It was exhausting trying to process it all. He needed to find something to talk about that was safe and neutral.

'How many times have you visited Scotland before?'

'This is my fourth visit. The other three times I was performing at the Edinburgh Fringe.'

'Did you get to see much of the city? Or visit outside?'

She shook her head. 'We were either on stage, watching other performances, or fighting for punters on the Royal Mile.'

'So, you're writing songs about the heart of Scotland, but your experience is limited to luvvies, tourists, and the odd Edinburger?'

'I went to a concert featuring twenty bagpipers in a room that held twenty-five. Doesn't that count in my favour?'

Jamie mouthed, *'So you're deaf then as well?'*

Sam giggled. 'Ha, ha. They actually handed out ear plugs at the door. The night was called "An Intimate Evening with Bagpipes".'

His shoulders heaved as he laughed and he shook his head. 'Jesus. I'm surprised you survived.'

'Only just. We staggered out afterwards and couldn't walk straight for a week. I was never the same woman again.'

'Do you want to see a bit of Kinloch? Maybe we could go for a stroll and I could show you some of where I grew up.'

'Now? Outside?' She was gazing out the window with a

frown.

'It's not raining. Are you outside intolerant as well as gluten intolerant?'

'I'm outside *allergic*—unless it involves the four S's.'

Jamie tried to work out what she was talking about. She had a cheeky smile on her face that he didn't trust. 'Sun?'

She nodded.

'Sea?'

She nodded again. His cock was rising with his heart rate.

'Sand?'

'Uh-huh. And the last one?'

He clamped his mouth shut as his brain screamed *'SEX!'* He shrugged, cheeks on fire. Sam dipped her head to one side. He swallowed.

'It's Sssssssangria.'

His shoulders slumped with relief.

'What did you think I was going to say, Jamie?'

He stood. 'Let's go out.'

THEY EXITED THE HOUSE DOWN THE BACK LANE TOWARDS the high street. Sam was wearing high-heeled boots, a tight skirt, and a tailored jacket. She looked a million dollars. Jamie felt like a dirty penny no one wanted to pick up.

'So, where are you taking me?' she asked.

'A place Zoe, Fi and I spent a lot of time when we were growing up. It's really beautiful and not far.'

A wind whipped around them and Sam shivered, hugging her arms across her chest.

'Are you warm enough?' he asked. 'Do you want my jacket?'

She stared at it and her cheeks pinked. She shook her head. 'I'm fine. Lead on, Macduff.'

He grinned and turned right down the hill. 'Okay, but you

know it's actually—'

'Yes, yes, "lay on, Macduff". But "lead on" sounds so much better.'

They smiled at each other and his heart jumped. He was outside, in public, with a beautiful woman. It was utterly new and completely surreal. He was desperate to hold her hand but knew he couldn't, so jammed his in the pockets of his jacket.

Enjoy what you can get.

He was going to show her something special to him, and he had her all to himself.

'Sam! Cooee!'

Oh, for fuck's sake.

Mrs McCreedie and her friends were blocking the road.

Sam stopped for a second and her body tensed. Then she smiled and carried on towards the matriarchs of Kinloch.

Mrs McCreedie was beckoning her as if she were a queen summoning her into the inner circle.

'Look who it is! Come here, dear.'

Jamie hung back as Sam was drawn into the middle of a squall of grey hair and glasses. Since the truck had crashed into the side of her house, Mrs McCreedie was living her best life. She'd been rescued by two young men and was the first person in the village outside of Morag's family to have met Sam—a bona fide famous person off the telly.

The women seemed to possess a gravitational field all their own as passers-by were sucked in. The group grew larger and Jamie was pushed further back.

'And, did you know that Wayne character waxes his chest! Tell them, Sam. Tell them what you told me. It's smooth as a baby's bum. Not like Morag's wee boy, Jamie.'

He cringed as Mrs McCreedie's voice carried over the crowd.

'No, young Jamie's got chest hair like a man.'

Like a man?

'But that's not all! Sam told me... What's his real name, lass? Ian? So, Ian—that's Wayne's real name—he also waxes...' She broke off and Jamie could see the grey heads leaning closer. '*Down there!*' Mrs McCreedie hissed loudly.

There was a sharp intake of breath.

'Why?' a couple of the women asked.

'Apparently, it makes *it* look bigger!'

'No!'

'Is that normal? Is that what all the young folk are doing nowadays?'

Seven heads swivelled in unison to look questioningly at Jamie.

'Mrs McCreedie,' Sam interrupted. 'Shall we take some more photos? We can use my phone and I'll email them to your grandson again?'

Jamie sagged against the wall of a shop. Was this what being with a famous person was like? Sam had been in his life for a few short days and yet at every turn he had to share her.

They should never have left the house. This was a mistake. Sam was smiling and chatting to everyone, the perfect example of confident sociability, whereas he felt like an awkward and grumpy teenager.

Spots of rain hit his cheeks.

Not now!

Sam extricated herself from the crowd and grabbed his arm. He couldn't breathe.

'Come on,' she whispered, dragging him away. 'Bye!' she called over her shoulder. 'See you again soon! Don't forget the concert next week!'

Jamie's stomach lurched. He'd forgotten all about it. Now he wanted to be sick.

Sam gazed at him with concern and dropped his arm.

'Sorry, I didn't mean to touch you, I was just trying to get away.'

He felt more rain. 'We should go back.'

'No, it's fine. We can keep going. Are we going to see the loch?'

He nodded.

She smiled brightly. 'I'm sure it's beautiful.'

They walked more quickly down the high street, then Jamie led her off to the right, through a gap in a stone wall and down to the rocky shore. The rain clouds were emptying themselves over the water. The only thing before them was a wall of grey.

Sam pushed a wet strand of hair out of her face. 'It's er, very, er... majestic.'

Jamie gritted his teeth. This was a woman who'd seen the world and he was showing her a whole lot of nothing.

'Is this where you bring all the girls?' She was still smiling, but the rain was running down her face and taking her eye make-up with it.

He jammed his hands deeper into his pockets. He didn't want to answer her.

'Were you ever interested in Zoe? Your mum said she wanted the two of you to get together.'

He stared at his feet.

'Did you ever kiss her?'

'It's none of your business. I don't want to talk about stuff like that. We're here to write music. That's all.'

Her laugh sounded flat. 'I'm not going to tell Mrs McCreedie your secrets. Don't you trust me?'

He glanced up. She was soaked through and had started to shiver.

'No. No, I don't. Come on, let's go. You look like a drowned rat.'

Jamie slept badly. Again. Even if he wasn't in the same room as Sam, he was aware of her. It was like the air was different or every room in the house suddenly seemed smaller. Nothing had changed in his immediate surroundings for as long as he could remember. That had always been a comfort, but now he felt restless.

He'd read his book to try and distract himself from the noises of Sam downstairs with his mum, and the sounds of her in the bathroom on the other side of the wall from where he lay. He'd finally fallen asleep facing the direction of her room and had woken late the next morning with a sore neck, lying in exactly the same position.

He rolled onto his back and stared at the ceiling, arms away from his body outside the covers. He refused to touch himself. He knew it would only offer temporary relief. Then the raging need would return like a spring tide.

He was torn between wanting to spend every moment with Sam and desperately counting the minutes till she was out of his life. As soon as she'd gone, everything could go back to normal. He could love her four times a week through the television.

There were footsteps on the stairs, then a knock on his door. He sat, bunching the covers over his lap.

'I'm awake. You can come in.'

Sam opened the door, her curves framed by the light outside. Why the fuck did she have to wear all those tight skirts? Why couldn't she dress more like Zoe?

'Are you okay?'

He realised he'd dropped his head into his hands and audibly sighed. 'Yeah, fine. Just didn't sleep well.'

'I wanted you to know I applied for permission to cook you breakfast.'

A smile spread across his face. 'Are you now in an appeals process?'

'Well, the committee of one did struggle to make a decision. However, I put in my request in front of a packed crowd in the post office and also volunteered the information that I spent three years as a short order cook in a greasy spoon café incident-free.'

Embarrassment burned through him. 'You asked Mum if you could cook *me* breakfast in front of *other* people? When?'

'About ten minutes ago.'

He glanced at the bedside clock, then clutched his head. 'Jesus Christ, no.'

'It's only eleven o'clock. It's not that bad.'

He groaned. 'It's a weekday. Fuck's sake. They're going to think the worst.'

There was silence. He looked up to see her leaning against the side of the door, her arms crossed. 'And what would "the worst" entail, Jamie?'

He was too hot. He needed to jump in a cold shower. Or the loch.

'Er.'

'Do you really think they're going to assume we've been at it like rabbits all night, and now you're so knackered I have to feed you up so you can get your strength back for round two?'

Fuck the cold shower or the loch. Now he needed a one-way ticket to the North Pole.

She sighed. 'The two of us know our relationship is purely professional. And I would never push myself on anyone who so clearly didn't want me that way.'

Misery seeped into his every cell.

'Except Brad Bauer, of course.' She winked. It felt like the slamming of another door between them. 'So, breakfast in fifteen minutes? Give you time to have a shower?'

She didn't wait for a reply, but left, closing the door behind her.

Fifteen minutes later Jamie was eating another perfectly cooked breakfast and reminding himself that none of this was going to last beyond the next week.

Sam was sitting across from him, her scrawled notes in front of her, gnawing on the end of a pencil and frowning.

'There's a pet shop in Inverness. We could get you a chew toy if you want?' he suggested.

She glanced at the savaged end of the pencil. 'I've used a baby's teething ring in the past. It's better than smoking or gum.'

'What's the problem?'

'It's this line. I can't get it to work.' She turned the paper around so he could read.

Scanning her notes, he couldn't think of anything but the truth burning inside him.

'The only thing I can offer is my heart and my life. I love you,' he said.

The pounding of his heart filled the silence. For a moment he thought her expression changed, then she grabbed the paper and scribbled the lyrics down.

'That's perfect. You should be writing these, not me. I can't believe you came up with that so quickly.' She pointed the end of her pencil at him, her eyes narrowing. 'Have you ever said that line to a woman?'

He hesitated. 'Once.'

'Ooh! Who was the lucky lady?'

'None of your business.'

She rolled her eyes. 'Oh yes, I forgot. You don't *trust me.*' She dropped her pencil to lift her hands and put 'trust me' in quotation marks.

He held her gaze, outwardly impassive, but inwardly calling her name, over and over. The kitchen door opened and his mother bustled in, holding a small padded envelope. She glanced around suspiciously.

'It arrived for you, love. Do you want me to put it anywhere?'

Sam took the package from her. 'Thanks, Morag, I'll keep it in the fridge for now. I was wondering if you had a pair of boots I could borrow and maybe a waterproof? I thought we might go out later and try to find some inspiration.'

'Aye, of course. Just come and grab me when you're ready.' She looked around the kitchen one last time, nodded at Jamie, and left.

Sam opened the fridge door and put the envelope inside.

'What's that?' he asked.

'None of your business,' she replied in a perfect and sullen imitation of his voice. 'I don't trust you.'

. . .

AFTER HE'D EATEN, JAMIE LOADED THE DISHWASHER AND they went back to his room. Part of him knew there was no reason for them to be there. His mum was in the post office and the house was empty. But having Sam there had now become more of a thrill than a discomfort. It was starting to feel familiar.

Sam settled herself at his desk and he sat on the edge of his bed. He'd never written music so fast in his life, but she seemed dissatisfied, as if only the unattainable was good enough. They had the shape of many songs but only 'The Heart of Scotland' was finished.

She encouraged him to be reckless, to try anything, and her energy and drive appeared limitless. She constantly kicked him out of his comfort zone and after a couple of hours they had two more songs they were happy with.

She went to the window. 'There's something very wrong with the sky.'

He got up and stood next to her, his body yearning to close the gap between them.

'It's this strange, uniform blue colour,' she continued. 'And there's this blinding light up there.' She pointed with one hand, using the other to shield her eyes. 'I think it's time to duck and cover. It's either nuclear Armageddon or aliens are landing. Whatever the case, it's the end of the world.'

'Ha, ha. You have no idea how beautiful a Scottish summer can be.'

She sighed. 'True, although I've heard the midges rather spoil the experience.'

'There's a bottle of Avon Skin So Soft in the bathroom. Mum swears by it to keep the buggers away.'

'Do you use it?'

'No. They don't seem to find me that attractive.'

Sam opened her mouth as if to speak, then turned away

and tidied the papers on the desk. 'I think we should go out. You're right. I don't know Scotland at all.'

'You sure? You did say you were "outside allergic".'

She grinned. 'I'm making an effort for the sake of the music. And this time I'm going to be prepared.'

JAMIE LEANED AGAINST THE KITCHEN COUNTER AND TRIED not to laugh. Sam was wearing his mother's walking boots and long khaki trousers with a shapeless long-sleeved jacket and a wide-brimmed hat covered in a net. Even her hands were lost inside net gloves.

'There we go, love,' said Morag, doing up the final zip and wrapping a scarf around her neck. 'They won't touch you now.'

'Thank you, Morag, but I think there's one thing you've forgotten.'

'Eh? What's that?'

'Could you dip Jamie in jam to act as a decoy?'

His mum hooted. 'Och, he doesn't need it, he's sweet enough.'

He pushed off the counter and grabbed his keys from a hook behind the back door. 'Come on, let's go.'

JAMIE DROVE SAM OUT OF KINLOCH ON THE ROAD NORTH. IT wound in tight curves around the glen, the sunshine making the greens, browns, and purples even more vibrant.

Sam had taken off her hat and gazed out the window as the landscape rolled by. He wasn't sure what to say, so remained silent. After fifteen minutes he pulled into a lay-by on the opposite side of the road.

'Where are we going?' she asked.

'You'll see.'

She pulled her hat on, secured the net over her face, and got out after him.

'We're going to follow a path up the glen along the stream. It's really pretty. I think you'll like it.'

'Will there be anyone else up there?'

'I don't know. Probably not. Why?'

She flapped her arms. 'Because I look like a beekeeper crossed with a rambler from the seventies. It's bad enough you're seeing me looking like a walking contraceptive, but I don't want to bump into anyone else.'

'Do you want sunglasses to help your disguise?'

'Do you have any?'

He shook his head and held his arm out so she could go first. She stomped up the path in front of him, chuntering away as she complained about the fact her boots didn't have a heel, how hot she was, and how annoying it was that he wore only a T-shirt. Jamie smiled. He had an inkling she was actually enjoying herself but didn't want to admit it.

Eventually, as the path got steeper, Sam stopped talking altogether. There was a stile up ahead and as she climbed over it she turned to face him. With the added height they were now eye to eye.

She lifted the net off her face. Her cheeks were pink and her eyes bright. He felt a sudden pang as if they were in a church and she was removing her veil. Everything tightened inside him.

'Are you okay?' He sounded out of breath, his voice gravelly.

Her eyes left his, jumping around like a cricket until they landed on her twisting hands. 'Yes, fine. I, er, just wanted to know how much further we're going, that's all.'

'If you're tired, I could always carry you?' The words were out before he could stop them.

She sat up, a look of surprise on her face, and her bottom slipped off the stile. As she fell backwards with a cry, he lunged to catch her, pulling her towards him. Suddenly she was in his arms, his hands on her back, her hot breath on his cheek.

They scrabbled to get away from each other, a hurried confusion of apologies and embarrassment. She yanked the net back over her face, hopped off the stile, and strode away up the hill.

He hung his head. *Way to go, Romeo*. He climbed over and followed. He needed to remember the only woman in Kinloch who wanted him to be 'an officer and a gentleman' was Mrs McCreedie.

When Jamie knew they were nearly there, he closed the gap between them. He wanted to be with Sam when she saw it. The ground was steep and uneven, and the sound of water was getting louder.

She rounded a corner and stopped abruptly, lifting the net off her face. In front of them, a waterfall cascaded into a small pool. The sunshine made tiny rainbows in the spray and everything glittered.

'Oh,' she said.

He ached to hold her. 'Do you like it?'

Her face shone brighter than the sun. 'Jamie, it's beautiful. How did you find it?'

He shrugged. 'I've always known about it. Fi and I used to come up here and swim. It's not deep. Mum would sit on the side and watch us and a couple of times she got in herself. I haven't been up for years though.' He felt a sadness, as if life had slipped by without him even noticing.

'Do you want to swim now?' Her voice was quiet, her eyes

searching his. 'I won't look.' She held up her little finger. 'Pinky promise.'

Heat, lust and raging need burned through him. He wanted to douse the flames that licked his skin, for the primal force of the water to counter the pull of her.

'I, I don't want to make you uncomfortable.'

'Jamie, I'm an actor. I'm used to being around naked bodies.'

'I'm not.'

She smiled. 'I can tell.'

She can? She knows? How?

'Look, I'll turn around and you can tell me when you're comfortable.' She didn't wait for an answer but walked away and turned her back.

He glanced at her, then the pool. He wanted to recapture his happy memories. Before he could second-guess himself, he stripped and entered the water, welcoming the cold as it pricked his skin.

Dipping under the surface, he swam a few strokes, then stood, eyes still closed, running his hands through his hair. It felt amazing. He heard a squeak and opened his eyes to see Sam staring at him, her mouth open.

'You said you wouldn't look!' he yelled, dipping back under the water. He'd been waist deep. *What else had she seen?*

She whirled back around. 'I heard a splash and wanted to make sure you were okay,' she blustered. 'And anyway, you didn't accept my pinky promise, so it didn't count.'

He sank back under the surface. He could hear the bubbling of the water as it fell into the pool. Did it really matter if she saw him half-naked? She'd seen him carrying Mrs McCreedie and it wasn't like she found him attractive.

Just get over yourself.

He lifted his head. She was still facing away.

'If you could stay there a moment, I'm just getting out.'

She nodded.

He stepped out of the pool, suddenly very aware he was completely naked, a few feet from the woman he loved. He shook his head, dried himself the best he could with his boxers, then pulled his T-shirt and jeans back onto his damp body. He lay his boxers over a stone and sat down.

'I'm decent,' he said. 'You can turn around now.'

She sat, far enough away it would be impossible for them to touch. He followed her gaze to his boxers.

'I didn't have a towel.'

Her cheeks reddened and she licked her lips. Was she embarrassed? Had he made a mistake?

'Do you want to go home?' he asked.

She looked at her watch. 'In a bit.' She gazed out across the water. 'It's so beautiful here. Can we stay a little longer?'

'Yeah, sure.'

They sat in silence, held in the web of sound from the waterfall, the faint rustling of leaves, and the trill of birdsong.

Jamie remembered talking to Rory about meditation, about being present in the moment. He let his senses take in every detail: the feel of the hard rock underneath him, the fresh smell of the water, the slight dampness in the air, the sunshine on his skin, the sight of Sam.

She made everything more alive and more beautiful. Was she the frame for this picture, or the picture itself? He wanted to hold onto this memory until it was the strongest image in his mind.

Eventually Sam stirred, stretching her arms and legs. 'Can we go now?'

He rolled his boxers up and put them in his back pocket, then waited for her to lead the way.

'I was thinking,' she said.

Uh oh. 'Ye-es?'

'You don't trust me.'

'Hmm?'

'But we have to trust each other when we play together.'

'O-kaay.'

'So, we should do a trust exercise.'

'A what?'

'A trust exercise. We did them at drama school all the time.'

'We're not at drama school.'

'Ugh, Jamie! These are done all the time as team-building exercises. Haven't you ever had team-building days at work?'

He shook his head, imagining paintballing with Callum and Hamish and the rest of the Neds from work. Jesus Christ. The only way that would happen would be if he swapped the paintball gun for a rifle he borrowed from Rory.

'I'm an electrician on a building site, not a civil servant,' he replied.

She unwound the scarf from her neck and tied it over her eyes. 'I'll go first.'

'What are you doing?'

'What does it look like? I have to trust you to lead the way. You take my hand and give me instructions.'

'I hold your hand?'

She gave an exasperated sigh. 'I don't have leprosy.'

She held out her hand and he stared at it. Could he do this? As their fingers touched, a bolt of electricity shot up his arm.

'Ow!' she cried.

'What?' Should he let go?

'Bloody man-made fibres. This suit is like a Faraday cage gone wrong.' She held him more securely. He could hardly breathe. 'Jamie?'

'Huh?'

'Lead me down the path.'

Her hand was so small in his. He couldn't stop staring at it.

'Jamie!'

'What? Yeah, okay. But it's really steep.'

'That's the point. I have to trust you.'

'Erm, okay, so you can start walking.'

She set off confidently and immediately tripped over a rock.

'Jesus!' He grabbed her, heaving her into his body.

'You were meant to tell me if there were any hazards!' she yelled.

'I didn't expect you to start bloody running,' he replied testily. He released her body but held on to her hand and arm, keeping her close. His heart was trying to hammer its way out of his body. 'Has Fi paid you to do this?'

'No, of course not.' She paused. 'Zoe did.' He flinched and she laughed. 'It's a joke!'

'Ha, ha.'

'It was actually Duncan.'

'Very funny. Right. Keep going, but slowly.'

'Or maybe it was your mum.'

'Come to the left a bit. That's it.'

'Or maybe it was Mrs McCreedie. She said she'd pay good money to see you naked.'

He stopped and sighed. 'Is this part of the trust exercise?'

'What?'

'The non-stop blethering?'

She giggled. 'Not really. When I get nervous I can't stop talking.'

'*You're* nervous? I'm the one leading a household name blindfolded down the side of a—*stop!* Okay, step down with your left foot. I've got you. Okay, now your right. This bit's really uneven. Take small steps. I've got you.'

Sam stayed quiet as he gave his instructions. The more

time passed, the more he could communicate with her through the subtle changes in the way he held her. Soon he hardly had to talk at all. It was like they were playing music again together. It was like they were one.

She stopped, let go of his hand, and pulled the scarf off. She blinked as her eyes adjusted to the light.

'Now it's your turn.'

'Me?'

'Of course. Trust works both ways.'

He looked down the slope. It was easier ground. But if he slipped, there was no way she could break his fall.

'But you're so small.'

Fire flared in her eyes. 'So?'

'It's not a criticism. It's just, if I fall, I don't want to take you with me down the glen.'

'You won't. Trust me. This is the whole point.'

What the fuck am I doing?

He took the scarf and wrapped it around his eyes, making sure he left a gap so he could see out the bottom.

She tightened it. 'No cheating now.' She took his hand and elbow. 'Start slowly; I'll tell you if the ground changes.'

Silent, he focused on his steps, on her beside him. The lack of sight ramped up his other senses. He could feel the way she was guiding him, her soft voice in his ear when a bigger obstacle presented itself.

The fear of falling gradually receded as he gave himself over to her. Even the stile was no issue. They walked a little quicker. He was actually beginning to enjoy himself.

'So, how did you manage to get time off work to come up here?' he asked. 'Your storyline is pretty full-on at the moment.'

'Oh, I told them my granny was dying. The old ones are the best—'

He tripped, pushing her away as he fell to the ground, rolling over and protecting his head with his arms.

'Jamie!'

He ripped off the scarf and stood.

'Are you alright?' Her hands were all over him. 'You've got some grass on your bum, let me get it off.'

Jesus!

She was red-faced and fussing, her fingers fluttering like a butterfly over his backside. 'Are you okay?'

He stumbled to get away. 'You told them your granny was *dying?*'

She hesitated. 'Ye-es, but—'

'Have you ever had a loss like that in your life? A loss that changes everything?'

She looked uncertain.

Fuck! Rein it in, Jamie.

He softened his tone. 'Come on, let's go home.'

❧ 11 ❧

Sam berated herself all the way back to Kinloch. She was so unstable around Jamie, like a pinball in a machine, constantly crashing into things and causing trouble.

She just couldn't work him out. She was used to actors, celebs, bankers, and wide boys. City boys with swagger and cut-throat charm. They knew the game and how to play it. But Jamie was from another planet. He had the body of a god, the voice of an angel, and the shyness of a schoolboy.

A shockwave of lust pulsed through her as she remembered him emerging from the pool, his eyes closed, his hands sweeping the wet hair off his forehead, the water dripping off the hard planes of his body. Holy fucking mother of God. He was like a supermodel on a porn shoot. She'd never had such a visceral reaction to anyone before.

Back in London, whenever she'd seen Zoe's videos and photos of Jamie, she'd felt a tug in her heart she tried to ignore. But now she was here with him, breathing the same air, and her heart kept threatening to stop and her ovaries explode.

Zoe told her Morag had tried to set her up with him when

she'd first arrived in Kinloch, so Sam knew he was single. But why didn't he have a girlfriend? And if he was gay, then where the fuck was a boyfriend? If Jamie lived in London, most of the people she knew would fight each other to the death for the chance to eat him alive.

She blew out her cheeks. If her life was different, if *she* was different, maybe it might have worked between them.

Dream on, Smulan.

As if he'd ever be interested in her. She'd fucked up so badly with him, again and again. God only knew what he thought of her now.

She stared out the window, her throat full of emotion. It was just like every other time she said or did something impetuous. The more nervous she got, the more her mouth ran ahead of her brain. Then she'd get angry when people looked down their noses at her and behave even worse—a great big 'fuck you' to everyone for their low opinions.

But the bravado couldn't be sustained. Every day felt like a performance whether she was on set or not. And at night, alone in her flat, she was exhausted with the effort of being what other people wanted, expected, or dreaded.

There were very few people who really knew and loved her. She knew her family did, but their love was tempered with a sense of bewilderment and frustration, and they were adept at pushing all her buttons. Out of everyone, Zoe was the only person she could truly relax around. Her best friend loved her unconditionally.

Sam pulled the net of the hat over her face so Jamie couldn't see her tears.

With Zoe gone from London it was like her anchor had been snapped. She was becoming more manic, fighting against the current to get to a better shore.

Breathe in, two, three, four, and hold, two, three, four.

She focused on the horizon through the screen of the net. One step at a time. Think of the music... and Brad. That was where her future lay.

He was the chance of a lifetime, and she couldn't blow it.

By the time they got back to Kinloch, Sam was on speaking terms with Jamie again, sticking to the safe topic of their music. She was glad to pull off Morag's midge costume and when she heard Zoe was in the living room with Fiona and Liam, she ran through to give her best friend a hug.

'We want to hear what you've been writing,' Zoe said. 'Your concert is next week.'

'Don't we just know it,' she replied. 'We've got three songs now, but it's not enough.'

'Can we hear them?'

Sam glanced at Jamie. He shook his head.

'For god's sake,' said Fiona. 'You've got to do it in front of the whole pub, and Brad Bauer. You might as well practice in front of a friendly audience.'

'Friendly? You?' Jamie replied.

Fiona threw a cushion at him and he threw it straight back, narrowly missing Liam's head. 'Oi! Watch our Liam, you big lump!'

Morag grabbed Jamie, pushed him to sit on the sofa, and plonked his guitar in his lap. Sam sat next to him.

He froze.

She leaned closer, her mouth right by his ear, and breathed in. He smelled so good. 'Please, Jamie,' she whispered. 'We can do this.'

He swallowed. 'Okay.'

Heart thumping, she pulled out her notes and flicked through them. Her mouth was watering. Being that close, feeling the heat from his skin, was almost painful. She wanted to climb onto his lap, wrap her arms around him, and never let go.

She cleared her throat. 'Okay, ladies and gentlebaby. Tonight, live and exclusive, we have the first ever performance from the band "name still not decided, all ideas welcome" of their amazing new music. So hot off the press, we're making it up as we go along.'

Morag, Fiona, and Zoe whooped and cheered. Jamie shook his head and began plucking a few chords.

'"Heart of Scotland" first?' she asked.

He gave a shrug and started the intro.

With the first few notes, a sense of peace settled through her. This music was theirs and it was right. The song was no longer about what had been, what might be, or what could never be. It was about the two of them in the ever-unfolding present.

As she sang the first phrase, the rest of the world faded away. There were no other complications, no other circumstances, no other people. It was just the two of them.

Jamie looked at her. Tingles fluttered in waves over her skin and joy filled her heart. She held his gaze as his voice joined hers. This was when she felt she truly knew him—the man underneath the shyness, grumpiness, and embarrassment—and when he knew the truth of her.

By the time the song finished, she'd forgotten where they were.

She jumped as the silence cracked with cheers, whoops, and whistles. She smiled at Jamie, seeing her own relief mirrored in his flushed face.

'More!' cried Morag.

He raised his eyebrows in question; she nodded and turned the page. They sang their songs into life, her confidence growing with every note. It was one thing for the two of them to believe in their work, but this was confirmation they were on the right track.

'Oh my god, that was incredible!' cried Zoe when they finished.

Fiona's gaze flicked between her and Jamie, a strange expression on her face. 'If that doesn't get you Brad, then I don't know what will.'

Jamie stood, turning away.

Shutters down, judgement back.

Pain and inadequacy smashed together, sparking a fire of fury. 'I hope so,' she replied, tossing her hair. 'I want to be sunning myself in LA by the end of the month.'

❧

JAMIE STOOD IN THE KITCHEN, THE STRIP LIGHTING SETTING his teeth on edge as it hummed and fizzed above him. His mum had refused to let him or Duncan change it, saying it wasn't broken, so didn't need to be fixed. He had the overwhelming urge to reach up with his guitar and smash it to pieces.

His sister entered the room, carrying Liam.

She shut the door behind her. 'You babysitting as normal tomorrow night?'

He shrugged. 'I guess.'

'You need to bring Sam.'

'I don't think it's her kind of thing.'

'You don't know that. Ask Zoe what her favourite food is and cook it.'

He put his guitar on the table and leaned against the worktop, arms crossed. 'Why?'

'Why do you think, you big lump?' she hissed. 'Impress her. Show her the real you.'

'Why should I bother?'

'Fuck's sake, Jamie. She likes you. You've got to make the effort.'

He shook his head. 'You have no idea what you're talking about. She's here for Brad. I'm just a means to an end.'

His sister advanced on him, jabbing her finger into the middle of his chest. 'Bullshit. Sam's been banging on about you to Zoe since last year. And I see how she looks at you. Brad Bauer's irrelevant. He's got nothing on you.'

'What, multimillionaire Brad Bauer? Hollywood superstar and every woman's dream? You've lost your mind.'

His sister let out a strangled scream. 'He's far too old for her and completely mental. It's never going to happen. And in her heart of hearts, Sam knows that too. Seriously, Jamie, what the fuck have you got to lose? She *needs* you to write this music. She's not going to bugger off if you make a crap joke or do your shite *Magic Mike* moves.'

'Hey, I can body-pop like the best.'

'Then show her. Stop being such a grumpy git. Stop being so afraid.'

The door opened and Sam poked her head in. 'Hi, er, am I disturbing you?'

'No, no, not at all,' replied Fiona with a big smile. 'Jamie usually babysits for Dunc and me once a week and I wondered if you were going to be coming too? It's tomorrow night. You don't get paid, but you do get fed and we've got a fifty-inch flatscreen TV.'

Sam smiled. 'That sounds amazing. What time do you want us there?'

❦ 12 ❦

Each morning, Sam woke thinking of Jamie, and every time, she had a different excuse as to why.

She was stressed and nervous and he was a safe distraction. She was projecting her fantasies of Brad onto him. He was a puzzle to be solved. He was a character study for future acting roles. He was objectively good-looking with an incredible physique. She was reading too many of Fiona's scorching hot romance novels before bed. She hadn't had sex for far too long.

Her legs twitched. She was tense and restless. Maybe she needed more magnesium? Perhaps she should go for a run? She shuddered at the thought of voluntary exercise.

When she sang with Jamie it was like they were soulmates. As if they'd known each other forever. But the rest of the time it was like living with a sullen teenager who didn't appreciate anything she said or did. She didn't know how to navigate around him and it seemed whatever she tried, she hit the same brick wall.

Hearing the shower in the bathroom next door, her mouth

watered imagining him in it. She'd already promised herself if their music worked on Brad, she was going to buy herself a bottle of his shower gel. She hadn't gone as far as using it herself, but still felt like an addict each time she flipped the lid to breathe it in.

Her nipples hardened under her pyjama top as desire tugged between her legs. She rolled onto her side and pulled out her phone to mindlessly scroll through social media. She would not touch herself thinking of the man on the other side of the wall.

AFTER BREAKFAST, THEY RETURNED TO HIS ROOM TO WORK on more songs. Jamie seemed in a better mood after the disaster of their walk the previous day. Sam had no idea what he'd been arguing about with Fiona, but it seemed to have lightened him up.

They laid out the bones of two more songs, then her stomach prompted her to check the time.

'Do you want to break for lunch?' she asked.

He stiffened. 'I have to go out for a few hours.'

'Oh. Where?'

His cheeks reddened and he shrugged. 'Just out. I've got stuff to do.'

Like a glutton for punishment, she pressed on. 'Can I come?'

He stood and stretched.

She repressed a whimper at the sight of his abs as his T-shirt rode up.

'You should stay here. Keep an eye on Mum.'

'Why? Does she start sniffing glue without adult supervision? Does she steal the pension money from the old folk of Kinloch to spend on fancy men?'

Jamie sighed. 'She likes you.'

Yeah, and you don't.

'Okay, so we'll forgo the glue this afternoon and just focus on the fancy men. I'm sure she won't mind sharing.'

He shook his head and left. As he jogged down the stairs, she touched the duvet where he'd been sitting.

'I'll see you later,' he called up the stairs.

She jumped.

'I'll be back by half four.'

'Okay,' she yelled back. 'But if the house is a smoking ruin when you return, it's all your fault.'

There was silence, then the back door shut.

DOWNSTAIRS, EVERYTHING WAS QUIET. OPENING THE fridge, Sam pulled out the package that had arrived the previous day, then emptied the contents onto the table: a plastic container holding a small vial, a pipette, and a large rectangular plaster.

She checked the temperature gauge on the outside of the container, then took out the vial, sucking the contents into the pipette and dropping the fluid evenly over the surface of the plaster. She rolled up her sleeves, inspecting the inside of her arms. The faint scars from previous treatments were still visible.

She chose a patch of skin she hadn't used before and pressed the plaster onto it. After a few minutes, the telltale itching started. She pursed her lips and exhaled a long, slow breath.

It was done. Now she just had to ride it out for a few days. It wasn't easy, but it was far better than the alternative.

Morag came through from the post office. 'I've got an hour. Fancy soup for lunch?'

'Yes, thanks, that would be lovely.'

'Where's our Jamie?'

'He had to go out for a bit.'

Morag shrugged and turned the stove on. 'All the more for us then. It's oxtail. My mother's recipe, though I've refined it. Now it only takes two days instead of four.'

She pottered around the kitchen, chattering away happily in a way that required zero response or input from Sam. It was very relaxing to be around someone who had no expectations of her other than being physically present.

'What do you think?'

Sam's focus snapped back. 'Spiced shortbread?'

'Yes, love. I wondered if you wanted to make a gluten-free version, seeing you can't eat the normal stuff?'

'Thank you, Morag, that would be lovely. Do we have time?'

'Aye, we do. You might have to take them out of the oven by yourself, but I'll set you up with a cooling rack. I've seen enough of your cooking to trust you to turn the oven off at the end.'

Sam grinned. 'I'm honoured.'

'It's lovely having you here. I hope you don't forget us when you're richer and famouser.'

'Never. I think most of my heart is in Kinloch.' She froze. 'And if I'm not godparent for Zoe's first kid, there'll be hell to pay.'

Morag turned the oven on and chuckled. 'Aye, I give it about six months before she's expecting. Fiona wants them to have a girl so she can marry her off to Liam.'

The two of them measured and mixed as the soup heated on the stove top. Morag showed her how to roll and cut the dough, then they sprinkled the biscuits with sugar, and put them in the fridge whilst they ate lunch.

• • •

MORAG HAD TO OPEN THE POST OFFICE AT TWO, AND DESPITE her earlier assurances, she popped back in when the kitchen was full of the fragrant smell of butter, flour and sugar to make sure the oven was off.

Sam didn't want to mope around the house waiting for Jamie and she knew Zoe was busy, so she strolled down to the shores of the loch. Now it wasn't raining she could appreciate everything Jamie had been trying to show her the other day.

It was beautiful, but not the kind of organised and controlled beauty she was used to. She'd grown up in London and the wildest countryside she'd ever encountered was Richmond Park. Even the occasional visit to see distant family in Sweden had been mostly city based.

Scotland was on a different level altogether. It was so bloody big. Sam felt small at the best of times, but here she felt tiny and utterly insignificant.

The sky was deep with clouds and the loch stretched out before her, its surface dark and rippled with grey light. She threw a stone at an angle into the water. It managed one bounce before sinking.

She picked up a handful and kept trying. When she'd achieved eight bounces, she sat on the shingle and hugged her knees into her chest.

Her mind was constantly pulled to Jamie, but she was adept at hiding thoughts of him under others. Right now, she was worried about being left in charge of a baby. Someone else's baby. How were they meant to keep Liam alive? In her opinion, babies were lemmings crossed with sheep, just waiting for the opportunity to kill themselves.

Her sisters were single and childless, and none of her friends had kids, so she hadn't the first clue what to do. Did they need to give him a bath? Did she have to put her elbow in the water first? How do you stop a wriggling, squidgy thing from slipping out of your hands and nutting themselves?

Then there was the bottom department... *Shit*. Thank fuck Jamie was going to be there. Liam was his nephew and therefore his problem. She'd supply the moral support and witty banter. *Yeah, he just loves it when I do that*. She scrunched up her face. She was the lemon in Jamie's life, and he'd rather sit and suffer in silence than try to turn her into lemonade.

JAMIE RETURNED TO THE HOUSE AT FOUR, EMPTY-HANDED. Whatever his 'errands' had been, he had nothing physical to show for it. He was even quieter than usual, avoiding eye contact and blushing whenever Sam tried to make a joke.

What had he been doing? Who had he been seeing? A secret girlfriend? She was annoyed he'd prioritised seeing anyone over writing music with her. *Get a fucking grip, Smulan*. He was the one doing her a favour. He could do what the fuck he wanted, with whomever he wanted, whenever he chose.

At twenty to five they left Morag's for Fiona and Duncan's house. Jamie was carrying his guitar, and Sam had their notes, a bottle of wine, and some gluten-free spiced shortbread in her bag.

They walked in silence. Sam was tired of trying to think of things to say. Tired of watching her jokes disappear like stones dropping to the bottom of the loch. Would she ever know what Jamie was thinking? Apart from all the negative stuff, of course.

'Are you okay?' he asked.

She nearly jumped out of her skin. 'What?'

'You sighed. Are you okay?'

'Er.' She pasted on a smile. 'Yes, of course. I'm fine.'

Fuck it! She stopped abruptly and he nearly bumped into her.

'Actually, no. I'm not one hundred per cent tickety-boo right now.'

He looked worried.

She squared her shoulders. 'What can I do differently to make you like me?'

Jamie's jaw hung slack and his cheeks reddened.

'I'm not expecting to be your best friend or anything,' she continued, 'and I know pretty much everything about me horrifies you, but I'm trying. I really am. Just tell me what I need to do.'

He looked stricken. 'I'm sorry.'

Sam bit the inside of her mouth. She would not cry. No fucking way would this big, awkward, teenager of a man make her cry.

'You don't need to do anything differently. You're, um...' He dropped his head. 'You're fine just the way you are,' he mumbled.

She dug her nails into her palms. 'Then why won't you talk to me? Why won't you look at me?' Her voice was wavering, and she clenched her teeth.

He lifted his head a fraction, his eyes so dark they appeared black. He held her gaze for a second, then looked back down.

'I don't know what to say. And I keep getting it wrong,' he said quietly. 'You're, I've never, um, it's just, er, you...' He broke off, rubbing his free hand across his hair. 'Fuck's sake.' He raised his head. 'I've never met anyone like you before. Everything about this is new for me. I'm sorry. I know it doesn't seem like it, but I'm trying too. Please believe me.'

She swallowed. 'So, you don't hate me then?'

He glanced away. A muscle was twitching in his jaw. 'Jesus

Christ, no. I don't hate you. I...' He exhaled a ragged breath. 'I—'

'Need a drink?'

He huffed. 'Yeah, I need a fucking drink.'

She sighed. 'Me too. Let's go and be drunk in charge of a baby.'

FIVE MINUTES LATER FIONA OPENED HER FRONT DOOR WITH a smile, a tumbler of whisky, and a glass of Prosecco.

'Welcome, welcome. It's tradition in the MacDougall-Sinclair household for you to have a drink before you enter our humble abode.' She passed them each a glass. 'Now down it, the pair of you. Jamie, you need it to show Sam you actually have a personality. And Sam, you need it because you're about to spend the evening with a baby... And Liam.'

'Ha, ha,' said Jamie as Sam snorted. He raised his glass to hers.

'Here's to surviving the evening,' she said as she chinked it. She necked the Prosecco and Jamie threw the whisky down his throat. Fiona took the glasses off them.

'Well done. You can come in now. Shoes go over there. Make yourself at home.'

Fiona led Sam into an open-plan room that spanned the length of the house. The living room area was dominated by a large sofa in front of a wall-mounted flatscreen TV, and the rest of the floor space was filled with brightly coloured plastic toys and a Jumperoo that Liam was sitting in.

The kitchen diner was at the other end of the space with a table, chairs and high chair. The walls were covered with photos from Fiona's and Duncan's wedding, and Liam. Duncan was in the kitchen and gave Sam a wave.

She took the wine and shortbread out of her bag. 'I know

it's a bit like bringing coals to Newcastle, but I brought you some shortbread. It's gluten-free, so you might think it's a bit crap compared to the real thing.'

'You're a sweetie, thank you,' said Fiona. 'Have you got enough at Mum's for you?'

'Tons. She made a double batch. And I wanted to bring something to say thanks for cooking for us.'

'Oh, we're not cooking for you. Jamie is.'

Sam glanced over at him. He was red-faced and rubbing the back of his neck as he avoided her gaze.

'But he can't cook.'

'Ah well, if you don't like what he gives you, there's plenty in the fridge.' Fiona poured her another glass of Prosecco. 'We're buggering off now. Have fun.'

'But what about instructions? I need to know what to do.'

Fiona went to the door and put her coat and boots on. 'It's easy. Give him more whisky. If he annoys you, tell him he's a dickhead. Come on, Dunc, time to go.' She pushed her husband out the door and closed it behind her.

The house was silent except for the sound of Liam bashing something that went 'squeak'.

Sam stared at Jamie. 'What the fuck just happened?'

He gave an embarrassed shrug. 'My sister happened. It's easier if you just keep your mouth shut and do what she says. At least, that's been my coping strategy for the past twenty-seven years.'

'But I don't have a clue what to do with a baby!' she cried, her anxiety levels rising.

'It's okay. I've got this. You don't need to do anything.'

'But apparently you're cooking. You can't do that *and* look after a baby.'

'I've done it at least twenty times before.'

Sam tried to keep her feelings off her face. *It doesn't matter what crap he gives you, just eat it and be grateful.*

She took a big gulp of Prosecco. Alcohol was going to get her through the inevitable shitstorm of an evening.

'Why don't you sit down,' he suggested. 'Put the telly on.'

She backed nervously away, skirting past Liam and perching on the arm of the sofa. Jamie lifted the Jumperoo with Liam inside and carried it to the kitchen, then went to the fridge and lifted out three plain blue plastic bags.

A takeaway?

'What are we having?'

'Thai. It's all gluten-free.'

She perked up. Thai was her absolute favourite and the ready-made sauces you could buy in the shops weren't terrible. Even a total moron could get it right. She watched as he brought out fresh herbs and vegetables, peanuts, chilli, ginger, chicken. Holy shit, was that galangal and tamarind? Thai holy basil? Where the fuck were the jars of sauce you plopped onto some cooked chicken?

She pushed off the sofa. 'Are you making everything from scratch?'

Jamie nodded, continuing to empty the bags.

'Where the fuck did Fiona get all this from?'

He stopped moving. 'I got it this afternoon. There's a good Asian supermarket an hour away.'

Sam's brain froze as it struggled to assimilate this information.

'But, er, do you know what you're doing?'

He nodded again, now arranging the ingredients. 'I've cooked Thai from scratch more times than I can count.'

'But, but, your mum?'

He finally turned around, his hands gripping the edge of the counter.

'My mum doesn't trust me in the kitchen, but Fiona does. Before Liam came along, I'd come over twice a week and cook for her and Duncan. Now I come over and also babysit if they want to go out. Fi said she wanted to try the new Italian in Inverness, so tonight I'm just feeding us.'

'You can actually cook?'

He grinned. 'I would withhold your judgement until after you've eaten it.'

Sam rubbed the holy basil between her fingers and brought it to her nose. 'I love this so much. After our final year at uni, Zoe and I went to Thailand for a couple of months. I did this crazy fast whilst Zoe stuffed her face and did yoga. Once I was eating again, we went on this amazing cookery course.' She picked over the ingredients and paused. 'What's on the menu?'

Jamie turned to the fridge and pulled out chicken and prawns.

'Pork and prawn spring rolls, chicken satay, pad thai, green papaya salad, green chicken curry, and sticky rice with coconut and mango for pudding.'

'That's literally a menu of my favourite Thai dishes ever.'

His eyes met hers and colour flooded his cheeks.

'I know,' he said quietly. 'I asked Zoe.'

❧ 13 ❧

Sam's mouth opened and closed like a drowning fish as her brain went from assimilation to overdrive to meltdown. Jamie pulled on a pair of disposable gloves, then grabbed a chopping board and started dicing shallots like a professional chef. Sam continued to stare.

'The gloves are so I don't have anything on my hands when I touch Liam. Chilli juice on a baby's skin would not be any fun for the wee man.'

Liam gurgled in agreement and Jamie wiggled his eyebrows at him. Liam's arms and legs kicked in excitement and Jamie blew him a raspberry. Liam cackled with laughter, so Jamie did it again.

Sam watched, incredulous.

Jamie went back to chopping as if he'd forgotten Liam was there, then suddenly turned.

'Boo!'

Liam shrieked with excitement.

Who the fuck was this man and what had he done with Jamie?

'Liam, I just want you to know, for future reference,' Jamie said. 'I'm currently chopping an onnnnnnnyyyyyyon.'

His impersonation of Sam's vocal warm up was so perfect she couldn't help but giggle. Liam laughed like a chipmunk.

'Oh, did you like that? Do you like a bit of onnnnnnyyyyyyyon?'

Liam was now laughing so hard his face resembled an over-ripe tomato.

Sam caught Jamie's eye and they smiled. Every cell in her body leapt up, then landed in completely the wrong place. What was going on? She felt like she was ten feet tall and made of rainbow marshmallows. *Stop grinning like an idiot!*

'How about Sam? Do you think she also likes a bit of onnnnnnyyyyyyyon?'

Jamie wiggled his eyebrows at her, and the rainbow marshmallows burst into flames.

Fuck, fuck, fuck, no!

She crouched in front of the Jumperoo, turning her back to Jamie.

'Liam,' she said. 'Have you ever considered galangal?' On the word 'galangal', she made her mouth wide like a letterbox and emphasised all the 'al' sounds. Liam stopped laughing and looked at her in surprise. 'Onnnnnnyyyyyyon or galangal?'

Liam snapped straight into a cackle so all consuming, Sam worried he wasn't breathing enough.

'Or maybe chilli?'

She said the word 'chilli' so high it sounded like a bat with a squeaky toy. She couldn't help but laugh as Liam lost his shit. *Jesus, if only all audiences were like this.* She sat on the floor in front of him.

'Right, little man. Let's see if I can amuse you long enough for your uncle to cook my dinner.'

. . .

SAM SPENT THE NEXT HALF HOUR MAKING LIAM LAUGH
whilst trying to ignore the sounds of Jamie moving around the
kitchen, chopping and preparing dinner.

It was like discovering the most tone-deaf person in school
was now an opera singer at La Scala. She'd spent so long trying
to figure him out, then he'd thrown her this complete curve
ball.

She heard the snap of a pair of gloves behind her, then felt
the heat of him.

A muscley set of arms reached down to pick up Liam. Sam
watched, her heart in her mouth and her ovaries rolling out the
red carpet, as Jamie held Liam to his chest and swayed from
side to side.

She'd been ambivalent about having children before, but
now every cell in her body was screaming *'Procreate! Procreate!'*
like a demented Dalek.

'Dinner's prepped and on. I'm just going to get Liam down.'

'Do you need me to do anything?'

'No, you put your feet up.' He pulled a bottle out of a
warmer on the side and dribbled a couple of drops of milk
onto the inside of his wrist. Liam grabbed at it. 'Get it down
you, champ.'

Jamie went with him to the door and disappeared up the
stairs.

Sam poured herself another glass of Prosecco and surveyed
the kitchen. True to his word, everything was prepared, but it
looked as if he was about to do a cookery demonstration.

Whenever a man had cooked for her in the past, she'd
wished he hadn't. In order to produce a meal that was merely
substandard, every pan and utensil had been used and half the
meal was plastered over every available surface.

The men then behaved as if they'd single-handedly

designed and built the Pyramids of Giza, sitting back with a beer and mansplaining that 'cook doesn't wash up'.

Wanting to do something to help, Sam found plates and cutlery. There were scented candles in the middle of the table, and she lit them before she could stop herself, justifying that she was helping remove the cooking smells.

On the kitchen counter was an old CD player containing a disc of *The All-Time Greatest Love Songs*. She put it on to play with a smile she convinced herself was ironic.

Just as her nerves were starting to get the better of her, Jamie came downstairs and turned everything to DEFCON four. How could he have become even better looking in the space of fifteen minutes?

His eyes seemed darker, his hair thicker, his jaw more stubbly, his shoulders broader. Had he been snorting testosterone? His forearms were corded with muscle, his hands, *oh fucking hell*, his hands... Sam wanted to weep with desire. *'Think of Brad!'* a tiny part of her screamed, whilst the bigger part yelled, *'Brad who?'*

Jamie turned his attention back to the kitchen.

'You sure I can't do anything?' she asked.

'You could pretend to like it?'

Sam sat at the table and allowed herself to ogle his backside as he worked. *You're pissed. Slow the fuck down.*

She pushed her glass of Prosecco away and tried to think of Ian Berresford as the ultimate passion killer. But every time she tried to imagine Ian's hairless, greased-up body sashaying towards her, the image disappeared like mist burned off by the sun.

Oh god. Now Jamie was singing along to the CD. *Fuck's sake!* His voice was quiet, but sooo good. As he sang 'I Wanna Sex You Up', her thighs involuntarily clenched and she shifted on her chair.

This was torture. The sooner she got to have sex with Brad, or anyone else, the better. She couldn't entertain thoughts about someone this special who didn't want her and would never be hers.

If waiting for the food was painful, then eating it was like being given a tour of heaven knowing you'd never make the grade to enter. Jamie looked uncertain as he dished up and visibly sagged with relief when she told him it was better than anything she'd eaten outside of the cookery school on Koh Samui. Despite the shortbread she'd eaten earlier, she was hungry and ate everything he put in front of her.

'So, you did a fast when you went to Thailand. Was that to prepare you for the cookery course?' he asked.

Sam shook her head, shaking up the memories. She wanted to hold back, but her stomach was contentedly full of food, and alcohol had made her blood run warm and slow.

'No, I had a lot of health issues growing up and it all came to a head during my final year at uni. The fast was a reset. It gave my system a break.'

'How long did you stop eating for?'

She pushed food onto her fork. 'Thirty days.'

There was a clatter as Jamie dropped his cutlery. 'A month?'

She nodded.

'Fuck. Did it work?'

She glanced up. 'Yes. It was the start of the healing process. It was the first step.'

He puffed out his cheeks. 'You're amazing. I get grumpy if breakfast is ten minutes late.'

'I thought grumpy was your default setting?'

He grinned. 'So I've been told.'

They continued eating in silence.

'So, the gluten thing,' he began. 'Is that to do with it?'

She nodded.

'Are you a celeriac?'

She snorted with laughter and started coughing as a bit of food went down the wrong way. Jamie passed her glass of Prosecco and she gulped it down, wiping tears from the corners of her eyes.

'Do you mean *coeliac*? Celeriac is a vegetable.'

Jamie blushed but still managed to grin at her. 'Fiona often says I've got less brains than a potato.'

'I'm not a coeliac. I have Crohn's. It's an inflammatory bowel disease.'

'Shit.'

She raised her eyebrows. 'That's one way to describe it.'

His face went redder and his eyes widened in horror. 'Sorry, I didn't mean that, I, shit, I mean, fuck, sorry.'

She giggled. 'It's okay. I've had many years of dealing with it and it's finally under control, touch wood.' She touched the table and Jamie patted his head.

'Are you on medicine for it?'

'I was. People present in different ways and have different triggers. Stress and diet are the biggest ones for me. That's why my final year was the worst. I nearly didn't graduate. And at times I didn't know if I would ever get better. I didn't know if I would ever be able to work or have a normal life.'

Jamie was quiet. His hand lay on the table, a couple of inches from hers. She wanted to reach out and hold it.

'I didn't get on with medication,' she continued. 'Surgery was looking like the only option, but I didn't want to lose half of my bowel with everything that entailed. So I ran away to Thailand with Zoe and stopped eating altogether. And when I started again, I went gluten-free.'

'And it worked?'

'Pretty much. I had two flare-ups after we got back. But

then I started Helminth therapy and I've been okay ever since.'

Jamie touched his head again and she smiled.

'What's Helminth therapy?' he asked.

She hesitated. Only her family and Zoe knew about it and her family had been less than impressed. What did she have to lose by telling him? It wasn't like she needed his approval. It wasn't like she would ever see him again after this. He could add it to his list of 'things I don't like about Sam'. One more wouldn't make any difference.

She pulled up her sleeve to show him the bandage on the inside of her arm. 'Helminths are parasites. I have a permanent colony of a human-friendly hookworm called Necator americanus living in my gut and top them up every year or so. Humans evolved with them and most of the world has them, just not us in the over-sanitised west. They have a symbiotic relationship with our immune system and help damp down the inflammatory response.'

'Oh.'

'They're not catching, if that's what you're worried about.'

He shook his head. 'Does it hurt?'

'No, but it itches like a bastard for a few days.'

'What does your family think about it?'

Her jaw tensed. No matter how many scientific papers she showed them, they refused to take it seriously. They refused to take *her* seriously.

'I think they see it on a par with my job. We don't talk about it anymore.'

She saw his hand reach towards hers, then he brought it to his glass.

'I think you're amazing,' he said, staring down at his drink.

Sam could hear her heart beating in the silence, then the faint sound of Liam crying upstairs.

Jamie pushed his chair back. 'Want to try out our latest material on the harshest critic in Kinloch?'

He got his guitar and Sam followed him upstairs with her notes, failing to avoid ogling his backside. Liam had pulled himself into a seated position and was looking tired and grumpy as he sniffled.

'Hey, wee man, want some music?'

'Dah,' Liam replied.

'Okay, well, just lie down then and we'll play your favourites and some new ones as well, eh?'

Sam bit her cheek as a wave of emotion rolled through her.

You're drunk. In a room with a cute man and a cute baby. It's hormonal kryptonite, that's all.

Jamie played quietly, his voice almost a whisper as he sang. The room was dark, lit only by a dull orange glow from a night-light. Liam's eyes opened as her voice joined Jamie's but soon fluttered closed.

It only took two songs for Liam's face to soften and his breathing become even and heavy. They let the song fade into silence and tiptoed out of the room.

❧

BACK DOWNSTAIRS, THEY FINISHED EATING AND CLEARED the table. Jamie felt fuzzy, as if alcohol and happiness had smoothed off all his sharp edges.

He enjoyed cooking for Fiona and Duncan, but he loved cooking for Sam. He'd done something right. Something that made her happy. And if she was happy, then he was fucking ecstatic. Her smile made his heart too big to fit in his chest and her laugh was like sparklers in his soul.

'Have you got any room for pudding?' he asked.

'It's sticky rice with coconut and mango. As long as I eat it slowly and don't attempt to move afterwards, there'll be room.'

'Go get comfy on the sofa and I'll bring it over when I've finished up here.'

'Let me clean up the kitchen. Cook doesn't wash.'

'Says who?' he said with a frown. 'You're a guest. And anyway, you don't know where anything is. Fiona drew me a full set of diagrams after I put the side plates in the wrong cupboard once.'

'Are you sure?'

'Yes. Go put your feet up. Their sofa is the best.'

He turned away to avoid watching her. She was so graceful. Every movement she made stabbed him in the heart or the groin.

He didn't know whether to clean the kitchen quickly or slowly. Did he want to keep his distance from her or close it? His heart beat loudly in his throat. He'd never imagined love could be so painful and so glorious all at once.

After giving the surfaces a final wipe down, he brought the pudding over to her and perched at the other end of the sofa. It was an L shape, almost as big as two single beds. Even though they weren't touching, it felt intimate. It didn't help that with each mouthful Sam ate, it sounded as if she was having an orgasm.

He shifted to a cross-legged position and put a scatter cushion in his lap, tightening his grip on the edge of the bowl and the spoon. *Think about the pudding*. He closed his eyes, tasting creamy coconut and the slippery sweetness of mango. Now he was on a tropical beach, licking up the inside of her thighs as she moaned and twisted beneath him. *Oh fuck*.

'So, do you think I can?' her voice interrupted.

'What?'

'See more?'

'What?'

'Of Scotland.'

'Er. It's a bit big.'

'So I've been told.' She grinned at him and blood continued to rush to all the wrong places. 'I wondered if I could fly from Edinburgh to Shetland, then back to Glasgow and look out the window. Would that do it?'

'Er.'

'I'm joking. I wish we had more time. I wish we could just get in a van and go on a road trip.'

'A van? You?'

She giggled. 'I'm not *that* much of a princess.' She waved her manicured nails at him. 'I only did this so I wouldn't bite them and I wear make-up because I'm used to it with work. If I didn't, I'd look shite.'

He shook his head. He couldn't speak. He didn't know where to start.

Sam put her empty bowl on the coffee table, flopped back and closed her eyes. 'That was the best. I could sleep for a week now.'

'Do you want me to sing you a lullaby?'

She smiled and snuggled further into the cushions. 'Yes, please.'

He took their bowls to the kitchen and brought his guitar back to the sofa. Sam was curled up on her side, her legs tucked underneath her, a strand of blonde hair falling across her forehead.

Jamie sat carefully, stretching his legs out across the cushions towards her, and started to play.

Her eyes fluttered open and her smile broadened. 'You're doing it.'

He nodded. 'What Princess Sam wants, Princess Sam gets.'

She snorted. 'First time for everything.' She hid a yawn behind her hand. 'Are you sure you don't mind?'

'It's not the first time my playing has sent people to sleep. Indulge me.'

She closed her eyes. 'I will indulge you, Jamie MacDougall.'

He pinched the bridge of his nose. *Fuck's sake!* With trembling fingers, he began picking out notes, trying to control his breathing. *Think about the music!* He closed his eyes, trying to erase the image of her soft body curled up in front of him, the sweep of her hip, the curve of her breasts.

His jaw was clenched so tightly he couldn't sing, so he hummed, his heart almost stopping as the corners of her mouth turned up and she sighed. Every muscle was wired and tense, but he focused on making his music as relaxing as he could.

He let the songs travel on, winding their way through verses and choruses, discovering hidden paths through extended instrumental breaks and meandering into codas he made up as he went along.

He'd spent so much time watching Liam falling asleep he knew when Sam had drifted off. He didn't stop playing but allowed himself to sing what was in his heart, telling her how he loved her.

There was a wonderful sense of freedom in this. He could hide behind the music and her sleep. If she was aware of anything, it would be tied up in her dreams.

Sam shifted position, her legs straightening and entangling with his. *Holy fucking shit*. His toes were now halfway up the inside of her thigh. He continued playing, but inside he was freaking out. Should he wake her? She made a little noise of happiness and her lips parted. He swallowed. Could he pull his legs back without her noticing? Nothing in his life had ever felt so right, but it also felt like he was taking advantage.

The front door opened and he held his finger to his mouth to tell his sister to shush. Fiona crept in, followed by Duncan, and they peeked over the side of the sofa.

Fiona clapped her hands to her heart. 'Oh, my god,' she whispered. 'Did you ever see anything so cute in all your life?'

Jamie stopped playing. 'I don't know what to do.'

'Pick her up and carry her home.'

'I can't do that!'

Sam stirred in her sleep. 'Jamie,' she moaned.

Fiona's eyebrows hit the roof and Duncan snorted.

Sam's eyes flickered open. She screamed, rolled sideways, and fell off the sofa.

❧ 14 ❧

Sam and Jamie walked home in silence. Fiona had made light of it, telling Sam she'd done well not to have fallen asleep in Jamie's company sooner, but he could tell she was embarrassed.

He was mortified. They'd been getting on so well, then he'd blown it. Again. When they got back, Morag had gone to bed and the house was quiet.

'Do you want to use the bathroom first?' he asked tentatively.

She shook her head, looking everywhere but at him. 'No, you go first. I want to take a shower.'

He swallowed, his throat tight. 'Okay. I won't be long.'

Jamie went up the stairs and into the bathroom, the sounds of his mother's snoring rumbling down the corridor. He cleaned his teeth, staring past his reflection to the shower behind him.

Sam was going to be taking a shower—naked on the other side of the wall from his bed. He closed his eyes and groaned.

His cock was still hard, pushing insistently against his

jeans. He rinsed his mouth and pulled off his T-shirt, then took a washcloth soaked with cold water and ran it over his face and torso, trying to shock the arousal out of him.

It was as effective as throwing an ice cube at an active volcano. He needed to get out of the bathroom and into his own room before she came upstairs.

He grabbed his T-shirt, opened the door and stepped straight into her.

'Oh.' She was staring up at him, holding a towel and wearing the fucking pyjama set that was his complete undoing. He fixed his gaze on a point an inch above the top of her head. In his peripheral vision, he saw her eyes flick down his body.

'It's all yours,' he said gruffly.

Her mouth opened.

He had to get away. He moved to the side as she mirrored him, her hot skin bumping into his.

'Sorry,' she gasped as she pushed past him, then slammed the door of the bathroom. He heard the scrape of the bin as she moved it against the back of the door.

He stomped into his room, stripped off his clothes, and sat on the edge of the bed, head in his hands.

❧

SAM STARED AT THE MIRROR, TAKING IN HER FLUSHED cheeks, her wide eyes, her breasts straining against the thin fabric of her pyjama top. Her body was needy, wanton, desperate. She glanced over her shoulder at the wall. It was the only physical thing between her and Jamie.

As for everything else that lay between them?

She sighed and concentrated on cleaning her teeth, scrubbing away the evening and starting afresh. She was undone, dismantled, taken to pieces by the quietest, shyest man she'd ever known.

She was meant to be in Kinloch for Brad and her career. But now nothing seemed more important than who was next door. *You've lost your mind.* Was this attraction so powerful because he wasn't interested in her? Did she only want what she couldn't have?

Jamie was a constant surprise. Grumpy and taciturn, then funny and engaging. A mummy's boy, then cooking like a pro. Inexperienced in life, then taking care of a baby. How Jamie was with Liam was enough to ruin Sam's underwear for life.

And she'd fallen asleep next to him. How had that happened? One moment she was listening to him play, the next she was dreaming of him naked and hard above her. What she didn't expect was to wake with Fiona and Duncan's faces looming at her over the back of the sofa. Ugh. Now *that* was embarrassing.

She rinsed her mouth and stepped out of her pyjamas. The gusset of the bottoms was already wet with desire.

Fuck's sake! Just have a shower and go to bed.

She turned on the water, letting it run over her fingertips. Droplets bounced off and up her arm. Her breasts ached. Her whole body was throbbing for the release she kept denying herself. If she made herself come whilst thinking of Jamie, she could no longer pretend she was only interested in him for his music. If she touched herself, she made it real.

She stepped into the flow. Sharp drops flicked against her nipples, drumming over her hypersensitive skin, shooting pleasure down her body. The water ran in rivulets between her breasts, over the swell of her stomach, coalescing in her curls, then running down her legs. She reached for the shelf with the shower gel.

Don't do it. Don't do it.

Heart thumping in her chest, she grabbed the black bottle, flipped the lid, and squeezed the gel into her hand. She rubbed it slowly between her palms, her nostrils flaring and her mouth watering as the scent filled the air.

She was going to do this.

Stepping back so the water hit the apex of her thighs, she stroked over her breasts. She circled them, teasing herself until she couldn't bear it any longer and rolled the tips between her fingers and thumbs.

Her eyes fell closed as she imagined Jamie behind her, cupping, stroking, kneading, pinching. Kissing and nipping her neck, biting the soft lobe of her ear and whispering her name.

JAMIE LAY IN THE DARKNESS, STARING UP AT THE SHADOWY ceiling, his hands clenched by his sides and his cock as hard as a rock. He squeezed his eyes shut as he listened to the sound of the water on the wall of the shower, as if by doing so he could block out the image of Sam naked and wet only inches away.

She was so fucking beautiful, so utterly intoxicating that she occupied his every thought. She was the brightest star in his sky, her light eclipsing everything and everyone else.

After the evening babysitting for Liam, he hoped she did like him a little more. But he wasn't stupid or arrogant enough to think she could ever feel any differently towards him. Her feelings for him would always be platonic.

He threw off the covers and knelt on the bed, facing the bathroom, resting his forehead against the cool wallpaper, the faint vibrations of the shower coming through the thin wall. They shivered down him, amplifying the fire burning through every cell.

He hungered for her with an intensity that was blinding. His right hand drifted to his cock and he sucked in a ragged breath as he touched the hard, pulsing heat. He stroked the thick length, shocks of urgent pleasure shooting through him, then rubbed the pad of his thumb over the head, spreading the slick precum.

In his mind he saw her in the shower, soapy bubbles clinging to her breasts, her nipples begging to be sucked. He swallowed, imagining his tongue around them, her soft voice moaning his name.

۞

'Jamie…' Sam exhaled with a sigh. She imagined his hard length rubbing up and down the crease of her bottom as she circled her clit and tugged on her nipple. The sensations rolled in rushes of boiling pleasure that pushed against the inside of her skin. She was frantic for more.

She grabbed the shower head from its holder, angling the jet of water directly onto the centre of her pleasure, gasping as the sensations rocketed higher. She spread her legs wider, imagining him behind her, the fat head of his cock pushing at her entrance. She leaned forward, opening to him, her left hand braced on the back wall, her fingers splayed as if yearning to reach through and clasp her hand with his.

۞

Jamie's nails dug into the wallpaper, every muscle in his body straining. His cock was weeping with need, the hard shaft slippery as he tugged in faster and faster strokes. He hissed each breath through his clenched jaw, imagining Sam in the shower, spreading her legs, beckoning him forward.

His climax coiled in tighter and tighter circles at the base of his spine, drawing his balls up, pushing him higher. He saw himself sink to his knees, pulling her onto his tongue, losing himself in her.

***

Sam gasped as she pressed her forehead against the wet tiles, trying to stay conscious as her breathing stuttered and her brain sparkled with stars. The water drummed against her clit, rushing her forward on the crest of an unstoppable wave.

She imagined him thrusting deep inside her and the wave broke. She cried his name as her orgasm crashed through her with rolling, flooding pleasure. She was lost to it, lost to him.

***

As Jamie imagined Sam climaxing on his tongue, he fell apart with shuddering jerks, his release shooting up the base of his spine, eviscerating everything in its wake. It was so all-consuming he lost all sense of self. Everything was blinding light.

He fell back on the bed, his breathing ragged, eyes wide but unseeing.

The only thing left in existence was her.

❧ 15 ❧

Over the next few days, Sam and Jamie seemed to settle into an understanding. Conversation centred around their music, personal subjects were avoided, and Morag was used as a buffer.

If Jamie had come out of his shell a little when they'd babysat Liam, he was now wedged so far back inside it even Hermit crabs seemed like extroverts in comparison.

Sam knew how badly she could be affected by anxiety before a live performance and was worried as Jamie got quieter and quieter.

Two days before the concert he was even more on edge. They'd just finished dinner and Morag had left the room to take a call. Jamie's knee bounced up and down. He kept swallowing as if he were trying to find the courage to speak. His hands were splayed on the table as if held there with superglue.

She inched her fingers towards his. 'Jamie, I—'

He leapt up as if stung, clearing the plates from the table. 'I want to take you somewhere tomorrow morning,' he said in a rush.

She sat back. 'O-kay. Where, when, why?'

He kept his back to her, loading the dishwasher. 'It's a surprise. I want to show you more of Scotland. We'd have to leave here at five a.m.'

'Five a.m.?'

He nodded.

'You'll have to give me more information than that before I say yes.'

He turned and allowed their eyes to meet before he glanced away again. His face was bright red. 'There's champagne.'

She perked up. 'How much?'

'You can drink mine if you want?'

His hands were clenched by his sides. He looked so nervous her heart melted. One day, some lucky, lucky lady was going to be loved by this awkward, beautiful man.

She sighed. It just was never going to be her.

'Will there be midges?'

He shook his head and smiled at the floor. 'I one hundred per cent guarantee there will not be any midges.'

She folded her arms. 'No midges and a double dose of champagne. I'm in.'

OH NO. OH NO. OH FUCKITY, FUCKITY, FUCK NO. SAM STARED out the window of the car, her heart in her mouth. She was going to vomit. Jamie was already outside, shaking an older man's hand and smiling as if he knew him.

Behind them in the wide-open field was a huge wicker basket. A burner was mounted on the top... filling an enormous red balloon.

So this was how Jamie was showing her more of Scotland. He looked so happy and excited. And she was about to crush all that joy out of him by telling him she was petrified of heights.

The condition was severe. She always requested seats in the middle of an airplane. She couldn't be in an office with floor-to-ceiling windows if it was above the ground floor. She couldn't even handle going on tall escalators in department stores.

There was no way in hell she was going to put her trust in a family-sized coffin made of twigs and a load of nylon and hot air.

And where were the other passengers? There was a van with a trailer and two men sporting more tweed and facial hair than she thought was possible. Had Jamie arranged this just for her?

She dug her nails into her palms, swallowed the rising bile, and focused on her breathing.

Breathe in, two, three, four, and hold, two, three, four...

Oh god. Jamie was walking back to the car with beardy-man number one. He opened her door.

'Sam, I'd like you to meet William, our pilot for the morning. William, this is Sam Adamson.'

The man extended a thick arm. 'Call me Billy. I'm the owner of Billy's Balloons. It's a pleasure to meet you.'

She wiped her clammy palms on the outside of her skirt before she shook his hand.

'I, I... I've never been up in a balloon before.'

'You're going to love it! It's perfect weather, and as there's only the pair of you...'

He broke off and looked around the empty landscape surreptitiously as if to check they weren't being overheard.

'You can have the bubbles during the flight,' he whispered. 'You don't have to wait until we land.' He waggled his eyebrows.

Sam glanced at Jamie. She'd never seen anyone look so

hopeful and expectant, like he was presenting her with a gift he'd spent a lifetime creating. And she was about to smash it to pieces under the heel of her boots.

'I can't wait,' she replied breathlessly. 'I've heard it's a once-in-a-lifetime experience.'

'Aye, that it is, lass. You'll be a completely different person in a couple of hours.'

Yes! A fucking dead one!

Sam laughed maniacally and two grouse bolted from the heather with a flurry and flap of their wings.

Billy led them to the basket and Sam crossed her fingers. She could sense Jamie staring at her.

'Are you okay?' he asked.

She opened her eyes wide and pulled the corners of her mouth up until her teeth were showing. 'Yes, of course!'

Her voice sounded as fake as her face felt. It was as if she'd been Botoxed into expression twenty-three: *'unbridled joy on opening the worst Christmas present ever'*.

'I couldn't get a plane to fly us to Shetland. So I thought of this.'

Sam nodded, the pain from her rictus grin helping mask the terror screaming up from her stomach. Where was the door to get into the basket? She could see what appeared to be foot holes in the side. Did she have to climb in?

Jamie was blushing. 'I forgot about this bit.'

He tentatively held out his hand. She took it, electricity shooting up her arm.

You can do this! Do it for him!

She reached her foot up to the first step, but her skirt was too tight. Billy was in the basket and looked at them over the side.

'Jamie lad, just lift the wee lass in.' He grinned reassuringly at Sam. 'We had someone who was one hundred and one in here last week.'

She glanced from his smiling face to Jamie's flushed one. She knew that holding her hand was already unwelcome to Jamie, and now Billy was suggesting *more* of his body come in contact with hers.

Visions of Mrs McCreedie in his arms came to her mind. She wanted him to hold her so much, but he appeared in physical pain at the thought.

She let go of his hand and pulled her skirt up her thighs. 'It's okay, I'll just hoick this up,' she trilled. 'I'll try not to flash my pants.'

Jamie's jaw dropped and he leapt forward, tugging her skirt down and sweeping her into his arms. Before she could comprehend what was happening, she was in the basket. He climbed in and stood on the opposite side from her, facing away.

Beardy-man number two presented her with a plastic glass. 'Hello, I'm Robert. Champagne?'

'We normally serve guests cava,' Billy whispered out of the corner of his mouth. 'But Jamie supplied us with the good stuff.'

She stared at Jamie's back. He seemed captivated by the view of a field and a van.

She took the glass from Robert. 'Heghlu'DI' mobbe'lu'chugh QaQqu' Heghwanl,' she said in a shaky voice before downing it.

'Is that Gaelic?' Billy asked.

Jamie turned around. 'Klingon.'

'Well, I never,' the man said, passing Jamie a glass. 'What does it mean?'

'Death is an experience best shared,' she said in a strangled whisper.

There was a beat, then Billy and Robert fell about laughing. Jamie passed his glass to her and she poured it down her throat. She hadn't eaten anything that morning and the alcohol was already punching its way into her bloodstream and fighting with adrenaline for control over her body.

Billy unsuccessfully tried to take the two glasses out of her hands. She didn't realise how strongly she was gripping them. He brought out the bottle and refilled them.

'It's always cocktail hour somewhere around the world,' he said with a wink.

There was a lurch and Sam squealed.

'Chocks away!' Robert cheered.

Sam drank her third glass of champagne and was halfway through her fourth when Jamie moved closer.

'Are you sure you're okay?'

She peered over the rim of her glass into his anxious eyes and nodded.

He handed her empty glasses to Billy and turned back to her.

Just focus on him. Pretend you're still on the ground. Everything's fine.

'Are you ready to have a look?' he asked. 'The view's better if it's not me.'

Wanna bet?

She held her breath and inched her body around, focusing on the weaved wicker side of the basket, the leather padding sewn around the edge. In her peripheral vision was the pale light of nothingness.

'It's so beautiful, Sam.'

Her name on his lips, said with such reverence, forced her eyes open.

Height, air, drop, death.

She turned back to him, burying her head in his chest, his

T-shirt scrunched in her fists, her breathing hot and fast as the blinding blackness consumed her.

'Sam!' His voice was in her ear, his arms around her, holding her tightly to him. 'I've got you.'

Her legs gave out, her body shuddering, but she didn't fall. She was held. She was safe. She forced herself to breathe in through her nose. The scent of his body wash and the innate smell of him was more soothing and intoxicating than anything from a bottle. She could feel the brush of his lips against her ear, the heat from his voice.

'I've got you. It's okay. Just breathe.'

She released her hands and wrapped them around his back under his jacket, burrowing her face inside so everything was dark. She felt one strong arm around her waist, the other stroking the back of her head and then... did he just *kiss* the top of her head?

Every hormone inside her was battling to the death, her mind a confused wasteland of fear, dreams, and desires. No, not possible. That was four glasses of champagne talking. She clung to him as if clinging onto life itself, her heart running so fast it kept tripping over itself.

'Just breathe.'

Everything was discombobulated and dizzy. She felt the hard muscle of his back beneath her palms, his flexed bicep against one cheek, the movement of his chest as he breathed.

She wanted to stay in his arms forever. It was like discovering heaven inside your worst nightmare. All she had to do was hold on and never let go.

THE LANDSCAPE DRIFTED ALONG BENEATH THEM IN QUIET perfection. Jamie kept his eyes glued to the distant mountains, bathed in the warm glow of the early morning light. Everything outside was calm and still. Everything inside him was an anarchic riot of thoughts and emotions.

He'd tried to do something special for Sam and had completely and utterly fucked it up. She was in his arms, clearly terrified of heights.

She was in his arms.

He'd kissed her. At her most vulnerable moment, when she was so fucking petrified she'd actually reached to him for help, he'd taken advantage. Nausea and guilt washed through him.

He was no better than Callum or Hamish. He just hadn't thought. His body had acted before his brain had a chance to vet his actions. And now, holding her to him, his happiness was tainted by self-loathing. He hated himself for how good it felt.

The basket floated on. Sam's breathing softened but she didn't let go. Billy and Robert couldn't see she was facing into him and not out. His body completely shielded hers. They were gliding through the air, suspended in time and space, far removed from any sense of normality.

Eventually Billy piloted the balloon towards an empty field where a car was waiting. Sam jerked as they landed, and he held her even tighter.

'We've landed,' he whispered. 'We're back on the ground.'

She stayed still for a moment, then slowly and stiffly disengaged, staring down at her feet. He was desperate to keep hold of her but jammed his hands in his pockets before they went rogue.

'I'm sorry,' she said quietly.

'Jesus, don't say that. *I'm* the one who's sorry. Sam, I'm so fucking sorry.'

'How was that then, ladies and gents?'

Sam glanced up at Billy, a forced smile on her face. 'That

was definitely a once-in-a-lifetime experience. Thank you both so much.'

A knife pierced his heart. She looked exhausted. She posed for pictures with Billy, then allowed him and Robert to help her out of the basket.

On the journey back to collect Jamie's car, she chatted away to the driver about everything she claimed to have seen, as the knife in his heart twisted and turned. Only when she was back in his car and he was driving away did the performance drop. Her eyes closed and a rush of air escaped her lips. She was so pale.

His throat was so tight he could hardly speak. 'I'm so sorry.'

She shook her head. 'You weren't to know.'

'I should have realised. I should have stopped it right at the start.'

'And ruin their happiness? Yours?'

He gripped the steering wheel tighter. 'Yes! Nothing is worth what you went through.'

Her eyes were still closed but she smiled. 'Well, now I've had my once-in-a-lifetime experience, I don't have to do it ever again.'

'I thought you were okay with heights.'

She raised her head from the headrest and stared at him. 'Huh?'

'That episode where you climbed out of the window to hide on the balcony after you were nearly caught in bed with...' He couldn't say his name.

She sighed. 'I was so petrified I fainted twice. Ian deliberately spun the scene out to make me suffer.'

'But, but, isn't he your—'

'Antagonist? Arch enemy? Nemesis?'

'Boyfriend?'

The colour came back into Sam's cheeks as she laughed. 'Oh, Jamie, I wouldn't piss on Ian Berresford if he were on fire.'

'But, but you're always pictured with him, and Mum's magazines say you're dating.'

She closed her eyes and exhaled. 'It's all bullshit to help our careers. It's not real. It's just work.'

THEY DROVE THE REST OF THE WAY HOME IN SILENCE. SAM was still pale and stumbled slightly when she got out of the car. Jamie rushed to help her, but she held up her hands.

'I'm fine. I just need to go lie down for a bit.'

He nodded, biting the inside of his cheek. He opened the back door to let her in and she took off her boots. She looked so small. So tired and vulnerable.

'Sam—'

'I'm fine. Give me a couple of hours and you'll be cursing my name again.' She smiled weakly at him and left the room.

❧

SAM LAY ON HER BACK ON TOP OF FIONA'S OLD BED, HER eyes open but unfocused, tears tracking down the sides of her cheeks and catching in her hair. She remembered being stuck at the top of a climbing frame, too terrified to move.

'Come on, Smulan,' her father had cajoled, his voice getting more and more exasperated.

She remembered passing out on a school trip when they climbed the steep steps to the top turret of a castle.

She thought back to the film crew. Only Shelley finally noticed how bad she was.

All the time she was an inconvenience, someone to get frustrated with. Someone who held everyone else up.

But Jamie? No matter how much he didn't want to touch her, he'd held her tightly for over an hour and hadn't once complained. He'd stopped her legs from giving way, calmed her down and made her feel safe.

Who had ever done that for her before? When had she ever felt so protected? So secure?

One day she would find someone like Jamie. Someone who'd care for her as he'd done. She'd settle for even half the support Jamie had shown her. She curled up on her side and wiped her eyes. The adrenaline and alcohol high was now wearing off. She needed to sleep.

Six hours later, Sam woke with a dry mouth, a full bladder, and a headache. She felt awful but much more normal. She propped herself up. On the bedside table was a pint of water and a note.

Jamie wants you to know it was me who brought you the water, not him. He wants to make it clear he is not 'some creeper who wanders into your room when you're asleep' (his words not mine). I told him you could work that out for yourself, but he insisted I let you know. Now he says I'm writing too much so I've stopped listening to him. You take your time getting up. Food is downstairs whenever you feel up for it. With love, your Scottish mum, Morag xxx.

Sam bit back a laugh that turned into a sob as her heart overflowed. She loved this family so much. She loved...

Snap out of it, Smulan!

She blew her nose, drank the water, then went for a shower.

. . .

By the time Sam got downstairs, Morag was making an early start on dinner. 'There you are, love. You feeling a bit better now?'

'Yes, thank you. Just hungry. I've only eaten champagne so far today.'

'Put some raw eggs in milk now and you're Marilyn Monroe.'

'Is that what we're having for tea?'

'Sadly not. You're going to have to put up with roast chicken instead.'

Sam's throat tightened. Before she could stop herself, she threw her arms around Morag. 'Thank you.'

Morag patted her back. 'There, there, love. Everything's going to be just fine.'

The back door opened and Jamie entered. Sam disengaged from the hug.

'You okay?' he asked.

'Yeah, yeah, just trying to persuade your mum to adopt me.'

'No persuading needed,' Morag replied. 'You can join Zoe as one of my honorary brood.' She turned to Jamie. 'Son, you still going to gymnastics tonight?'

There was a beat as his face went bright red. 'Mum!'

'What? It's gymnastics tonight. Isn't it?'

Sam failed to hide her grin. 'Gymnastics?'

'Och yes, he's been going for years now. Apparently he's quite good. But he never lets me come to their show.'

Jamie was now staring at the ceiling.

'A show?'

'Aye, where they demonstrate all their skills.'

'Oh, Jamie,' Sam said. 'I can't believe you don't let your own mother come and watch your gymnastics show.'

She could see a muscle twitching in his jaw.

'Do you have a leotard?' she continued. 'Ribbons? A hoop and ball? Or do you use the rope and clubs?'

He sighed. 'Do you know how strong male gymnasts have to be?'

Her tummy did a salto-forward-tucked tumble with a half twist. 'No?' she replied innocently.

He lowered his eyes from the ceiling to hers. They were burning.

'Strong,' he replied, his tone laced with fire.

Her stomach added a salto-forward-piked turn for good measure.

She shrugged. 'If you say so.'

Jamie looked her up and down, and suddenly she couldn't breathe. It was like he'd stripped off all her clothes and was about to eat her alive.

'I could show you.' His voice appeared to have gone down several octaves.

'Really, now?' Her voice had gone the other way.

'Outside.' He strode out the back door.

Could he be any hotter? The commanding tone in his voice had created such internal heat her pants had melted and her nipples were sparking.

Morag took off her pinny and bustled out of the kitchen. 'Come on, Sam! Now, this I *have* to see.'

Jamie was outside in the street, shaking out his shoulders, his jaw set with determination.

'You don't think gymnasts are strong?'

Sam shrugged, her heart hammering, one beat away from combustion.

'Can you make your body tense?' he continued.

Her mouth dropped open. *Whaaaaaat?*

'Stiff?' he asked. 'Hard?'

'*Gah…*'

He must have taken her response as a 'yes' as he moved closer.

'Ready?'

She nodded. She had no idea what he was about to do, but right now she would say yes to anything.

He reached down and grabbed her, balling his hands in the bottom of her skirt and the back of her top. Before she knew it, she was lying horizontally across the back of his shoulders and he was standing. She screamed with nervous laughter as Morag whooped in the background. Jamie took a breath and she tensed.

Before she could blink, he shoulder-pressed her above his head. By now she was hysterical and convinced she'd just climaxed.

Then she was falling. He caught her in his arms and she reflexively held around the back of his neck. They stared at each other, breathing hard.

'Oh my giddy aunt! Jamie, ma wee boy, that was amazing!'

He started as if woken from a dream and let Sam gently to the ground.

'I've even got it videoed on my phone. Come and see.'

Jamie shook his head and went inside the house, returning with a gym bag and his car keys. 'I'll see you later.'

'But son, what about dinner? You don't have to leave yet.'

'I'll eat later, don't worry about me.'

He walked off hurriedly and Sam watched him go.

❄ 16 ❄

B y the time Jamie returned from gymnastics, Sam was reading one of Fiona's romance novels in bed with the accompanying noise of Morag's snoring rumbling down the corridor.

She'd deliberately chosen a story with a blond alpha billionaire in an attempt to draw at least some of her cognitive function away from Jamie. But despite how much she tried to get into it, she was irritated by the male lead's high-handed arrogance and what a doormat the female main character was.

She put the book down as she heard Jamie in the shower. Her mouth ran dry as she imagined the water sluicing over the muscles she'd felt earlier.

He was the quietest, yet most powerful man she'd ever met. And despite his shyness, the way he'd stared at her, the way he'd said the word 'strong', she was in absolutely no doubt should Jamie choose to unleash his passion, he had the ability to be her complete undoing.

She shivered, remembering the way Rory had gazed at Zoe. She'd seen the same intensity in Jamie's eyes. It was just a shame that intensity had been motivated by annoyance, not lust.

She turned off the light and let her hands trace over her pyjama top. She knew he thought she was crazy, but he definitely didn't think she was cute. Her fingernails dragged over the fabric, pulling it across the tips of her nipples. Her soft sigh filled the darkness as pleasure rippled through her and she let herself drift into fantasy.

It was still dark when Sam woke. She checked her phone.

After over a week of writing songs almost non-stop with Jamie, the day of the concert was finally here. Nausea rolled in her stomach.

What had she done? She'd turned their lives upside down and for what? An insane notion that the world's most famous movie star would notice her, fall in love, and whisk her away to LA?

Sleep was now an impossibility, as everything inside her was scratchy and irritated. She flung off the covers and tiptoed out of the room. She needed a cup of tea to calm herself down.

Descending the stairs, she could see a faint light coming from the kitchen. Jamie was sitting shirtless at the table, his head in his hands.

He glanced up as she entered. His eyes widened.

'Um.' He looked panicked. 'I'm wearing boxer shorts.'

Sam sat opposite him. 'I didn't think you were naked.'

He stood. 'I should go.'

'Ugh, just sit down. I don't care that you're only in your underpants. I've only got one more item of clothing on than you and you're not bothered.'

He swallowed. 'Do you want a cup of something? Kettle's just boiled.'

'Sit, I'll get it.'

She made herself a cup of tea and sat opposite him. 'Can't sleep?'

He shook his head.

'Me neither. I get so nervous before a live performance.'

His jaw was tense. A pulse beat fast in his neck and she could feel vibrations through the table as his leg bounced up and down. He swallowed, his eyes shifting around as if looking for something.

'I'm so nervous I think I might have a panic attack,' he said quietly.

'Have you had one before?'

He nodded.

'How did you deal with it?'

He cleared his throat. 'I waited until I passed out.'

'Oh, Jamie.' She pressed her hand to her chest as if trying to keep the pain she felt for him from spilling out. 'Can I teach you a breathing technique that helps me?'

He shrugged.

'My teacher called it "battlement breathing". You breathe in and out through your nose a really small amount of air. You breathe in for a count of four, hold your breath for four, breathe out for four, then hold your breath again for four. You also make sure you only breathe with your belly.'

His forehead creased.

'Okay, I'll show you.'

She sat up straight, putting one hand on her stomach, the other between her breasts.

'Look at my chest and my tummy.'

He kept his eyes glued to hers as the colour rose in his cheeks.

She blushed. 'Okay, maybe we should try this another time.'

He nodded and gazed out the window, then cleared his throat. 'It's a starry night. Do you want to go out for a bit? I could take the guitar?'

'Do you have anywhere in mind?'

He nodded.

'Will my feet stay on the ground?'

He smiled. 'Aye, they will.'

TEN MINUTES LATER THEY WERE DRESSED AND DRIVING OUT of Kinloch. There were no other cars and Sam felt like they were the only people left in the world. After a few minutes Jamie pulled up by the side of the road and cut the engine.

They got out and stood in the silence, looking up. They were encased in a bowl of stars that stretched from high above them to every point on the horizon. Sam had never experienced anything in nature so profound and all-encompassing.

'It's so...' She broke off, lost for words.

'I know,' he replied softly. He slung his guitar case and a bag over his shoulder. 'It's not far, but the ground is a little bumpy.' He paused and she saw him swallow. 'If you like, I mean, if you need to, you could hold my hand?'

She tried to speak, but her throat was squeezed so tightly shut she couldn't even breathe. She nodded and slowly extended her arm towards him.

His fingers caught hers in a warm grip that stopped her heart. His eyes were darker than the night sky. He smiled at her and her heart tripped back to life. He squeezed, and pleasure pulsed through her.

'Shall we go?'

She nodded again and they set off.

Her body felt so alive at his touch, as if energy were flowing between them, connecting every cell and completing a circuit. Every nerve seemed rerouted to her palm, every part of her yearning to be touching him.

Even though his legs were so much longer than hers, he matched her stride. It was so right, so perfect, she wanted to weep.

He squeezed her hand, then let go to open a gate.

'We're here.'

Without his touch she felt bereft. They entered a small field, in the middle of which was a circle of standing stones.

'Are we going to travel back in time?'

He smiled. 'Maybe we already have?'

She turned her head. Apart from the modern gate, the landscape around them was timeless.

'Have you ever brought a woman up here?' she asked.

'Once,' he replied.

He turned and went into the middle of the circle, taking a blanket out of his bag and laying it on the ground.

'I thought we could have our final practice here. Or you could lie back and I could play you "Twinkle, Twinkle, Little Star"?'

'Or "Lucky Star" by Madonna?'

He grinned. 'Moby's "We Are All Made of Stars"?'

'"Starman" by Bowie?'

'Deal.' He took out his guitar and sat down to tune it.

Sam sat next to him, watching his hands on the strings, his fingers tightening the pegs. Lust coursed through her so sharply her eyes fluttered closed. She lay down and let the night sky fill her vision.

He started to play. *Hey now, now. Oh, oh, oh...*

Her eyes pricked with pain and the stars blurred into a hazy light above her. As he sang the chorus, she wanted to join in but knew she couldn't hold her voice steady, so dug her nails into her palms and let Jamie's voice wash over her.

'...He knows it's all worthwhile.'

Was Brad worthwhile? Was he really the Starman waiting for her at the end of the day? She wanted to scream at herself. What the fuck was she doing? Everything was such a mess.

Jamie carried on singing and she listened. Even when he started playing their songs, she didn't join in. She just inched her hand towards him and touched the side of his leg.

He shifted a millimetre closer and her heart skittered in her chest. He hadn't moved away. When he'd played through their songs twice, he let the guitar fall silent. She stared up at the stars and the moon shining through a gap between the stones.

Would she ever be anyone's world? Someone's sun, moon, and all their stars? Another poem came to mind and before she was even aware, she was speaking the second half out loud.

'I fear no fate...'

She trailed off and Jamie took it up, his voice low and hesitant. He knew all the words.

She let her voice join his for the final line.

'I carry your heart (I carry it in my heart).'

Silence hung heavy between them. 'I didn't know you knew E.E. Cummings,' she said.

'We did it at school and I remembered it.'

'Have you ever said it to a wo—'

'Once,' he replied, cutting her off. He packed his guitar away. 'We should get going. Try and sleep a bit before...' He sighed. 'Before later.'

Sam sat up. 'Yeah, sure, good idea,' she replied brightly as her heart cracked open with questions of who this woman was who had stolen his heart.

After they got back to the house, Jamie had tried to rest but instead oscillated between anxiety-fuelled nightmares and living his fears fully awake. When his mother called them down for breakfast, Sam was as grumpy and snippy as he was.

It didn't help that the previous day, Rory had gone full Hulk and thrown Brad in the loch. It was all over the internet and TV, and the speculation was that the two men were in a love triangle with actress Kirsten Bjorkstrom.

Sam was now fretting Brad wouldn't show up that night to their concert. Zoe soon arrived at the house, followed by Fiona and Liam. When they'd all finished eating, Morag brought in the morning's papers.

The press had gone to town, with pictures of Kirsten in her costume looking scarily like Zoe, Rory topless in a kilt and wielding a broadsword, and Brad his usual perfect self.

Jamie knew it was all bollocks, but part of him wished it was true and that Brad's amorous attentions were directed elsewhere. He knew he didn't have a chance with Sam but felt ill at the thought of her throwing herself at Brad and having her feelings reciprocated.

'Kirsten Bjorkstrom declined to comment,' Zoe read out loud. 'But a source close to the production said it was clear Miss Bjorkstrom and the earl shared an intense connection.' She threw the paper down. 'I'm going to kill her.'

'Oh, it's not her fault, love,' Jamie's mum interjected. 'Rory's just a little possessive over you, that's all.'

'That's not the half of it. He went mental because he'd just found out Brad's been, er, Brad is...'

Jamie watched Sam as she leaned in closer, her eyes wide. 'Brad has been *what* exactly?'

Zoe blushed. 'He is, erm, in a relationship with Barbara,' she mumbled.

What the fuck? Rory's mum?

Sam blinked rapidly, as if trying to turn Zoe's words into a statement that made sense.

'What kind of relationship?' she demanded.

Zoe looked down. 'A, erm, sexual one.'

Jamie's heart flooded with relief as his sister howled with laughter and his mother repeated 'No!' over and over. Sam was arguing with Zoe, refusing to believe it.

'I saw her coming out of his room in the middle of the night,' Zoe told her. 'He was naked, and they kissed. It's definitely sexy sexual.'

Jamie's relief bubbled up into laughter. The concert was unnecessary. He clapped Sam on the back.

'Well then, no reason to do the gig tonight, is there? I'll ring Clive and cancel it.'

She turned to him, eyes flashing. 'Over your dead body, Jamie. We're doing the gig and that's that.'

Anxiety roared back through him, slapping him around the face and kneeing him in the nuts.

'Well thank goodness that's not in the papers,' said his mum. 'Once again they've got the wrong end of the stick. Poor Kirsten—she must be mortified.'

Zoe snorted. 'By the time I'm finished with her, she'll wish she'd never been born.'

'What?' asked Fi as the room fell silent.

Zoe fiddled with her knife. 'Last night someone told Rory I was coming back to the castle. So he stayed and went to sleep. In the middle of the night, he woke to find Kirsten in bed with him.'

'Nooooooooooooo!' shrieked all the women around the table.

Jamie forced a hollow laugh. 'That's priceless! I'd pay good money to be woken up like that.'

Sam glared angrily at him and his mum slapped him across the back of the head. 'Son! That's enough.'

'What did Rory do?' asked Fiona.

'He leapt backwards out of bed and into the side table. He's got a black eye and a massive cut above his eyebrow. He came to the cabin in the middle of the night covered in blood, looking like he'd been mugged. It was awful.'

Sam's mouth was open, her cheeks pale. 'Is he alright?'

Zoe nodded. 'I think so. He had an army first aid kit in the truck, so he gave himself some stitches, then sealed the rest up with Steri-Strips.'

Jamie shook his head. 'Bugger me, he's bloody Rambo.'

JAMIE SPENT THE REST OF THE DAY WISHING DUNCAN WAS around or Liam was twenty years older. Having Sam, Zoe, his mother, and his sister together was deafening. He volunteered to take Liam out for a walk but they all clearly thought he might do a runner as they kept finding reasons why he had to be in sight at all times.

Eventually he retreated to a chair in the living room, watching the clock tick down, his nerves spiking with every second.

He'd played a couple of times in the pub and once a few months ago for Brad Bauer. After that experience he swore he'd never do it again. But here he was. About to play, not only for Brad, but as many of the village that could fit in the pub.

With brand new music.

And Sam.

She dominated his consciousness. She was stuck to his every thought like glue, interwoven tightly into the very fabric of his being.

Late afternoon she disappeared upstairs with Fiona, returning an hour later transformed from a goddess into the whole of existence itself. She was dressed in an off-the-shoulder skintight gold dress that finished just below her knees, and her blonde hair was tied up with tendrils curling around her neck. She glimmered and glowed brighter than an Oscar statuette, and he was blinded by her beauty.

He stared at the floor as Zoe and his mother fussed around her. He couldn't ignore her. He had to say something. But what?

'Well, son, what do you think of our Sam? Doesn't she look an absolute picture?'

He glanced at Sam and swallowed. The room fell silent. He could hear the ticking of the clock getting louder and louder.

Think!

Sam was looking expectantly at him.

'Erm. You look very nice.'

Her face fell a fraction.

Embarrassment burned through him. 'Like a movie star.'

Her expression froze.

Nooooooooooo!

'Absolutely. You could give Kirsten Bjorkstrom a right run for her money,' added Fiona, making everything a million times worse.

He stood. 'I'll take a quick shower and change.'

Running up the stairs, he swore at himself under his breath.

How could he have been such a fucking idiot? Sam acted in a UK soap and dreamed of Hollywood. In two sentences, he'd not only reminded her that she wasn't where she wanted to be, but his sister had rubbed salt in the wound by bringing up Kirsten Bjorkstrom—a blonder, thinner, younger version of Sam who was starring in a blockbuster and already had an Oscar to her name.

Jamie was completely out of his depth. He wanted to say or do something to make it better, but knew he couldn't be trusted not to make everything worse.

The one thing he could do was show up for her. Doing the concert was the only concrete way he wouldn't let her down.

JAMIE SAT ON A CHAIR, HIS GUITAR ON HIS LAP, AS IF FACING a firing squad. The biggest room in The King's Arms was packed with people he didn't know, acting like they would have been the most important person there had the King of Hollywood not been in attendance.

Brad Bauer sat at the front, legs spread, smile wide. Kirsten Bjorkstrom was next to him, revealing most of her thigh through the split of her dress, her arms squeezed into the sides of her chest to emphasise her cleavage.

She stared at Jamie and rippled her fingers in a coquettish wave. He was going to be sick.

Fiona pushed her way through the crowds and stood in

front of him, blocking him from everyone's view. She was carrying a wastepaper basket lined with one of Liam's nappy sacks. Jamie glanced gratefully at her, took the basket, turned his back and threw up in it.

When he'd finished, with the efficiency of a new mum, she handed him a glass of water, tied a knot in the top of the bag, pulled it out, replaced it, and carried his offering out of the room.

Sam was standing slightly in front of him, adjusting her microphone. She moved it so she stood directly between him and Kirsten. Kirsten forced another person to change seats with her. Sam changed her position again and took the mic off the stand.

'Ladies, gentlemen, commoners and the legend that is Mr Brad Bauer, welcome to this very special concert put on tonight for you by myself, Sam, and my right-hand music man, Jamie!'

Everyone in the room cheered and clapped. She was dazzling.

'Jamie and I have been inspired by Brad and his master-piece to write the music you will hear tonight. Count your-selves lucky, ladies and gentlemen; you are the first, the very first, to have heard these songs.'

'And they're bloody brilliant!' yelled his mother from the back as everyone laughed.

'So, without further ado, we're going to start with the title track from the album, "The Heart of Scotland". This one's for you, Mr Bauer.'

She turned to Jamie and gave him a wink. This was it. He looked down at his guitar and closed his eyes. Everything was quiet. It was just him and Sam and their music.

He could do this.

As Jamie plucked the first notes, Sam's heart started beating again. No matter what happened after tonight, they'd done it. They'd written an album in just over a week and Jamie had stuck with her every crazy step of the way.

She sang with relief, joy, and gratitude. The faces in front of her faded as his voice joined hers. It was perfect. She moved to the side so she could see him better, not even worrying about Kirsten Bjorkstrom anymore. She performed to the crowd, but she sang for him.

When 'The Heart of Scotland' finished, she watched his eyes snap open as the room erupted. He held her gaze and smiled, a still point of connection amidst the chaos. Brad was on his feet, punching the air and yelling 'hot damn!' over and over.

She laughed, the sound lost under the screams and whoops, and Jamie's smile got wider. She gave him another wink and turned back to the mic to introduce their next song.

In the end, they'd managed to complete nine songs altogether. They played 'The Heart of Scotland' twice as an encore and by the second time, the audience was singing along with every chorus. Sam's eyes pricked with tears as she watched the biggest men in the room crying and hugging each other. She knew it wasn't just the free bar Brad had provided that had brought out this emotion.

She and Jamie had done this.

As they stopped playing for the last time, their chorus continued like a rugby chant. Brad sprang forward like an overexcited panther, his assistant following with a notebook and pen.

He was the whole reason Sam had started this insane journey and yet now he was in front of her, she couldn't remember why she'd ever thought he was the answer to any of her prayers.

He was gesticulating like a conductor on amphetamines and spouting superlatives like an out-of-control thesaurus. For only the second time in her life, she was lost for words. Luckily Brad was supplying all the words anyone could ever need and then some extras he appeared to have made up on the spot.

'Man, you squeezed that fucking lemon till the pips squeaked. It was so sick it was fa-sheezy. Man, my fucking heart stopped.'

He punched the middle of his chest so hard she wondered if he was attempting defibrillation.

'You got me here!'

Jamie was still seated and Brad pulled him to his feet, holding him and Sam together as if fusing them together for life with the power of his touch. His dark eyes flicked between them, holding them prisoner.

'I'm not just saying "hell, yeah" to the two of you. No.' He broke off and shook his head, his nostrils flaring. 'You're getting a "fuck, yeah" from me!'

Sam was only barely taking in what he was saying, but the gist was he thought they were the best thing since sliced bread and he wanted their music in *Braveheart 2*.

She managed to stammer her contact details to his assistant, then Brad was on his way, high-fiving everyone as he swaggered through the pub.

She turned to Jamie and they stared at each other.

What now?

Before she could reach him, the crowds piled on, separating them. Suddenly she was back being Bethany from *Elm Tree Lane* with people wanting selfies and some of the more confident and inebriated men taking their tops off and asking her to autograph their chests. She usually didn't mind dealing with fans, but right now she needed to know Jamie was okay and wanted to share this moment with him.

Glancing over her shoulder and deflecting another huge man who wanted to tell her exactly why she needed to date a Scot, she saw a flash of blonde hair and Jamie's guitar.

Without thinking, she pushed through the crowds to see Kirsten Bjorkstrom sitting down with Jamie behind her. He was showing her how to play a few simple chords. The blinding pain of insecurity and hurt roared through her.

Zoe and Fiona were standing off to the side, Zoe's arms crossed as she watched them. Sam stomped over.

'What the actual fuck does she think she's doing with him?' she demanded.

Fiona downed a shot. 'Why do you care? It's not like you're interested,' she replied mildly.

Sam's jaw worked up and down, but no sound came out.

'But Fi, look what she did to Rory!' exclaimed Zoe. 'Do you want her as a sister-in-law?'

Fiona shrugged. 'She'd get him out from under Mum's feet, plus she's loaded. I always said my brother would ruin some poor woman's life, so he might as well ruin hers. I'm going to get another drink. Want one?'

She walked unsteadily towards the bar.

Sam turned to Zoe. She was so angry she didn't know whether to scream or cry. How fucking dare Kirsten go anywhere *near* Jamie.

'If you don't do something, I will,' Sam hissed, her jaw beginning to wobble.

Zoe cracked her knuckles and nodded. Sam felt an overwhelming rush of love for her friend as she stalked with murderous intent towards Kirsten and Jamie. They both glanced up and Kirsten's face blanched.

Jamie lifted his guitar off her and placed himself between

her and Zoe, giving Kirsten the chance to flee the pub. Sam watched as Jamie pulled Zoe in for a hug, a big smile on his face.

She swallowed. Her throat felt too full. Why did Jamie never pull *her* in for a hug? Why did he never look this relaxed and happy when *she* was around?

This was meant to be one of the best moments of her life. She'd done something amazing. Rather than simply reading out the words of others, she'd created some of her own.

She gazed around the pub. Everyone was laughing. Everyone was happy.

All Sam felt was the familiar twinge of inadequacy and emptiness. She would never be good enough. It didn't matter what she looked like or what she did.

Brad Bauer didn't want her... and neither did Jamie.

Clive rang the bell for last orders and people began to stagger towards the door to leave. Morag had already left, and Fiona had her coat over her shoulders as she wandered to Sam's side.

'Well done, hen. You did good. I'm proud of you.' Fiona leaned in and hugged her, her mouth right by Sam's ear. 'Do you want me to walk you home? Maybe give Jamie a bit of space to go up to the castle, eh? He can play Hide the Haggis with Kirsten.'

Fiona snorted at her own hilarity and Sam froze.

'I think he's pulled. Whaddya think?' Fiona didn't wait for a reply but pushed herself off Sam into a vaguely upright position and gave her an exaggerated wink. 'Kirsten and Jamie, sitting in a tree, k-i-s-s-i-n-g.' She laughed again and stumbled out of the pub.

. . .

THE NIGHT AIR WAS COOL AS SAM WALKED BACK DOWN THE hill with Jamie towards the post office, but inside she was burning. He'd tried to engage her in conversation, but after a few curt answers, he'd given up. He unlocked the door and she put her hand on his to stop him.

'Are you sure you want to do this?'

He frowned. 'Do what?'

'Go in. Wouldn't you rather be somewhere else?'

'Er.' He paused, as if trying to work out the answer to a trick question. 'Be where else?'

'The castle.'

His forehead furrowed. 'Why?'

She crossed her arms. 'Don't act all innocent. You know why.'

'I do?'

'Fuck's sake, Jamie. *Kirsten*. She wants you. You clearly want her, so—'

Jamie shook his head, pushed the door open and entered the kitchen. He put his guitar on the table and took off his boots.

'Do you want something to drink?' he asked. 'Glass of water or anything?'

'Don't ignore me. I'm trying to be nice. If you fancy her, then go for it.'

He stared at her and her heart skipped a beat. 'I'm not interested in Kirsten.'

Emotion boiled inside her. *Do not cry. Do not fucking cry!*

'Of course you are,' she huffed. 'She's beautiful, talented, famous, and rich. Even Fiona said you liked her.'

'Fi said *what*?'

'You like each other.'

Jamie shook his head. 'She's pissed and full of shit.'

He poured out two glasses of water, put one on the table next to her, drank his, then refilled the glass.

'I'm going to bed,' he said.

He left the room and she followed him up the stairs.

'Jamie!' she hissed. 'Don't ignore me.'

He stopped outside his room. They could hear Morag snoring loudly down the corridor.

'I'm not ignoring you. I heard you, but you're not listening to me. I don't want Kirsten.' He sighed and ran his hand into his hair. 'I want—'

'What? What do you want?'

'I want to go to bed.' He pushed open the door, put his glass of water on his bedside table and flicked on the side light.

Sam followed him, closing the door and slamming her glass on his desk. Drops spilled out.

Jamie sat on the edge of his bed, hands clenched by his sides, his head bent.

'Why don't you want Kirsten?' she demanded.

Silence.

He exhaled. 'She's not you.'

'What's that got to do with anything?'

His dark eyes met hers and she froze. He looked in pain.

'Sam, I want *you*.'

Her heart leapt off the blocks at a hundred miles an hour.

'W-what?' she stammered. 'What do you mean? In what way do you want me?'

There was a pause. His gaze was desperate.

'In every way,' he finally replied.

❦ 18 ❦

Blood roared and crashed in Sam's ears, a pounding surf of white noise. She struggled to explain Jamie's words away, to find an explanation that fitted her narrative. But the way he stared at her stopped every thought in its tracks.

He looked at her the way Rory looked at Zoe. As if she held his life and his happiness in her hands.

Sam, I want you.

With those four words, he'd opened himself up. He'd laid out his heart and it was up to her to take it.

She closed the distance between them as he stood. His pupils had turned the irises to night. They pulled her in, drawing her to him. Every nerve was trembling with anticipation. She reached her hands to his and he took them. He leaned down and her eyes fluttered closed.

Cool air ghosted between her lips, then warmth as his brushed softly against hers. They traced her skin with sparkles of light that spun in circles, lifting her higher each time his skin touched hers. She squeezed his fingers, anchoring herself before she floated away.

Every kiss was a caress. Each slow pass of his lips made her hungry for more. Desire shivered through her, drawn to the heavy heat between her legs. She pressed herself against him, feeling his breath catch.

He released a hand from hers and threaded it into her hair, groaning against her open mouth. She sucked his bottom lip between hers and he jerked as if shot, pulling away, his forehead on hers.

'Jesus, Sam. Fuck, I...'

Happiness bubbled inside her. This strong, silent man was falling apart with a kiss. She scored a fingernail up the crease of his spine. With every inch, his breath quickened, his grip tightening on her. She grabbed his hair.

'Kiss me, Jamie.'

He cradled her head, kneading her scalp as his lips grazed tantalisingly across hers. She was filled with honey and caramel. Drugged with pleasure. The tip of his tongue traced each lip, and she clutched his T-shirt, needing him closer, needing him inside her. She opened wider, pressing her lips against his, gasping as his tongue swept into her mouth.

Electricity arced through her, sharp prickles of pleasure overriding all thoughts except those crying out *more*. His kisses were hot and urgent, his tongue stroking hers as if emboldened each time she pulled him closer.

She tugged his top from his trousers, greedily stroking the hard expanse of his back, feeling the movement of his ribs as he dragged air in and out. He felt so good. Everything felt so good. She broke the kiss, pushing him back so she could pull his T-shirt up. He didn't move to help. He just stared at her as if woken confused from a dream.

'Take it off, Jamie.'

His breathing was ragged, his cheeks flushed. He paused as if uncertain what to do, then ripped it off and threw it to the floor.

Sam stared.

He was incredible. So big and solid. His muscles rippled under the skin as he breathed. Dark hair graced the centre of his chest and ran from his navel into his jeans.

She swallowed. Despite her denial, she'd thirsted after him for months and now she was going to drink him in. She zeroed in on the huge bulge in his jeans and wet her lips. Her fingers darted to the waistband, but his hands covered hers.

'Sam.'

'What?' Her breathing was frantic, a desperate drawing in of oxygen to fuel the fire raging inside her.

'I... Can we go slow?'

What? 'Why?' She wanted him now. She felt like she'd waited half a lifetime for this moment, but the intensity in his gaze made her pause.

'I want this to be good for you.'

She huffed out a laugh. 'You have got to be kidding me, Jamie MacDougall. This *is* good. It's the best good I've ever had. Now take off your clothes before you drive me insane.'

His eyes flickered, then he shook his head. 'No.'

'What?!'

Morag's rumbling snore from the other room suddenly stopped. The silence was deafening. They froze.

Morag started up again and they released a collective breath. Sam wanted to laugh, but when Jamie's eyes returned to hers, all she saw was blistering heat. She surreptitiously tried to free the top button of his trousers.

He raised an eyebrow and shook his head.

She giggled. 'And how are you going to stop me?'

There was a rush of air as her feet left the floor, then she was on the bed, his body half on hers, his arms bracketing her head.

He blinked as he stared at her. As if he'd lived all his life in darkness and had just stumbled into the light.

Her throat tightened. She felt so cherished. So seen. So wanted.

His lips lowered to hers, his head slanting to deepen the connection as his tongue caressed her mouth. She clung to his broad shoulders, rolling waves of pleasure crashing through her.

Each kiss was more intense, more perfect than the last. He responded to every movement she made, every moan, as he rocketed her higher. Her orgasm was shaking inside her, desperate to escape.

She pulled back, and he gazed at her, concern etched into his forehead.

'Are you okay? Is it okay?'

Her cheeks flushed. She was suddenly shy as if she couldn't voice the words ricocheting around her head—the words begging him to fuck her hard and fuck her *now*. She cupped the side of his face.

'It's incredible, Jamie. I just want more.'

'Tell me what you want.' He looked desperate, as if wanting everything but afraid to ask.

Her heart was thumping in her chest, her breasts aching to be free. She swallowed and hooked her fingers under the top of her dress. He pulled back, watching, his hands clenched into fists on his thighs.

She'd never felt so aware of her body before. She slowly pulled the dress off her shoulders, down over the swell of her breasts.

His eyes widened, his breath coming faster.

Her head was dizzy as she worked the dress lower. She

wasn't wearing a bra and the edge of the fabric snagged on her nipples, sending darts of pleasure through her body. She sucked in a breath and let her breasts spill free.

He stared, his knuckles white, all his muscles strained as if fighting to hold himself back.

'Tell me what you want.' His voice was a question and a command, so low it was almost a growl.

She reached out, unclenching his fist. He watched, mesmerised, as she dragged his fingers to her breasts.

'I want you to touch me.'

As he grazed her taut nipple, she let out an involuntary cry, her hand jerking off his to cover her mouth. She closed her eyes and let him lead.

Sensation tingled through her as he rubbed the swollen peak between his finger and thumb. She arched up to him as he circled and rubbed her nipples, drawing out pleasure that coiled and spun, then lashed out inside her.

'Oh god, Jamie, Jamie, Jamie...'

She whispered his name like an invocation, urging him on, begging for more. She felt the heat from his breath on her puckered skin and opened her eyes to see his face at her breasts, watching as he rubbed her nipples.

He looked up, his gaze heavy with lust. His tongue wetted his lower lip, and she groaned.

'Yes, Jamie. Please.'

He lowered his head and sucked the nipple hard into his mouth.

Sam crashed back into the pillow, biting the side of her thumb to muffle her cry. If Jamie had been taking it slow, he'd just shot up to fifth gear. He held her tight to the bed as he sucked and licked and nipped at her breasts and she thrashed and moaned beneath him.

She'd never experienced anything like this. Her body fizzed

and popped with pleasure, endless bubbles of light expanding inside her. Her arousal was slick on her inner thighs as she squeezed them together, her clit burning and aching with need. The pleasure was so intense it was almost unbearable.

She grabbed one of his hands, pulling it away from her breast. His head shot up.

'What's wrong? Do you want me to stop?' He was out of breath, his eyes unfocussed.

She tugged his hand between her legs, inside her dress, and thrust his middle finger deep inside her.

'Fuck!' Jamie's head fell to her chest, his breath harsh and out of control. 'Jesus Christ! Oh god, Sam.'

She held tightly, squeezing her muscles around his thick finger and rocking her hips against him.

'Fuck, fuck, fuck, fuck, fuck!' he cried.

She stroked into his hair with her other hand.

'Are you okay?' she whispered.

He looked at her, his eyes wild. 'You're...' He struggled for breath. 'You're not wearing underwear.'

'I didn't want any VPL in this dress.'

'What?'

'Visible Panty Line. Don't you know anything about women's underwear?'

He dropped his head and huffed a laugh between her breasts. 'Not a thing.'

'Well, that's your first lesson done. Now, er, if you wouldn't mind, erm...'

He glanced up and her heart skipped a beat. Another finger pushed inside her to join the first, his thumb now circling her clit.

She gasped.

He raised an eyebrow.

'Er, yes, er, that,' she said.

His fingers slipped free.

'No! Don't stop!'

He brought them to his mouth and sucked, his eyes still on hers.

Holy fucking shit.

He growled and her heart hammered out of control. Without breaking eye contact, he knelt. He spread her legs, pushing her dress over her thighs, opening her completely to him. He stroked slowly up and down the inside of her legs, going a little higher each time.

'Tell me you want this, Sam.'

She nodded, swallowing rapidly as her mouth watered. 'Yes, yes, yes. Please yes, Jamie.'

His gaze tracked a path down her body, stopping when it reached the apex of her thighs. His cheeks flushed and he blinked.

'You're so fucking beautiful.'

Sweet pain flooded through her chest. Had anyone ever looked at her the way he did? Had anyone ever touched her like this?

He shifted down the bed, hooking her knees over his shoulders. He spread her open with a long slow lick and she slumped back into the pillows, scrunching the sheets in her fists, trying to anchor herself. He groaned into her, the vibrations spreading out in trembling waves, then lapped at her clit.

Sensations fluttered up inside her like firebirds, scorching the inside of her skin. He hummed into her, holding her tighter as she rocked against him. Her orgasm was building like a storm on the horizon. Every sound he made was the low rumble of thunder, every flick of his tongue the first drops of rain.

She heard herself keening as the sensations whipped higher.

She pulled a pillow over her face, moaning into the softness, falling into the feelings.

She'd never known pleasure like this. Every lick, every suck, every kiss felt wholly part of her. His tongue was insistent now, a steady, rhythmic pulse. She kept one hand on the pillow, muffling her cries, and threaded the other into his hair.

His groans were shaking her body, each stroke of his tongue sweeping the flames higher. Her breath was ragged as she ran towards the storm. His tongue raced with her, urging her forward, until her orgasm split her apart like lightning, thundering through in an unstoppable wave.

He held on as her hips bucked, pleasure shaking and battering her, roaring through her body like a tornado. As her climax slowly subsided, she felt like she was floating above an empty landscape. Every thought, feeling, and memory had been obliterated. The only thing left was Jamie and an eternity of pleasure.

He licked her again and fireworks flickered above her. She clenched her fist into his hair. Her hips took over, grinding into his mouth as he increased the pace of his tongue. She stiffened as everything exploded, crying his name into the pillow as another release blazed through her.

When she finally got control of her breath, she tossed the pillow to one side and pulled on his hair to bring him up. He lay on his side gazing down at her, his cheeks flushed, eyes dazed. He stroked her hair, and her heart squeezed.

'Who taught you all of that?' she whispered.

He looked shell-shocked, as if he wasn't quite sure where he was, or what had just happened.

'My sister.'

'Wha—'

'Oh no! Shit no! Not like that!'

What the fuck?

He leaned over the side of the bed, grabbing something out from under it.

'I read these.'

Sam took the book. 'You read your sister's romance novels?'

He nodded. 'She has too many to keep at her house so she keeps bringing them here and I, er, borrow them.'

'Your incredible sex skills were learned from *romance* novels?'

He blushed.

She bit the inside of her cheek. He looked so earnest, so unsure. She couldn't laugh. She examined the cover. '"Ensnaring the Earl"?'

'Don't be fooled by the cover. It's, erm... it's... er, a bit racy.'

She kept her face straight. 'A bit *racy*?'

He nodded. 'They're really graphic.'

She tossed the book to the floor. 'Well, now you know about VPL, I think your education is complete.'

She tugged her dress off and pulled her hair free. He stared at her as if his brain had frozen. She pushed him onto his back and straddled him.

'So... am I allowed to take the rest of your clothes off now?'

He swallowed. 'Are you sure?'

She flicked open the top button of his jeans.

'Oh yes. I'm very sure.'

She forced her shaking hands to be still as she unzipped his trousers. The material was soaked through. Had he come already? She heard his breathing stop, saw his hands clenched by his sides, the knuckles white.

Don't say anything.

She pulled his jeans apart and tugged his boxers down, reaching inside and pulling out—

'Holy shit, Jamie.'

'What's wrong? Is it okay?'

She stared at his cock in her grip. Her fingers and thumb didn't touch as she encircled it. It was long and thick, hot and hard, the slit weeping precum.

She swallowed.

'Jamie, I, er.' She giggled. 'I think you just might have the perfect penis.'

His breathing restarted, then hitched as she twisted her hand up his length.

'Oh god, Sam, Jesus.'

His jaw was clenched, the tendons in his neck strained as he fought for breath.

'Do you have a condom?' she asked.

He looked blankly at her and shook his head.

'Hang on.' She vaulted off him. 'Get undressed. Back in a sec.'

She ran out of the room, stifling her giggles as Morag's snoring filled the corridor. She grabbed a box of condoms from her suitcase and tiptoed back.

Jamie was sitting on the edge of the bed, naked, his hands gripping the edge, his cock huge and ready. He looked terrified. She sat on his lap.

'Don't look so worried. I may be small, but if other women have survived an encounter with the Kinloch monster, then I'm sure I will.'

He swallowed. 'Sam. I—'

'Let me do the honours.'

She tore a packet with her teeth, pulled the condom out and unfurled it over him. A nervous giggle escaped.

'Jesus, Jamie. You're so big.'

She straddled his lap, her heart jumping inside her chest.

'You ready?' she asked breathlessly.

'Not really.'

She stopped moving and searched his face. His cheeks were

red, his breathing unsteady. Had she pushed him into this? Did he even *want* to have sex with her?

'We don't have to do this, Jamie.'

She moved to get off, but his hands clamped to the outside of her thighs, pinning her in place.

'Sam, I...' He swallowed. 'I want to do this. More than anything in the world. Please.'

'Are you sure?'

He nodded. 'Yes.'

She cupped his tense jaw and kissed him.

'Alrighty then,' she whispered.

She deepened the kiss, her tongue tangling with his. Sparks of light rained down through her, meeting the tip of his cock as she slowly stretched him into her body.

He groaned into her mouth, his breathing hard and fast. He clasped one hand behind her back, the other diving into her hair, holding her tightly as she worked herself deeper.

Yes, yes, yes, yes.

He felt so good. She moved up and down, every thick inch gradually filling her, then broke the kiss, resting her forehead on his and panting.

'Oh god, Jamie.'

'Are you okay?'

She nodded. 'It's incredible.' She rocked deeper onto him. 'Are you okay?'

'Yeah.'

She lifted her head to look at him. 'Is that a "yeah", a "hell, yeah", or a "fuck, yeah"?'

The intensity of his gaze stopped her smile. He brushed a strand of hair off her forehead and tucked it behind her ear.

'It's a "where have you been all my life?" yeah.'

Her heart squeezed up into her throat.

This man.

She pulled his mouth to hers as she finally took everything he could give. Pleasure shivered through her body, pulsing stronger each time she lifted and dropped down. She clung to him, circling her hips and grinding into him as stars danced behind her eyes.

He tore his mouth from hers, dipping his head and sucking on her nipple. She groaned, raking her nails over the hard planes of his back, feeling him shudder beneath her. Another orgasm was uncoiling deep inside her.

How is this happening?

Nothing could ever compare. There was sex, then there was this. He thrust his hips up to meet her. Pleasure arced through her, fracturing into spinning vortexes as his fingers rubbed against her clit.

It was too much. It wasn't enough. Her breath was frantic as she rode him, the release rushing unstoppably towards her.

'Jamie, I'm going to come!'

He lightly bit on her nipple and the orgasm slammed into her like a freight train, knocking out her breath. Convulsing waves of pleasure collided inside her, shot through with rushes of light as he thrust up.

He cried her name, his body shaking as his own climax consumed him. She held tight to him, her breathing ragged, her vision gone. There was only him.

She floated back down to earth, his arms clasped around her. He was trembling. She stroked his back, soothing him as she tried and failed to process what had just happened.

It can wait.

Right now, she needed to make sure he was okay. He was slumped under her as if completely spent. She eased herself up and pulled off the condom. He looked up and she kissed him.

'I'm just going to get rid of this.'

He held on as if reluctant to let her go.

'I'll be back. I promise.' She kissed him again. 'Get into bed.'

She slipped out and went to the bathroom, disposing of the condom and staring at her reflection in the mirror. She looked tousled and alive, her cheeks pink and her lips swollen. Joy burst out of her in a giggle, and she skipped back to his room.

Jamie was lying in bed on his side, the covers open for her. She dived in and he held her so tightly she could hardly breathe. She wrapped her arms and legs around him, feeling his heat, hearing the thud of his heartbeat. She had so much she wanted to say, but suddenly the words were lost under a wave of tiredness.

She closed her eyes, fighting to stay afloat, before sinking into sleep with a sigh.

Jamie stared at the ceiling as the early morning light moved across the ridges of Artex. Last night he'd dropped into a dreamless sleep, only to wake a couple of hours later. Sam had gone. The room was the same as it had always been. The sounds of his mother's rhythmic snores still percolated through the far wall, but everything inside him had changed.

Had it really happened?

The experience seemed so cataclysmically unreal he'd turned on the light, searching for evidence he hadn't lost his mind. On the floor were his jeans, the front still damp from his first embarrassment, and an empty condom wrapper.

Christ.

No matter how far up the river of denial he was frantically paddling, it *had* happened. He'd had sex. With Sam. Each time he blinked, a new memory shocked through him to squeeze his heart and swell his cock.

It was one thing to read about sex in a book or see it on

screen. It was a completely different matter to actually experience it.

He felt a yearning pain in his chest, a sadness that it had taken him until the age of twenty-seven to do what kids ten years younger than him were doing in the backs of cars in Inverness every night.

He hadn't chosen abstinence. It had just never happened. He lived in a sparsely populated part of the world. He was quiet. He was shy. He was working. He was playing his guitar. He was at gymnastics. He was with his family.

The excuses were more familiar to him than the back of his own hand. And the older he got, the more difficult it was to address. How do you explain to a potential girlfriend you'd never even kissed a girl?

He squeezed his eyes shut and rubbed his forehead. *Sam*. She was his sun, his moon and all his stars. His everything. Kissing her, touching her. It blew his mind. Fuck, he'd come in his jeans feeling her fall apart under his tongue. Had he been good enough for her? Would she ever want to do it again?

She was leaving in two days. After that he'd never see her again. He was just a night of fun, the consolation prize for not winning Brad Bauer. He was deluded if he thought she'd ever want more.

But how was he meant to act towards her now? He had no fucking idea what to say or do. And what if his mum had heard them? His heart hammered in his chest. How could he face either of them?

Panic consumed him, clutching at his throat. He threw back the covers. He couldn't do this. He needed to go.

S AM SLEPT IN, WAKING WITH A STRETCH AND A DREAMY smile. She ached in all the right places and her tummy fizzed with excitement.

Who knew Jamie MacDougall was a secret sex god? She'd never felt like that with anyone before. Sex with him was like surfing the perfect wave on the shores of heaven and she was desperate to ride it again.

She checked the time. Could she sneak into his room for round two? She'd left his bed because she didn't want him to be embarrassed in front of his mum. Morag would be in the post office by now, so the coast was clear.

She tiptoed into the bathroom to clean her teeth, then knocked quietly on his door.

Silence.

Without Morag's snoring, the corridor seemed very quiet. She knocked again, a little louder. Still nothing. She pressed her ear to the door but couldn't hear anything. She slowly pushed it open. The room was empty, his clothes from last night still on the floor. Was he downstairs?

She walked through the silent house, pausing at the door to the post office. She could hear Morag laughing with a customer on the other side. She went back upstairs to get dressed and put on make-up. She was uneasy and unsure and needed her face on to hide her feelings.

In the kitchen there was no sign Jamie had eaten breakfast. She didn't have his number so couldn't ring him.

What now?

Indecision gnawed at her until she went back to the post office.

'There's the wee superstar! How's your head? Did you sleep alright?' Morag's face was open and bright. There was no sign she'd heard them the night before.

Sam forced a smile. 'Feeling great, thank you. I was just wondering if you'd seen Jamie this morning?'

Morag frowned. 'No, love. I thought he was still asleep. Give me a moment.'

She finished with her customer, then took out her phone and dialled. She stared at it in confusion as it went to voicemail.

'Hi, son, just wondering where you've got to. Give us a ring when you've got this, eh? Love you.'

Sam could recognise a fake smile at a dozen paces and Morag's looked like it had been drawn by a child.

'He's probably forgotten to charge his phone, silly boy. I bet he's nipped out to get you some fancy pastries for breakfast so you can celebrate. He won't be long.'

Sam went back through the house and out the back door. Jamie's car was gone. She made herself breakfast and turned on her phone. It vibrated non-stop with messages and notifications.

Her stomach sank. She was all over Brad Bauer's Instagram feed from the concert. This was not the right way to keep a low profile.

A text from Ian Berresford came in, asking how her dying granny was doing. *Fucker.* She ignored all messages except one from Crystal, Brad's main assistant.

Her pulse quickened. Brad was serious about wanting their music for *Braveheart 2*. This changed everything. He wanted them to send him their tracks so he could give them to a string arranger, then book into a studio in London within the next three weeks to record them with an orchestra.

He was promising to use at least three of their songs and offering a fee of forty grand for each one. Crystal wanted an answer now and the tracks by the end of the day.

Sam rushed back to the post office. She had to talk to

Jamie. Morag was on her phone, facing away. 'I've no idea where he's got to, Fi,' she said. 'The last time I saw him was in the pub. What's going on?'

Sam made a noise and Morag whipped around, her cheeks colouring.

'Ah, hello, Sam,' she said loudly. 'Okay then, Mr Smith,' she enunciated into the phone. 'I'll be sure to telephone you right away if the package turns up. Good day.' She ended the call with a flourish and raised her eyebrows theatrically. 'Customers. Can't live with 'em, can't live without 'em.'

Sam wasn't sure whether to laugh or cry. Jamie was officially AWOL.

❧

THE WATER FELL, CRASHING INTO THE POOL BELOW WHERE IT bubbled and flowed out into stillness. The sight and sound were hypnotic, taking Jamie's attention away from his empty stomach, his sore muscles, and what the fuck he was going to do next.

He'd driven mindlessly for hours before ending up at the start of the track to the waterfall. There were no other cars, so he knew he'd be alone. He didn't check his watch, but could tell the time passing with the changing position of the sun. How long could he stay out here? Could he sleep in his car?

A stone dropped into the water beside him. Duncan was standing a few feet away.

'Alright, mate?' Duncan pulled out his phone, tapped the screen and put it to his ear. 'Yeah, I've got him. You can call off the hounds and stop your mum dragging the loch.' His face crinkled with a smile. 'I can't promise that, but I'll ring you when we're on our way home. Okay, love you, sweetheart.'

He put the phone away and sat next to Jamie.

'I don't want to talk about it.'

'Talk about what?' Duncan asked.

Jamie's shoulders hunched higher. 'Don't be a dick, Dunc. You know.'

His friend picked up a stone and skimmed it across the surface of the pool.

'You're between a rock and a hard place, Jamie. You can either talk to me or your sister. And as much as I love Fiona to the moon and back, if I were you, I'd talk to me.'

Jamie picked up a stone and threw it angrily into the water. 'I don't know what to say.'

'Then can I ask you a question?'

He shrugged.

'What happened between you and Sam last night?'

'Fuck's sake, Dunc, push me in at the deep end, why don't you?'

Duncan raised his hands in supplication. 'Mate, I'm trying to make this easy for you. Do you want me to dance around the elephant in the room until you're ready to talk? I've spent all day trying to stop your mum and sister calling everyone from the police to NATO, then finding your sorry arse. I care, Jamie, but I'm also hungry and want to go home.'

Duncan skimmed another stone across the water.

'Did you have sex with Sam last night?'

Jamie nodded.

'Halle-fucking-lujah. Your sister owes me twenty quid.'

'What the fuck? This isn't a joke.'

'Calm yourself down, Jamie, it's only between me and Fi.'

'She told Sam I fancied Kirsten,' Jamie said angrily. 'Why? Is this some kind of game to her?'

'Of course not. She did it to force Sam to make the first move. She knew pigs would fly through a freezing hell before you did anything.'

'Does Mum know?'

'No. She thinks you've just freaked out because Brad wants to give you a hundred and twenty grand to use three of your songs.'

'What the fuck?' He leaned forward, his head spinning.

'Just breathe. It's all okay. Sam's dealing with it.'

Jamie raked his fingernails across his scalp, trying to remember the breathing exercise she'd taught him. *Breathe in, hold, breathe out, hold.*

He kept going until his head cleared, then rubbed his face as if he could wipe all the stress away.

'Are you ready to go back yet?' Duncan asked.

Jamie shook his head violently.

'Why not?'

He shrugged.

'Okay, I'm going to try and find the right words here, so bear with me.' Duncan sighed. 'Last night, with Sam…'

Jamie tensed, dreading what might be coming next.

'Did she, um, *enjoy* herself?' Duncan's face was as red as his felt. 'Did, er, you manage to—'

'Jesus, Dunc! Fuck's sake! I "managed" to make her "enjoy" herself three times. Happy?'

Duncan slapped him on the back. 'Fair play, mate, fair play. I owe Fi another twenty quid. Those sexy books of hers must have done the trick.'

Jamie scrambled to his feet, his hands clenched into fists.

'What the fuck? What the fucking fuck?'

Burning embarrassment and shame raged through him.

Duncan stood. 'That came out wrong. Jamie, I'm sorry.' He ran his hands through his hair. 'Look. Fi worries about you. I don't care that you've never had a girlfriend, but she does. She thought reading those books might give you a bit of confidence. That's all. She wants you to be happy.'

'I am happy.'

'So you'll stay living with your mum all your life?'

'She needs me.'

Duncan rolled his eyes. 'Whatever, Jamie. Look. If it went well with Sam, then what are you doing here?'

He shrugged.

'Fuck your insecurities. What do you think's been going through Sam's mind today? How do you think she felt waking up to find you'd gone?'

'Why would she care? I bet she does this all the time.'

Duncan shoved him in the chest. 'Don't put your shit on her.'

'Fuck off.'

'No, *you* fuck off. You're being an arsehole. Sam's awesome. She wouldn't jump into bed with someone she didn't care about.'

'Brad Bauer?'

'Don't be such a dick. She would never have shagged him. He's just an excuse to try and make more of her life. She's clever and funny, cool and pretty. Do you think she really wants to spend her life playing a tart on *Elm Tree Lane*?'

'If you like her so much, then why don't you sleep with her?'

The sudden silence slapped him in the face.

Duncan turned on his heel and stalked off, shaking his head.

'Dunc—'

'Get to fuck, Jamie.'

Jamie bent forward, his hands resting on his thighs as if he'd been punched in the stomach. He'd been so caught up in his own feelings it never crossed his mind Sam might be having any of her own.

Duncan was right. He'd been a total fucking dick. He jogged after him.

'I'm sorry. I didn't mean it.'

His friend changed from a stride to a jog, his feet crunching on the loose stone, sending shale tumbling down the path.

'Dunc, wait up.'

He ignored him.

'Dunc, please. I don't know what to do!'

Duncan stopped and faced him, breathing hard. 'No shit, Sherlock.'

'I'm sorry. I don't know what to say, how to act with her, anything.'

'Mate, just be yourself.'

He shook his head. That would never be enough.

'Can I come back to yours for a bit?' he asked.

'You'd rather face the Fiona inquisition than see Sam right now?'

He hesitated, then nodded.

Duncan shrugged his shoulders. 'Your funeral. Don't say you haven't been warned.'

THAT AFTERNOON ZOE CAME AROUND TO MORAG'S, SO SAM spent the afternoon and evening using alcohol and her best friend as a distraction from the fact that Jamie had disappeared.

Morag kept leaving the room with her phone. When she finally returned with a smile, Sam knew he'd been found and was okay.

After Zoe left, she stayed up with Morag, the two of them sneaking glances at the clock as if in the next five minutes Jamie might appear. Eventually they gave up and went to bed.

Sam lay in the darkness, hurt and confused. Had she pushed herself at him? He was clearly very familiar with a woman's body, yet he'd been reticent with her.

Finally she heard his footsteps on the stairs. He paused outside her room. Her heart beat loudly in her throat. Was he going to come in?

She sat up, smoothing her hair, then heard his bedroom door closing. She curled up on her side, facing the wall, biting her lip to stop the tears.

SAM DREAMT SHE WAS ON SET. WITH HER, AS WELL AS THE cast and crew, were her family, Zoe, Rory, Morag, Fiona, Duncan, Brad, and Jamie. She was as small as a mouse, running around, trying to make herself heard.

Brad was telling Zoe he was taking Jamie to LA. Jamie was between her sisters, his arms draped over their shoulders as they stared adoringly at him. Morag was feeding her parents shortbread and crumbs were dropping to the floor, hitting her like rocks.

No one noticed her.

Now they were all walking towards Brad's private jet. She ran behind them, yelling at them to stop, to wait for her. But they didn't.

A knocking sound woke her, and she flailed in the covers, orientating herself. *Morag?*

'Come in, I'm awake.'

The door opened. It was Jamie, holding a mug of tea. She sat up, running her hands through her hair and across her face.

'The tea's for you, if you want it?'

Sam swallowed. She didn't know what to say. The last time

she'd seen him, they'd both been naked. He seemed as unsure as she felt, the colour rising in his cheeks.

'Can I come in?'

She nodded and scooted back, pulling the duvet up under her chin.

He placed the mug on the bedside table and stood at the end of the bed as if he were a footman awaiting instructions.

'I want to apologise,' he said. 'For yesterday.'

She stayed silent, not knowing where this was going.

'I want to, er, explain.' He rubbed the back of his neck. 'Can I sit down?'

She nodded and hugged her knees to her chest. He perched at the end of the bed, as far as he could from her without falling off the end. This didn't bode well.

His hands were clasped in his lap and he stared at them, taking breaths as if about to speak, then sighing them out. With each exhale, Sam's anxiety increased until she couldn't bear it anymore.

'For goodness sake, Jamie, if you're trying to let me down gently, I'd rather you just put a pin in it, rather than drawing it out like a bad soap storyline.'

'What?'

'It wasn't what you really wanted. You didn't know how to tell me. You want us to be "just friends". Blah, blah, blah. Jamie, my career is based on constant rejection. I've got my big girl pants on. I can cope. Just get on with it.'

He stared at her, his mouth open. If she wasn't so upset, she would have laughed.

He cleared his throat. 'Um, that's not what I was going to say.' He took a big breath. 'Is that how *you* feel? You, er, don't want it to happen again?'

She hugged her knees tighter to her chest and shook her head. 'No, no, no. You don't get to turn this back to me. You're going to put your big boy pants on and tell me why you walked out without a word and didn't come back until after midnight.'

He swallowed and pulled at the front of his T-shirt. There was a faint sheen of sweat on his forehead, as if he'd been running for his life only to end up between a wall and a firing squad.

'I, er, I've never, erm. It was the first time I've ever...' He gulped in a breath. 'And you're, you're... I freaked out. I didn't know what to do. I'm sorry.'

Relief started trickling in. 'So, you don't regret it?'

'God no. It was the best thing that's ever happened to me.'

The relief was now a flood. 'Thank fuck for that.'

'So, you don't mind that I've, I've never—'

'Jamie, look at me. I'm just a person.'

He shook his head vehemently and her heart did a pirouette.

'Just because I'm on the telly doesn't make me any different. I don't care you've never had sex with someone famous. Kinloch's hardly LA.'

'No, that's not—'

'Actually, you're right. Kinloch's currently got more stars per square mile than LA. I'm just a forty-watt bulb in comparison.'

'No. You're not. You're everything.'

Her heart was so puffed up, there was no room left in her chest for her lungs to work properly. He was gazing at her with such desperate intensity her skin felt on fire. She dropped the duvet and knelt on the bed.

His eyes flicked to her chest and he sucked in a ragged breath. His gaze held so much heat, it crackled down her body. She wanted him so much it hurt.

'Do you want it to happen again?' Her voice was breathy with longing.

He nodded.

She held his gaze and slowly pulled one of the thin straps of her pyjama top off her shoulder.

He blinked, his breath coming faster.

She hooked her finger under the second strap. 'How much do you want it, Jamie?'

He opened his mouth to speak.

'Kids!' Morag's voice boomed up the stairs.

Sam froze.

'Breakfast's almost ready.'

Jamie went to the door and opened it. 'Thanks, Mum, give us five minutes.' He closed it again and stared at her. 'Get the pillow.' His voice was a growl.

She pulled it from behind her without thinking, her heart stuttering.

'W-why?' she stammered.

'Just in case.'

He stalked towards her, grabbed her ankles and tugged her down the bed. He yanked her pyjama shorts off, spread her legs and buried his tongue inside her.

Sam pulled the pillow over her face to stifle the scream. Stars exploded in the blackness as he zeroed in on her clit with fast hard licks. There was no easing in, no gradual ramping up. He turned her from simmering to combusting in a heartbeat.

His strong hands held her tight as she jerked beneath him, fighting to contain her cries and breathe through the pillow. Her orgasm was hurtling towards her.

His fingers pushed inside her and she started shaking. He thrust them in and out, raking them against the top wall, his tongue fast and furious. Her orgasm slammed into her, knocking out her breath with a silent scream. She convulsed beneath him, her body falling apart with pleasure.

The sensations carried on and on in wider and wider waves

until they rushed back together with a roar for a second climax almost painful in its intensity. Sam was lost, shivering and shaking, blinded by feeling. As she floated back to earth and her breath returned, she felt his fingers slip free.

He gave a long, slow lick up her length, then pulled back. She took the pillow away and stared up at him. He was standing, the bulge in his jeans huge. She could see a wet patch on the fabric.

Holy shit. He'd come just by bringing her off. His hand stroked his shaft through his trousers, outlining how hard it still was. He was breathing heavily.

'That's how much I want it, Sam. That's how much I want you.'

❧ 20 ❧

Sam was grateful for Morag's constant chatter. It was a soothing balm of white noise that required no input from either her or Jamie to keep it in perpetual motion.

She was used to putting on a face, adopting a role, playing a part. However, trying to hide her thoughts and feelings when her body was still unsteady with pleasure was impossible.

It didn't help that Morag had cooked them the biggest sausages she'd ever seen. Sam couldn't look at Jamie without blushing, and when she glanced at her plate, the fire in her cheeks only intensified.

Suddenly she was aware of silence.

'What do you think? You going to try them?' Morag repeated.

'Er?'

'The sausages. I picked them up this morning from the butchers. They're gluten-free.'

Sam cut the end off one neatly and put it in her mouth.

'Robbie brought out two new varieties after Rory threw

poor wee Brad in the loch. He's made a turkey chipolata called "The Bauer", and an extra-jumbo sausage with haggis called "The Earl". What d'you both think of Rory's sausage?'

Jamie dropped his knife and fork with a clatter, and Sam started to choke. He leapt to her side and passed her a glass of water.

'You okay?'

She nodded as she coughed. Jamie rubbed her back as his mother laughed.

'Oh, I've been waiting to make that joke all morning!'

'Mum!'

'What? You need to try something new once in a while. You never know if Rory's sausage is for you unless you try it.'

'Have you been drinking?'

'Och no, you're just too easy to wind up. You youngsters are so straight-laced.' Morag wiped the corners of her eyes with her pinny. 'Have you told Sam about tonight?'

Jamie shook his head and sat down. Sam looked at him and raised her eyebrows.

'It's the last day of the shoot and they're having a ceilidh up at the castle to celebrate,' he said.

'That sounds amazing. Can we go?'

He nodded. 'I, er, erm... wondered if you would be up for something?'

Her cheeks heated.

'I thought, at the end as a surprise, maybe we could perform "The Heart of Scotland"? I know the band, so we could teach it to them this afternoon. If you like?'

Sam was stunned. 'You're actually *suggesting* we perform?'

'Well, you'd be out front and I'd be hiding at the back. I just thought it might be something people might, er, enjoy...?' He trailed off, his face red.

She reached across the table towards his hand, then hesitated. 'I think it's a brilliant idea.'

'Woo hoo! I can't wait to tell everyone,' said Morag excitedly.

'Mum! How is it going to be a surprise if you do that?'

'Ah, you're right, son.' She looked at their plates. 'Are you both done?'

They nodded. Morag grabbed the half-eaten sausage from Sam's plate.

'Well, you might not appreciate Rory's sausage, but I certainly do,' she said, biting off a chunk and giving them a wink.

❦

THEY CLEANED UP THE KITCHEN AS MORAG POTTERED around downstairs, doing laundry and vacuuming. Jamie was conscious of each moment, wanting to spend every second he could with Sam before she left.

Tomorrow she'd go back to her life and he'd go back to his. His heart ached for what could never be. How could anything ever work between them? Their lives were poles apart in every way.

'Did your mum tell you what Brad wants?' Sam asked.

'She said something crazy about a hundred and twenty grand for three songs?'

She nodded, her eyes sparkling. 'Yes. He wants three songs, maybe more. And we get forty grand per song. That's sixty grand each, Jamie.'

He thought about what he could get in Kinloch for sixty grand. About the money he'd been saving to maybe buy a house. With this he could afford a small place almost outright.

'So, we just need to record them and send him a copy, and he'll give us a hundred and twenty grand?'

She laughed. 'If only it were that easy.'

His stomach twisted with embarrassment.

'We need to record them now and send them to Brad. He's getting an arranger and producer on board, and we'll record them again in London in a couple of weeks.'

'What?'

'It's going to be amazing.' She smiled at him. 'And we can hang out together.'

'How long will it take?'

She shrugged. 'It's usually two to three days per song, so maybe a week to ten days if we're quick.'

'To record less than fifteen minutes of music?'

The ground was shifting under his feet. Had he ever spent even a night away from home before? What about his mum?

'What about work?' he asked.

'I'm sure your boss would be cool with it. It's not that long.'

'I've already been away from site for nearly two weeks. I can't take any more time off. They need me.'

Her smile faltered.

'And what about your job?' he added. 'How are you going to swing more time off?'

She chewed her lip. 'I don't know. I'll find a way.'

'Another dying granny?'

Her gaze dropped to the floor. 'I think I'm maxed out on them now.'

He turned back to washing the dishes, trying to think clearly, to weigh up the pros and cons. The pros were spending time with Sam and the money. The cons were the more time he spent with her, the deeper he fell in love and the more memories he made to stab him in the heart when it was all over.

'How would I get down there? Where would I stay?'

'Oh, Brad will pay for everything. He'll fly you down and put you up in a hotel. But...'

He felt her hand on his arm. Electricity sizzled across his skin.

'You could always stay at mine? With me?'

He lost himself in the blueness of her eyes. How could he refuse? Love started and ended with her. Maybe he should just take whatever she gave and be grateful for it.

He took the tea towel from her and dried his hands.

She swallowed.

He ran his fingers down the curve of her waist until he reached her hips. Her tongue ran out to wet her lips. He lifted her onto the counter and she gasped. He spread her legs and she pulled him against her with her heels.

The door banged open and Morag backed in with the vacuum cleaner. They sprang apart and Sam leapt to the ground. Jamie plunged his hands into the washing-up bowl.

Morag clattered past. 'You not done yet? Don't you need to record your music and send it to wee Brad? You're already a day late.'

'Yes, no worries, Morag,' said Sam. 'We're going to do it after we've done this.'

His mum pulled Jamie away from the sink. 'Don't waste any more time on this, you get going.'

Sam glanced at him through her eyelashes, a smile tugging at the corners of her mouth. 'Thank you, Morag.'

She went to the stairs, and he followed.

'Where are you going?' Morag asked.

'To Jamie's room?'

'Don't be daft, I've just tidied the lounge for you. I want to listen in.'

Sam's face fell and Jamie fought to remain calm.

'My own private concert. I can't wait!'

JAMIE DIDN'T KNOW IF SEXUAL FRUSTRATION MADE FOR better music, but he knew their performance was faultless. He was desperate to get everything right the first time so he could get his mother out of the way and be alone with Sam.

He hadn't kissed her for nearly thirty-six hours and was desperate to feel his lips on hers, her tongue sweeping into his mouth. They sang with their eyes locked on each other, raw emotion binding them together.

When they'd finished each song, they checked the recording, then emailed them directly to Brad's assistant, Crystal, from the laptop. It had taken a while to set up the microphones, so by the time they were finished they only had an hour before they were due at the castle for the band rehearsal.

Sam stood. 'Thank you, Morag. What are you up to now?'

His mother blew out her cheeks. 'Not sure, love. I might watch some telly?'

'That sounds a perfect idea. I think I'll go upstairs and pack. Jamie, would you be able to give me a hand?'

'Oh, I can help—' Morag said.

'No, I'll do it,' he said hurriedly. 'You put your feet up.'

Sam dashed out of the room and he followed her into the kitchen before his mother could say another word. He closed the door behind them and tugged her to him, cradling her head as he brought his lips to hers with a groan.

A loud knocking at the back door jumped them apart. Zoe barrelled in, her left arm outstretched, an enormous ring on her fourth finger.

'I'm engaged!' she screamed.

. . .

By the time the rehearsal at the castle was finished, Jamie was at his wit's end. There wasn't a moment he could be alone with Sam. Everyone wanted to talk to them. If he was shy and antisocial before, now he was a Trappist monk with an attitude problem.

Even on the walk to and from the castle they were accosted. He had to keep biting his cheek to stop himself telling everyone to fuck off and leave them alone.

Back at the house, his mum cooked them dinner and his sister arrived to monopolise Sam, dragging her upstairs to select an outfit for the night. He stomped after them, crashing about in the bathroom and banging his wardrobe door like a petulant teenager as he got dressed.

There was a knock at his door.

'What?'

Sam poked her head in. 'Are you nearly—*holy shit*.' Her eyes raked over him. 'Jamie MacDougall. Oh my good god.'

Heat rose through him. 'Is my sister out there?'

She shook her head. 'She's downstairs with your mum.' She stepped into the room and closed the door.

'Jesus, Sam,' he groaned.

She wore a black dress that hugged and caressed her curves. It was strapless, held up by the magical power of her incredible breasts. He itched to pull it down and suck them into his mouth.

She stepped to him and bunched the sides of his kilt in her hands, finding his skin and following it up to his hips. Her eyes widened and she gasped.

'You're not wearing any underwear!'

'I didn't want any VPL.'

She giggled and made small circles with her fingernails. He bucked towards her and she moved to his front, stroking his cock with one hand and rolling his balls with the other. He closed his eyes tightly and let his head fall back, his breath hissing in and out. She gripped harder.

'Jamie, you're so bloody big.'

'Kids! Come on, it's time to go!' Morag yelled up the stairs.

'Fuck's sake!' he growled.

'What was that, love?'

Sam released him and went to the door. 'Nothing, Morag. We're just coming.'

He stared at her. 'Are we?'

She smirked. 'Well, maybe later?'

THE GREAT HALL IN KINLOCH CASTLE WAS PACKED AND buzzing. The band had already set up at one end and the bar staff were rushed off their feet at the other. Jamie stuck to Sam like glue, his hand itching to reach out to hers. She was alive with excitement, smiling and chatting with everyone.

It couldn't be clearer how different they were. This was his turf, yet she was playing on it like a pro whilst he stood on the sidelines.

Fiona thrust a glass of whisky into his hand. 'Cheer up, Jamie. Might never happen.'

'It already did.'

He drained the glass and Fiona took it from him.

'It's not over till the fat lady sings.'

He stared at her. 'You're full of it tonight.'

She grinned. 'It's going to be okay. I promise.' She glanced past him and pulled a face. 'Don't look now, but I think Kirsten wants another crack.'

He shuddered as he felt a cool hand on his arm.

'Hey, Jamie.'

Before he could turn around, warm fingers interlaced with his, tugging him away.

'Come along, darling,' said Sam. 'There's someone you just *have* to meet.'

She dragged him through the crowds with the determination of a honey badger. His heart turned over and he smiled. He was being rescued by the princess. She pulled him out of the hall and down the corridor.

'Where are we going?'

'No idea.'

She kept her hand wedded to his as she pushed open doors and looked in. The corridors were getting narrower, the ceilings lower, and he had to duck his head.

'Aha. This will have to do.'

She dragged him inside a room and closed the door, turning a big iron key in the lock. He only had a second to realise they were in an old storeroom before she grabbed him, her mouth finding his, her kisses hot and hungry.

He wrapped his arms around her, groaning as his tongue met hers.

Finally.

Her touch was fire, scorching through him, turning everything to light, heat and need. He squeezed her bottom as she ground against his cock, threading the fingers of his other hand through her glorious hair.

He sucked down her neck as she mewled in his arms, stretching back, opening her body to him. He glanced hazily over her shoulder and lifted her, carrying her to an old wooden desk.

Shuffling off his jacket, he placed it over the top as she tugged to undo the buttons of his shirt. He sat her on the desk, cradling her head, his kisses deep as she worked his shirt open and he dropped it to the floor. His cock jerked painfully as she raked her nails down his chest.

She grasped his length through the kilt and he cried out,

pulling away, his hands gripping the side of the desk, the muscles of his arms strained to breaking point, eyes tightly closed.

'Fuck!'

He opened his eyes to see Sam pull a condom from the top of her dress.

She giggled. 'I thought you'd never ask...'

He shook his head with a laugh. 'You're, you're—'

'Well prepared?'

He took the condom from her and put it on the desk. He swallowed, still out of breath. 'You're everything.'

Her cheeks turned a deeper pink and she smiled shyly at him. He trailed a finger down the line of her neck and across her collarbone. With each rise of her chest, his cock swelled harder. He hooked inside the top of her dress and she gasped.

'Fuck, yes,' she breathed.

He could feel goosebumps prickle under his touch and his mouth watered. He worked her dress lower, the sound of their desperate breaths filling the space. Her breasts fell free, the nipples hard.

'Jesus Christ, Sam.' He stared, frozen, his heart beating out of control.

She arched towards him. 'Please, Jamie.'

He fell on her breasts, licking, sucking, rolling the pebbled ends as she cried out. Every sound she made was the sweetest music to his ears. He drew his hips back. He couldn't have any friction, or it would be game over. He didn't want to come until he was buried inside her.

She clutched his hair, gasping his name, pulling him closer. He ran a hand up the outside of her thigh, letting out a guttural cry as he discovered she wasn't wearing underwear. He sank to the floor and pushed her legs apart, hooking under her thighs and pulling her onto his mouth, licking into her hot sweetness.

'Jamie, Jamie, Jamie, oh god...'

Each time she moaned his name, blinding light rushed through him. He'd never felt so good, so powerful, so right. He sucked her clit and she cried out.

'Yes, yes, Jamie, yes.'

There was no need to be quiet—no one could hear them. He wanted to make her scream. Her legs were trembling, and he gripped them tighter. He fucked into her with his tongue, as deep as he could go, then flicked her clit with fast licks. He sensed she was close when her legs shook and her voice went higher.

He shook his head, growling as his tongue vibrated. She clamped her thighs to his head and screamed his name, convulsing around him, her orgasm pulsing against his mouth. He held her, licked her, loved her as she undulated beneath him. When her legs went soft, she pulled on his hair.

'Jamie, I need you inside me.'

He stood, unbuckled his kilt and let it drop to the floor. She rolled the condom over him. His breath hissed through his clenched teeth. He had to control himself. He had to make it good for her. He lifted her and she wrapped her legs around him.

She tugged his mouth to hers, her tongue diving in as she positioned herself and sank her weight down. He broke the kiss with a cry. The feeling was overwhelming. She was so tight, so sweet.

Her body entwined around him, taking him until he thought he would go blind with pleasure. He backed her against the nearest wall, one hand behind her back, the other under her bottom. The scrape of the old plaster against his forearms, the abrasion, helped distract from the feelings of her squeezing his cock.

She was circling him, trying to pull him deeper.

'Jamie, more. Please.'

He held her to him and thrust. She gripped around his neck.

'Yes!'

He pumped up into her, again and again, harder and harder until she was shaking and tightening. He pounded against the wall, hanging on by a thread, the fuse lit, a line of fire burning its way to the base of his spine.

'Fuck! I'm going to come. Jamie! Oh god, Jamie.'

She bit his neck and screamed as she stiffened around him.

He let go with a roar, pumping his release deep inside her. Light shot up his spine, obliterating everything in its path. Her muscles milked him dry, contracting around him, pulling out every ounce of pleasure.

'Sam, Sam, Sam.' He could hear his own voice, but it seemed far away.

I love you, I love you, I love you.

His eyes were pinched shut with pain. How could he live without her? How could life ever be anything but empty without her?

Hold it together.

He drew in shuddering breaths, stroking her hair, raining soft kisses down the curve of her neck. She pulled back, looking stunned.

'Jamie, that was...' She shook her head and let out a laugh. 'Fucking hell, Jamie. I think you've broken me.'

He smiled. 'I think you broke me the first time we met.'

She giggled. 'A wee lass like me?'

'You're small but you're mighty.'

She grinned. 'Says the man who's holding me up.' He gently

pulled out of her and put her to the ground, then went to take the condom off.

'Jesus, Jamie!'

His forearms were streaked with blood. They glanced at the wall where lines of livid red brushed against the rough whitewash.

'Oh.' He laughed. 'My first ever sex injury.'

She found a roll of blue paper towels and pulled sheets off, gently patting them against his arm. 'You okay?'

He smiled. He'd never felt better. 'Yeah, I'm grand.'

She gazed at his neck and her forehead creased.

'What is it?' he asked.

She blushed. 'Erm, I might have, er, bitten you.'

Heat rushed to his cheeks. 'Oh.'

'I'm sure it'll be fine once your shirt is back on.'

It took ten minutes for Sam to straighten Jamie out. His hair was defying gravity, he'd lost two buttons from his shirt, and his arms had to be bandaged with paper towels to stop the blood from seeping through and staining the fabric. His collar only just hid Sam's bite—he was glad that on stage later he'd be hiding at the back.

They strolled slowly through the dark corridors, their hands intertwined. She let go outside the main door to the great hall and part of his heart fell away.

It's not over yet.

He pushed open the door for her and they entered a world of light and heat and noise. Zoe rushed over and grabbed Sam, and Jamie let her go, going over to the band who were having a break.

Donnie, a fiddle player a couple of years younger than him, waved him over.

'I've got you a beer.'

Jamie took it. 'Cheers.'

'I didn't get a chance to speak to you earlier,' Donnie said. 'But have you thought about how you're going to get your music out?'

'Out?'

'Into the world. Get yourself a deal.'

'A record deal?'

'Yeah, what else? A buy one, get one free deal from Iceland?'

'I hadn't thought about it.'

Donnie shook his head. 'Well, you should. You need to speak to Campbell King. He's the big man at Ness Records. He's sound. Really decent bloke. You must have heard of him?'

Jamie shook his head. 'You know me, I don't get out much.'

'Well that's about to change now Brad Bauer's all over you like a rash.'

Jamie gazed out into the crowds. Brad was talking to Sam and Zoe. He gesticulated wildly, then pulled them both in for a hug. Rory was standing to one side, a muscle twitching in his jaw.

I know how you feel, mate.

'Don't you think?'

He turned back to Donnie. 'Sorry, think what?'

'This is your ticket out of here. See the world. Get paid for doing what you love. Live the dream, Jamie.'

He shrugged. 'I don't think that's my dream.'

Donnie looked at him askance. 'Then you need your head examined, mate.' He drained the bottle. 'Come on, you're up next.'

. . .

WHEN IT WAS JUST JAMIE AND SAM PLAYING THEIR MUSIC, IT was powerful but intimate. But in such a big space with the ceilidh band, it was immense. The crowd roared when Sam strode onto the stage. Brad hadn't been told they'd be performing, and he absolutely lost it, jumping up and down and whooping.

Jamie couldn't help but grin. Brad was like a kid on Christmas morning who'd already worked his way through an entire selection box and the liqueur chocolates meant for Grandma. His enthusiasm was infectious and soon everyone was stamping on the wooden floor, cheering and clapping.

Sam was incandescently bright. Whether singing or talking, she whipped everyone higher and higher. They played 'The Heart of Scotland' three times at the end of their set, and everyone joined in.

Jamie tried to take mental snapshots of what he knew would be a once in a lifetime experience. The stuff of legends and tall tales. A story you told your kids and grandkids.

His heart pinched.

Or the stories he would tell Liam, and Liam's kids. Without Sam, a family was a path he knew he'd never take.

THEY ALL STAYED UP TILL THE SKY WAS TURNING PALE AS IF trying to deny the night its closure. Jamie passed out in his bed and Sam slept for a few hours in Fiona's old room. By the time he woke with his throat scratchy, Sam's hire car was outside the back door, her suitcases inside.

Zoe, Fiona, and Morag were tired and emotional, hugging Sam goodbye and crying. Jamie stood in the doorway watching, rubbing at the bristle on his chin.

Sam broke away and put her arms around him. He patted her back awkwardly.

'See you in a couple of weeks?' she asked.

He pulled away and nodded. 'Safe trip home.'

She smiled and got in the car. He stood with the others, his hand raised as she drove away.

Sam Adamson was gone, and his life would never be the same again.

21

Sam closed her eyes as hands came to the back of her shoulders. The man kissed her neck and she repressed a shudder.

'Babe,' he said huskily. 'I'm gonna light your fire.'

She froze. What was she meant to say? There was an awkward pause, then she shook Ian off and glanced up.

'Sorry, Tamsyn. Can you just give me a minute?'

'No worries. Okay, everyone, quick break. Don't run off anywhere.'

Sam turned away from the crew and sat on a sofa, looking out of a window with a painted view behind it. Ian slumped next to her, manspreading. She crossed her legs away from him.

'How's your granny?' he asked. 'Is she dead yet, or do you need her to hang on until you've finally banged Brad Bauer?'

'bIjatlh 'e' yImev, Hab SoSlI' Quch!'

'Eh? Is that Scottish or more bloody Klingon?'

'It means "shut up, your mother has a smooth forehead".'

'That's true. I pay for her Botox. You should try it. Brad

might have given you a go if you weren't such a sour-faced old cow.'

'Eat shit, Berresford.'

He stretched his arm along the back of the sofa.

'I'm going to be kissing shit in a minute,' he replied. 'If you remember your lines, that is.'

Being back in London was jarring. Sam had lost her mojo and even the ability to fake it. Her flat was too quiet and lonely and the set of *Elm Tree Lane* too busy and loud.

She missed the distant rumble of Morag's snoring, her soft hugs and her laughter. She missed Zoe and Fiona. But most of all, she missed Jamie.

It was a pain she tried to ignore. They had no future. She was an actress and he was an electrician. Her life was in London and his was in the Highlands of Scotland.

After they'd recorded the music for Brad, they'd nowhere else to go together. What was the point in even thinking about him?

Still, she kept checking her phone for messages. She'd rung Jamie's boss and explained who she was and that she'd pretended to be a registrar. They'd actually had a lovely conversation. It was clear Gregor thought the world of Jamie.

Everyone thought the world of Jamie.

After that conversation, he'd texted.

> Jamie: Thank you for speaking to Gregor.
> Hope you got home okay.

She'd tried to engage him in conversation, but it appeared he was as quiet over text as he was in real life.

Brad had put her in touch with the producer, and they'd agreed to try and get all three songs recorded within a week.

The producer would lay down the backing with the orchestra on Monday and Tuesday, and she and Jamie would add their voices and guitar over the last three days. Jamie let her handle everything, telling her he'd fly down on Tuesday and go back Sunday.

Her heart ached. It felt like they'd gone back to square one, that the intimacy they'd shared never existed. Jamie had said she was his everything, but now she was reduced to nothing. As significant as a biscuit crumb left on a plate.

She'd had to ask Sandra, her agent, to get her another three days off work for the recording. Then a journalist rang wanting the inside scoop on what she and Jamie were doing with Brad Bauer.

If they hadn't been plastered all over Brad's Instagram feed, she could have tried to lie. She had to keep control of the message, so agreed to meet the journalist with Jamie when he was down.

Sam lay in bed, unable to sleep, the blue light from her phone filling the darkness as she mindlessly scrolled through social media and waited for texts from Jamie that never arrived.

The phone ringing shocked her. It was her sister.

'Esther, you okay?'

'Yes, of course I am. Are you?'

'Um, yeah, fine.' There was an awkward silence. 'Mum and Dad okay?'

'Yes, fine. I just wanted to remind you about Anna's birthday next Thursday. Remember?'

'Er, um, yes of course. I don't think I can come. I've got Jamie stay—' She paused. 'The guy I wrote the music with is coming to London to record it.'

'Bring him along. We'd all like to meet him.'

'I can't bring him to a family meal.'

Esther gave a short and efficient laugh. 'Why not? It would be nice to have someone there to delay the conversation turning to the latest advances in sutures and the GMC.'

Sam smiled. 'I thought you loved talking about that stuff.'

'Well, it's nice to have common ground with Dad, but sometimes it gets a bit much. It's like he's testing me all the time. Sometimes I just want to have a drink and talk about rubbish on the telly.'

Rubbish like Elm Tree Lane.

Sam bit the inside of her cheek. 'Okay, I'll bring him. Text me the details, okay?'

'Sam, I didn't mean—'

'Gotta dash, another call coming through.'

She cut her sister off, threw her phone across the room, and curled up on her side, making herself as small and insignificant as she knew she was.

THE FOLLOWING TUESDAY, SAM TOOK A TAXI FROM THE studio to the airport to meet Jamie. He was expecting to meet at her flat, but she wanted to surprise him.

She'd scrubbed off her Bethany make-up, and Shelley had blow-dried her hair. She was sick with nerves, her stomach churning. It reminded her of the worst days of her Crohn's, and she had to stop and do her breathing exercises to calm down and remind herself how much better she was now.

She stood back from the barrier in arrivals, not wanting to draw attention to herself. Her heart jumped each time the doors swished open, discharging more people.

Where was he? Had she got the time wrong? Her heart stopped as he strode out, a holdall over one shoulder, his guitar case in his hand. His hair had been cut and he looked like a model-turned-rock star.

Sam's head was dizzy. Jamie was stupidly handsome. And he was *here*.

He stopped, looking around as if to orientate himself. She ran over, pushing herself into his eyeline. He stopped and stared at her, blinking, as if his brain had stopped and was restarting.

'Jamie. It's me.'

'What are you doing here?' His voice sounded choked, and he cleared his throat, colour rising into his cheeks.

'I thought I'd surprise you.'

He looked blankly at her.

'Did it work?'

He swallowed and nodded. She tried to keep her smile in place, but inside she was crumbling. Why did she have to fuck everything up?

He started. 'Sorry, erm.' He put his bag and guitar case down and held his arms out stiffly.

Sam hesitated, but the lure was too strong. She melted into him, snaking her arms inside his jacket and burying her head into his side, inhaling citrus, sandalwood and *him*. He folded her into his body, holding her tightly and nuzzling the top of her hair.

'It's so good to see you again,' he breathed.

She could hear the fast beat of his heart, feel the rise and fall of his chest. She pressed herself closer. She could feel—

She giggled into his jacket. 'Jamie, is that an earl's sausage or are you pleased to see me?'

He huffed into her hair. 'I'm sorry. I didn't mean for that to happen.'

Sam pulled her head out of his jacket and grinned. 'I'm not sorry. I thought you'd forgotten all about me.'

The colour in his cheeks deepened, and his eyes darkened.

'Never.'

They took a taxi back to her flat in Shepherd's Bush. Jamie had worried about the cost, but Sam told him they could charge it to the *Braveheart 2* production.

She knew it was a legitimate expense, but she would have paid it anyway. She didn't want to share Jamie with tube and bus passengers. She kept her fingers threaded through his. His eyes kept moving from the window to her as if he couldn't decide what to look at.

'Have you ever been to London before?'

He shook his head.

'Did you remember your passport?'

'I don't have one.'

Her mouth opened and she shut it again. *Think before you speak, Smulan!*

'Well, in honour of your first visit to our great nation's capital, I've created a packed schedule.'

He looked panicked. 'You have?'

'It's fine, it's nothing much,' she lied, inwardly cringing. 'We're recording tomorrow through to Friday. Thursday night we're going for a meal to celebrate my sister Anna's birthday and Saturday night we're going to the soap awards.'

Seeing his expression, she decided it was probably best not to mention the interview she'd lined up with the journalist.

'Your *family*? The *soap* awards?'

'Don't worry, they're not like me. You'll be fine.'

He pulled his hand from hers and rubbed his face. His breath was changing, speeding up. She touched his thigh.

'It'll be okay, I promise. I thought you could be my date?' She let the question hang, watching his cheeks colour. 'I don't have anyone to go with and I don't want to be anywhere near Ian Berresford right now.'

At the mention of Ian's name, she felt his thighs stiffen.

'I'll do it,' he said gruffly.

She breathed again.

'But I don't have anything to wear.'

Sam squeezed his leg. 'I'll take you shopping on Saturday. My treat.'

THE TAXI PULLED UP OUTSIDE A LARGE WHITE TERRACED house on a quiet street and Sam and Jamie got out.

'Is it all yours?' he asked.

'God no, I'd need to sell off every organ to afford that. I've got the ground floor flat. I think it's the best. I don't get heights, but I do get the garden.'

Sam unlocked the main door, then the one to her flat. She was suddenly shy. What would Jamie think?

'So, shoes can go there and let me give you these before I forget.' She pressed a set of keys into his hand. 'This one is for the main front door and these two are for the flat.'

'Why do I need these?'

'So you can come and go as you please.'

'But won't I be with you all the time?'

'Yes, but if I'm asleep and you want to pop out you can. Visit Buckingham Palace or something.'

'Is it close?'

'What?'

'Buckingham Palace?'

She started to laugh, then stopped. He looked mortified.

'It's not walking distance, but we can go there on Saturday, if you want?'

He shrugged.

'So, do you want the grand tour? I'm afraid I'm all out of guidebooks, but I can answer any questions as long as they only pertain to the content, not the fabric of the building.'

Sam hadn't meant to go for Scandi chic when she decorated, but her upbringing had obviously rubbed off on her.

The first room they entered was the living room. It had polished wooden floors, white walls and a large bay window facing the street. A gilt mirror hung over the fireplace with photos stuck inside the frame.

The colour in the room was provided by the furniture, including a shocking pink velvet sofa that ran along the length of one wall.

'Wow,' Jamie said. 'If Fi could see that.'

'It was my first big splurge purchase after the flat. I got it from Heal's on Tottenham Court Road. I wanted something that even Zoe would get lost in.'

'Heels? Sounds like your perfect shop.'

'Ha, ha. H-e-a-l-s.'

Jamie inspected the photos she had displayed. He grinned as he saw the ones of Sam and Zoe at uni.

'Is Zoe dressed as a tiger?'

'Yes. It was a "law of the jungle" party.'

'What did you go as?'

'Darwin.'

He snorted with laughter and her heart leapt.

'I knew it was a long shot, but I thought I'd make a statement about the survival of the fittest and all that.'

His eyes crinkled with amusement. 'I never thought I'd ever be attracted to someone with a beard.'

Sam's pulse quickened. She took his hand. 'Come on. Let me show you the rest of the place.'

Next to the living room was a bathroom, then down two steps was a large kitchen full of light from the wall of glass that looked out onto the garden. Jamie shook his head. 'This is like something out of a magazine.'

Sam squeezed his hand. 'Help yourself to anything. The bedrooms are this way.'

She led him out of the kitchen into a small corridor with two doors. She pushed open the first one. The space was filled with boxes and junk, but there was a double bed in the middle that had been cleared.

'This is the spare room.' Her hand was suddenly clammy with nerves. 'I didn't know whether you wanted to sleep here, or...'

He was silent.

She didn't look at him but went to the next door and opened it. Her room was dominated by a wooden sleigh bed. Pink fairy lights trimmed with marabou looped around the headboard and large pink sheepskin rugs covered the floor.

'Or if you wanted to sleep here. With me.'

He brushed his hand down the side of her cheek and tilted her chin so she met his gaze.

'I always want to be with you.'

Sam clamped her jaw shut to stop it trembling. The way he looked at her made her heart weep.

There it was. She hadn't imagined it.

No one had ever looked at her like that before. Even the best actors couldn't fake this depth of sincerity, this depth of lo—

She blinked, steering her mind back to the physical sensations of his thumb rubbing circles into her palm, his fingers stroking down her neck.

'Sam.' The way he said her name was a caress.

She whimpered. Jamie ran his hand up into her hair, holding the back of her head as she reached up to meet him with a kiss. As their lips touched, sparks flew like the tail of a comet across her skin. She grabbed his head, pulling him closer, the flick of his tongue into her mouth making her groan.

He clasped her bottom, roughly pulling her against his thick length. She undulated against it, feeling him fighting for breath until he pulled away with a harsh cry, resting his chin on top of her head. She licked his neck and he jerked away.

'Sam.'

'Yes, Jamie?' She reached for his trousers and undid the top button.

He covered her hand with his. 'Stop, please.'

Worry knifed through her. 'What's wrong?'

He cradled her head, kissing her. 'Nothing's wrong, I just want to love you before I take any clothes off.'

She tried to pout but couldn't stop the smile from spreading. 'But where's the fun for you?'

He rubbed his cheek against hers. 'Believe you me, the pleasure is all mine.'

She clenched her thighs, her body pulsing with need.

'So, er, when I've had, erm, my fun, do I get to take your clothes off?'

'You can do whatever you want with me,' he replied. 'I'm yours.'

'Really?'

He tugged her earlobe into his mouth and bit down gently. She gasped.

'Although I draw the line at ninety-nine per cent of what went on in that billionaire bondage novel Fiona was raving about,' he whispered.

She giggled. 'What's the one per cent you'll allow?'

He licked circles on the sensitive skin of her throat. 'The food. They ate some posh nosh in that book.'

She swallowed.

'So, do you accept my terms?'

Her tummy tripped over itself with excitement. 'One hundred per cent.'

Jamie didn't take his time undressing her. He made short work of removing her clothes and laying her out in the centre of the bed. Only when she was naked did he pause.

His eyes raked across her, fanning the flames that licked at the inside of her skin. The intensity of his gaze made her suddenly shy, and she moved to cover herself. He shook his head and she stopped.

'Don't ever hide who you are. You're incredible.'

She blinked, the edges of her eyes prickling.

'You're everything.' He covered her with his body, bracketing her head with his arms, slanting his hot mouth over hers, their tongues tangling.

Her body shorted out, nerves firing and misfiring, setting up chain reactions that flickered and fizzed through every muscle. His hand found her breast and pleasure shot down between her legs. Her toes curled as she arched up to him.

How could he be so good at this? There was literally no other comparison she could make. She couldn't even remember any other sexual encounter, any other men when he was with her. It wasn't just the way Jamie touched her, it was the emotional energy that poured off him in waves. He was an ocean of passion, and all that power and strength was directed solely at her.

Sam closed her eyes as his mouth trailed a hot path down to her breasts, his fingers exploring her wetness, then plunging deeply inside her as her hand covered his. She rocked against him, holding his head to her nipple, his fingers inside her, his thumb rubbing circles of light over her clit.

Her body vibrated with tension, her sharp cries a counterpoint to his growls as he sucked her deep. The pleasure was whipping in tighter and tighter circles inside her, squeezing her lungs, wringing her muscles, until everything compressed to a diamond point of light and shattered.

Her eyes rolled back, her mouth opening wide as every part of her exploded. Her body convulsed, arching up, then thudding back to the bed. She was lost inside the blinding light of her climax as it took her to the edge of the stars, then beyond.

Her breath returned in gasps, her fingers trembling. She tried to find a coherent thought, something to say, but then his head was between her legs, his hot tongue plunging inside her, and the only word she could cry was his name.

Jamie was ferocious, licking and sucking until another orgasm crashed through her. She was utterly discombobulated and out of control. She needed to find her centre, remember who she was, but he didn't let her.

He pushed her forward into another orgasm, then another. Her heart couldn't take it. It opened itself up like a flower, the petals delicate and fragile. She curled up on her side and he lay behind her, holding her tightly. She squeezed her eyes shut and held her breath, pushing all the emotion back down.

His breath was ragged in her ear. 'You okay?'

She nodded.

'You sure? I didn't hurt you?'

Sam finally let go of her breath with a laugh. Her heart was retreating into comfortable territory.

'You're a sex god, Jamie MacDougall. Actually, that's not true. We live in a monotheism. You're *the* sex god. The one and only. Forever and ever, amen.'

He hugged her tighter. 'I'd do anything for you.'

She turned her head. 'Ah, yes. Now I'm revived from my sex coma, it's my turn to play.'

He froze. 'What do you want me to do?'

She rolled over to face him. 'Stand by the side of the bed and take off all your clothes.'

He swallowed. 'All of them?'

She nodded. 'Especially your socks.'

He sat on the edge of the bed and took them off first, showing them to her before dropping them to the floor. She giggled and propped up on her side. He pulled off his shirt, and her mouth watered. He shucked off his jeans and boxers and stood before her.

Sam swallowed, and it turned into a cough. 'Fucking hell, Jamie.'

She ran her eyes lasciviously over his broad shoulders, the ridges of his abdomen, his thick muscled thighs, his huge hard cock.

'Don't move.'

She crawled towards him and sat on the edge of the bed. He moved away and she shook her head, pulling him towards her.

'What are you doing?' His voice was breathy, his eyes panicked.

Sam squeezed his shaft. 'Are you going to do what I say, or not?'

'Um, yes, but, er.'

She arched an eyebrow and he swallowed.

'What are you going to do?' he asked again.

Leaning forward, she and licked the end of his cock.

'Jesus Christ!' Jamie jerked away from her, his hands fisting on his thighs, all the muscles in his neck strained.

'Jamie?'

He stared at her, his gaze desperate.

'I really want to do this,' she said. 'But if you don't want me to, I won't.'

His mouth opened and shut as he drew in ragged breaths, trying to speak. 'I do want it, but I won't last long.'

She grinned. 'I'd be disappointed if you did. You've set the bar pretty high with your oral skills and I don't want to fall short.'

He shook his head vigorously. 'Never.'

'So, let's find out then, shall we?'

She pulled him back towards her, one hand holding the base of his shaft, the other cupping his balls. She held his gaze as she circled the head with her tongue. His eyes were wide, his mouth open, his cheeks flushed as he watched her. Her cheeks hollowed as she sucked.

'Oh god, Sam. Fuck!'

A thrill raced through her. She wanted to pleasure him as he'd done for her. She took him deeper, twisting her hand up his shaft. His hands fluttered uncertainly to her head, threading into her hair, following her movements. She sucked and licked, tugging on his balls, gripping him tighter as she pumped his length.

She felt him start to lose control. She knew he would want to pull out, so she grabbed his backside, digging her nails in, holding him in place.

'Jesus, Sam! I'm going to, you don't have to, I, I—'

She took him deeper, stroking harder as he let go with a roar. His body shook, his release pumping at the back of her throat. She swallowed it and sucked harder.

He folded forward over her, gasping and trembling. She licked and kissed his cock, then moved away so he could fall forward onto the bed. She lifted his legs to the mattress and cuddled him from behind.

'That was...' he began. 'That was unbelievable.'

She nibbled his earlobe. 'Welcome to London, Jamie MacDougall.'

That evening felt like the calm before the storm. Sam and Jamie got takeout and ate it in bed with a picnic blanket laid across the duvet. They didn't discuss music or what was going to happen next. They kept their world small, just the two of them.

Overnight, Jamie kept waking, disorientated. Sam held him close as he fell back to sleep, wondering if he'd ever spent a night away from home before. As the predawn light filtered in through the windows, they made love as if for the last time, holding each other tightly. As they left the bed, the silence grew like a wall between them.

Sam didn't know what to say to lift Jamie's mood, as she was as nervous as he looked. To protect him from the strangeness of a new city, she ordered another cab to take them to the studio and gripped his hand as they drove from Shepherd's Bush to Hampstead.

When they exited the taxi, he faltered. 'It's a church.'

'It *was* a church. This is Air Studios. Scores for everything from *Harry Potter* to *Wonder Woman* have been recorded here.'

'Fuck.'

'It's okay, Jamie. We've got this.'

He shook his head. '*You've* got this. I haven't.'

'Jamie, you have. Just close your eyes and imagine you're back in Kinloch.'

He stared up at the building, a muscle twitching in his jaw, then took a big breath in. 'Okay. Lead on, Macduff.'

She smiled at him. 'Not "lay" on?'

'You were right, "lead" on does sound better.'

They entered through the big doors into the central atrium, stopping as the enormity of the space hit them. It was vast, the vaulted roof reaching up to the sky, the floor filled with chairs and music stands.

Sam gazed at their faces reflected in the long piece of glass that separated the studio from the control room. They looked like deer caught in the headlights of a truck.

Jamie squeezed her hand as a tall, slim man with short white hair strode towards them. His eyes were bright.

'Sam, Jamie, I'm Chris, your producer. Great to finally meet you.'

They each shook his hand.

'We've had a fantastic couple of days,' he continued. 'Your songs are just beautiful. We've got all of them laid to a click track now, so we'll be ready to go in half an hour or so when the band arrives. Is this your first time at Air?'

They nodded.

'Great. You can put your guitar and bags down there and I'll show you around.'

He was chatty and affable as he took them around the studio. Sam kicked her social skills into gear, drawing on her experience and training to smile and nod in all the right places.

Chris tried to draw Jamie out, but he was quiet and pale, walking around like the newly undead, unsure of who or where he was. By the time they arrived back in the central atrium, it was full of people and instruments.

'Band?' Jamie croaked.

Chris laughed. 'Ah, yes, we call them a band, but it's really a full orchestra of a hundred players. Well, one hundred and two with you.'

Sam grabbed Jamie's hand. It was cold and clammy.

'You'll be out the front, near me,' Chris continued. 'Grab a seat and we'll get your mics set up.'

He strode off and they sat as engineers fiddled around them. She held onto his hands. 'Do you want to breathe with me?'

He shook his head.

'We can do this, Jamie. Just close your eyes and imagine you're playing for Liam.'

He nodded, but his face was grey and perspiration was breaking out across his forehead. Sam got out his guitar and passed it to him, giving him something to focus on whilst the room filled up.

She was used to the pressure of a performance but had never done anything like this before. Her heart thumped in her chest as her head flicked around the room, catching people's eyes.

They all knew each other and were relaxed. She was so wound up she was about to snap. All of this was happening because her mouth had run away with her, and Jamie had sweetly played along. She owed him everything.

Chris stood on a low podium. He tapped his baton on a music stand and the room fell silent.

'Morning, everyone. I'm delighted to welcome Sam Adamson and Jamie MacDougall, the writers of these stunning songs, who will be joining us for the next three days.'

The room filled with applause. Sam felt like she was going to burst into tears. Jamie looked like he was going to be sick.

'We've got plenty of time to play around, so let's get started with "The Heart of Scotland".'

There was a rustle of sheet music behind them and the sound of an oboe as everyone tuned their instruments.

Chris turned to them. 'Okay, so we've laid everything to a click track, so if you pop your headphones on, you'll hear what you're playing and be able to follow along in time.'

They put them on and Sam moved her chair closer to Jamie, touching her foot to his. He looked at her and tried to smile.

'Right, guys, let's take it from the top. Nadim, are you ready for us?' Sam saw a thumbs up from inside the control room. 'Okay, everyone.'

Chris lifted his arms and caught their eye. They jumped as a loud robotic clicking sounded in their ears, followed by the sound of the strings playing.

Chris lowered his arms and everything fell silent. 'Sorry, Jamie, my fault. I should have explained, you start after the first four clicks. Let's go again.'

They stared up at Chris as the clicks started. Jamie began on time but stumbled over the chords. Sam sang but it sounded false and stilted. By the end of the first chorus, they were almost a beat behind everyone else.

Chris stopped everyone and they went again. Sam watched a bead of sweat run down Jamie's temple. This was *not* what she'd expected. If she was struggling, then how the fuck was he going to cope?

Chris seemed laid-back, but after half an hour they hadn't managed to get to the end of the song in time. Jamie's breathing was quicker, his fingers starting to shake.

'Let's try one more, then have a break, shall we?' said Chris.

The click started and Jamie's head dropped forward. Sam grabbed the guitar out of his trembling grip. He ripped his headphones off and walked unsteadily away, breaking into a run as he reached the door. She ran after him, pushing through into a green room as he staggered to the floor on his hands and knees.

'Jamie!'

She could hear him fighting for breath, wheezing in and out as he swayed, then he crashed to his side, his hands twisting and spasming. She grabbed his head. His eyes were wild and unfocused, his lips pale.

'Jamie! Look at me! Breathe with me! *In, two, three, four and hold, two, three, four!*' She kept going, shouting instructions as she dragged him out of the darkness.

When his breathing quietened, he closed his eyes. She took his hands, massaging them, getting the blood flow back. Her cheeks were wet and she swiped the tears angrily away.

'I'm so sorry, Jamie.'

The door opened and Chris appeared. Sam shook her head at him and held up her hand, the digits splayed to indicate five minutes. He retreated.

She held Jamie to her, laying his head on her chest, stroking his hair until he finally stirred.

'I'm sorry, Sam.' His voice sounded lost and far away.

She sniffed. 'No, Jamie. *I'm* sorry. It's all my fault. I should have known what I was dragging you into.'

The door opened again and Chris came in. He sat on the floor next to them and Jamie pushed himself into a seated position.

'How are you doing?' Chris asked.

Jamie shrugged. Sam pulled a tissue out of her pocket and blew her nose.

'Have you ever played with a drummer before?' Chris continued.

Jamie shook his head.

Chris rubbed his jaw. 'I can't remember the last time I worked with an acoustic set-up like this, especially someone who hasn't worked to a click track or drummer.'

'Sorry.'

'God, don't apologise, Jamie. This is entirely on me. We're going to ditch the click track and work from the two of you. The engineers will route whatever you're playing to me and the rest of the band. You'll set the tempo and we'll follow. Does that sound like something you can work with?'

He nodded.

'Chris, can you give us half an hour?' Sam asked.

'Sure, of course. I'll make sure you're not disturbed. Take as long as you like.'

He left the room and Sam wrapped her arms around Jamie. 'You don't have to do this if you don't want to.'

He dropped his chin with a sigh. 'You want this.' It was a statement, not a question.

She didn't reply.

'I'll do it,' he whispered. 'I'll do my best.'

Sam's heart howled. She knew what she was asking Jamie to do, but equally she couldn't bear the thought of this chance passing her by. Her tears splashed onto his hand and he glanced up.

'Hey, don't cry. Please don't cry.' He looked in so much pain as he wiped her cheeks. 'I'm choosing to do this. It's okay. I promise.'

He drew her onto his lap and rocked her as the sounds of the musicians outside filtered through the door.

When they finally came out of the room and put their headphones back on, there was nothing but blissful silence awaiting them. They angled their chairs so their legs were touching, and Jamie closed his eyes.

As he plucked out the first notes of 'The Heart of Scotland', the music wound its magic around them, lifting them. After the first take, the room erupted with stamping feet and cheers.

Chris was grinning from ear to ear. He spread his arms wide. 'And the Oscar goes to... Sam Adamson and Jamie MacDougall!'

Sam smiled at Jamie, relief flooding through her, and he smiled tentatively back.

'Okay, ladies and gents,' said Chris with a big smile. 'Let's go again. Whenever you're ready, Jamie, take it away!'

THEY ARRIVED BACK AT SAM'S FLAT LATE, HAVING STAYED after the session ended to grab some food with Chris. When they got in, Sam sat an exhausted Jamie in front of the television and went to make him a cup of tea.

When she returned, he was asleep, his face finally soft and calm. She arranged pillows at one end of the sofa and carefully rolled him onto his side, covering him with a blanket. He didn't stir.

Sam turned everything off, leaving the light in the corridor on, then went to bed. She managed five minutes of well-practised self-loathing before sleep stole her.

❧ 23 ❧

Jamie woke and enjoyed a brief moment of bliss before reality hit like a collapsing wall. Memories of the previous day tumbled onto him, brick by brick, until he couldn't breathe.

Everything was new and utterly overwhelming. Sam, sex, London, recording. Just one of those things on its own would have been enough, but together they were paralysing.

He'd slept all night, fully clothed on the sofa, but didn't feel rested. His body and brain were in meltdown.

There was a knock on the living room door.

'I'm awake.'

Sam entered, already dressed. 'The taxi is due in half an hour. I didn't want to wake you until the last possible minute. Do you want to have a shower or anything?'

He sat up and rubbed his face.

'Yeah, I do. Are we going straight from the studio to the restaurant for your sister's birthday?'

She paused. 'Er, kind of. I'm meeting a journalist friend beforehand for a quick drink.'

'Do you want me to clear off when you do that? Do I need to pick something up for your sister?'

'No, it'll be good you're there and I've got Anna a card and present. I'll be in the kitchen if you need anything.'

She disappeared and Jamie's head dropped.

You can do this.

SAM WAS AS QUIET AS JAMIE AS THEY DROVE TO THE STUDIO. He now knew what to expect. As long as the two of them could hold it together, the recording would be done in less time than allocated. He decided to approach the day as he approached his work on site: head down, focus, get the job done.

With his eyes closed and Sam's leg touching his, he felt centred enough to lose himself in the music. If he stayed present, moving from note to note and not thinking past the next bar, he'd be okay.

By mid-morning Chris and the engineers were happy with the second song, and by 3.00 p.m. the third was in the bag. They had a quick break whilst the mixes were patched over to Brad in LA, and shortly afterwards Chris told everyone that Brad was a 'very happy bunny'.

Everyone clapped and cheered, but Jamie sank deeper into his chair. He was drained and empty, all his reserves of energy spent.

He'd never felt like this before, even after a workout on the rings when all his muscles were twitching. It was as if every cell in his body had curled up and was refusing to work.

Sam packed his guitar away, laughing and joking with everyone, then called them a taxi. He let her lead him away and slumped in the seat, his eyes falling closed.

She didn't speak, but held his hand in hers. Finally, they

were done with recording, the film, Brad, and all other distractions. He wasn't flying back until Sunday afternoon, so they had nearly three days with each other. For the first time since they'd met, they could be together without any other purpose guiding them.

He squeezed her hand. Maybe then he could work up the courage to tell her how he felt and see if there was any chance she might one day feel the same.

Sam's phone rang.

'Hey, Sandra, how are you?... Yeah, all good here. We're done already, so I can go straight back to set on Monday... Tomorrow? Yes, what time... Okay, I'll see you then. Bye, bye.' She ended the call. 'That was my agent. She wants me to go in tomorrow for a meeting.'

'Is everything okay?'

She tossed her hair and smiled. 'Yeah, probably something big. She always likes to deliver the good news in person. We can go on from there to see Buckingham Palace if you like? Or wherever you want to go.'

'I don't mind. Maybe see Big Ben? Harrods? Tower Bridge?'

She snuggled up to him. 'We can see it all.'

THE TAXI DROPPED SAM AND JAMIE OFF IN SOHO OUTSIDE AN independent coffee shop that looked like a funeral parlour run by hipsters. The outside was entirely black except for the name 'Coffine House' painted above the door and across the windows in gold letters.

Men wearing jeans three sizes too small and sporting beards four sizes too big bustled about serving customers crammed around tiny tables on the pavement outside.

Sam led Jamie inside to the back where a woman waited for them in a private booth. She was small and glossy, with shiny red nails that matched her perfect lipstick. Her green eyes flicked like a snake between him and Sam, and Jamie's brain started scanning for the nearest exit.

Sam was drawn in for air kisses.

'Saaaaaaaaaam, darling, it's been just too long.'

'Karen, this is Jamie MacDougall who I wrote the music with.'

'Well, hello, handsome.'

Nervous heat rose through his body as he took the woman's hand. It was cold and dry. He swallowed.

'Aren't you a glass of smoky single malt?'

Jamie didn't know how to reply, or when he could let go of her hand.

'Does he speak?' Karen whispered to Sam.

Sam laughed, pulled Jamie away and sat him down. 'He's a man of few words.'

Karen slid in opposite them and took out her phone. 'Well, let's see if I can coax a few out of him.' She winked at Jamie, and he blinked back.

Sam ordered coffee and Karen set her phone to record.

What the fuck is this?

He felt Sam's hand on his thigh, gently squeezing.

'So,' Karen began. 'I've been following this story via Brad's Insta and I'm just so *intrigued*. Sam, you're in the middle of the most exciting storyline *Elm Tree Lane* has had all year, and now you're a singer-songwriter providing the music for *Braveheart 2*?'

'Well, Karen, not *all* the music—just three songs.'

'But how did this happen? And how did you meet Jamie?'

Sam took a sip of coffee. 'Just one of those magical twists of fate. I was in Scotland on a family matter and met Jamie through my best friend—'

'The Countess of Kinloch?'

'They're not married yet, but when they do, yes, she'll be the countess. Anyway, she's very close to Brad Bauer—'

'Yes, and we're debating exactly *how* close after the earl went on his well-documented rampage.'

Jamie bristled and felt Sam stiffen beside him.

'They're simply friends,' she said firmly. 'Zoe showed Brad a video she took of me and Jamie playing. Brad asked us to compose some music for the film, so we did.'

'What a wonderful story.'

There was silence. Karen's eyes bored into his. Jamie felt like she was preparing to strike.

'So, Jamieeeee. Tell me more about you...'

Panic slashed through him. Anything he said would be twisted by her into a knife with which to stab him. He would trust the Neds at work before he gave up a piece of himself to her.

He shook his head. Sam reached across the table and paused the recording.

'Karen, Jamie has Selective Mutism Disorder. I need to make it absolutely clear that under no circumstances should you mention this in your article or to anyone else.'

Karen's eyes bugged out of their sockets and Jamie looked down. What was Sam doing? Even if he wanted to talk, now he fucking couldn't.

'Yes, of course. How about I treat you as the Penn and Teller of the music world?'

'Sounds perfect.'

A red fingernail inched across the table and resumed the recording.

'So, Sam, are you and Jamie dating?'

He froze. If he'd been on high alert before, now he was running for the bunker as nuclear warheads rained down.

Sam laughed, and the sound gouged deep fissures into his chest.

'No, Jamie and I are just friends.'

Jamie's heart bled out. He stumbled to his feet and strode off, pushing open the door to the men's toilets. He went into a stall and locked the door, sitting on the seat and dropping his head in his hands.

How could he have been so stupid? As if Sam Adamson would ever want anything more than a casual shag from him. He thought he'd been pretty clear with her how he felt. He'd told her she was his everything. But what was he to her? Nothing more than a means to an end.

Time passed, but he didn't move. He was desperately homesick. He saw himself back in his living room singing with Sam, his family and Zoe around them. That was where he felt safe and happy. Right now, he was at the bottom of a well of misery.

He heard the door to the bathroom open.

'Jamie? She's gone.'

He unlocked the stall door and went out.

The smile had fallen off Sam's face. 'I'm sorry, Jamie. I should have known better. I was just trying to control the message and she's been good to me in the past. I'm sorry.' She looked small and tired. 'We're meeting my family in twenty minutes. Do you mind walking? I need some air.'

As they left the coffee house, Jamie held his guitar between them and Sam crossed her arms in front of her. With every step, the silence became more painful.

Was this what love was? Unearthly joy, then hellish lows? He'd never had a girlfriend before, so had no template to hang upon whatever he and Sam shared. Were they 'friends with benefits'? 'Fuck buddies'? His stomach rolled.

He'd once hoped to find love, but now it had found him, he wasn't sure if he wanted it anymore.

Sam's phone rang, jolting him back into the moment.

'Hey Crystal, how's it going?' Sam laughed as if she hadn't a care in the world. 'I'm so glad he likes it. Yes, we're super pleased with how it all turned out.'

She listened to her phone, then glanced up at Jamie, her eyes dancing. She mouthed, *'oh my god'* at him.

'Uh-huh, yes, absolutely. We'll be there. We can do eleven thirty? Yep, I know where that is... Amazing. Thanks Crystal, speak soon. Bye, bye.'

She snapped the phone shut.

'OMG, Jamie! The studio behind *Braveheart 2* wants to sign us to their music division. They're offering us a record deal!'

He stopped. 'But—'

She put her hands on his arms and he felt her energy jumping into him.

'I know, I know, we need to read the small print, yada, yada, yada, and we need to make this work around the rest of our lives, but... Jamie! This could be it! The chance of a lifetime!'

Sam was bouncing with excitement, throwing scenarios at Jamie that sounded like they belonged to a different person in another life. He couldn't take any of it in. He'd reached capacity.

And now it was time to meet her parents.

They stopped outside an old Georgian building with ornate stone carvings around the entrance. The restaurant was so upmarket it didn't even have a menu displayed outside. Instead stood two doormen who looked like they modelled for Armani when they weren't being hitmen for the mafia.

Sam faced him, her forehead creased. 'Look, I know I haven't told you much about my family.'

'They're all doctors. Your dad's Swedish and called Leo. Your mum is Jennifer, and your sisters are Esther and Anna.'

'Yeah. They're perfectly pleasant, but just don't be put off if all they talk about is medicine. And don't ever admit you've got something wrong with you or Anna and my mum will take your trousers down and make you cough.'

He sucked in a shocked breath and started choking.

'Jamie, that was a joke!' She held his arm. 'I'm sorry. I love my family, but I find them hard work. Just bear with the Adamson family for a couple of hours, then we can go home and talk. Okay?'

Jamie wasn't sure what to expect, but it wasn't a group of glamazons. Sam's family were all tall, blonde, and beautiful. Sam's mum was the smallest but even she was as tall as Zoe. Anna and Esther were both over six feet and Leo was as tall as Rory.

Jamie glanced between Sam and her family as his brain struggled to add her to the group portrait. They were clearly genetically related, with the same blue eyes, high cheekbones, and naturally blonde hair. But either the rest of them had taken growth hormones, or Sam had been shrunk.

'Smulan!' said her father, enveloping her in a hug.

Sam's smile froze.

'Come sit next to me.' He extended his arm to Jamie. 'I'm Leo, nice to meet you.'

Her father led the introductions and Jamie sat between Sam and her brain surgeon sister, Esther. It couldn't be more different to the family mealtimes he was used to, with all of them crammed around the dining room table, shouting over each other.

Sam's family were so well-mannered. They listened to each other and didn't interrupt. If he'd ever harboured hopes he could have a relationship with Sam, the image of their families meeting was the final nail in the coffin.

'So, Jamie. You're an electrician?' asked her mother.

He nodded.

'What does that involve?'

He hesitated. He couldn't exactly say he spent his days on a building site, dusty and dirty, trying to control a couple of useless, porn-addicted Neds.

'I work on new-build projects. Small housing estates, doing both the first and the second fixes.'

'And what does a first and second fix entail?'

'Er, the first fix is the preparation work. The cables and wiring, back boxes and so on. The second fix is what you see after the plastering has been done. The light fixtures and fittings, sockets, consumer units.'

'Fascinating. And how long did you study for?'

'Three years.'

Her mother smiled at Sam. 'The same as you, darling.'

Leo nodded. 'But working with electricity is far more dangerous and takes more skill. If Smulan forgets her lines, no one is going to go up in a puff of smoke.' He laughed at his own joke.

Sam leaned back to speak to a waiter. 'Could I have the gluten-free menu please?'

Her father ruffled the top of her head. 'Come on, Smulan. Live a little.' He broke open a bread roll, scattering crumbs over the table.

Sam flinched and brushed them away from her plate.

'I *am* living, Dad. More than I was before.'

'Did I tell you my paper on surgical interventions in epilepsy has been accepted into the International Conference on Neurosurgery and Brain Repair next month?' said Esther loudly.

Her parents lit up.

'Darling, that's wonderful news,' said her mother.

'About time too. What took them so long?' grumbled her father.

'Well, I had to go through peer review, which took longer than expected because the procedures are so groundbreaking.'

Anna raised her hand to high-five her sister. 'Well done, sis, you so deserve this. Where is it?'

'Los Angeles.'

'Smulan, maybe you'll be there at the same time?' her father asked. 'Have you and Jamie finished working on the Scottish film now? Will you be going to Los Angeles?'

Sam shook her head. She seemed to be sinking lower in her chair, getting smaller and smaller with each moment.

'No, we're done now. We finished recording the songs today.'

Her mother raised her glass. 'Well then, this is a double celebration. For Anna's birthday, and Sam and Jamie finishing their songs for... what was the film again, darling?'

'*Braveheart 2*.'

Her mother frowned. 'But didn't William Wallace die at the end of... No matter. Congratulations!'

They clinked their glasses and Jamie tried to smile. He'd never seen Sam so subdued. At the first meal she'd shared with his family she'd been throwing her voice and taking the piss in Klingon. What had happened to *that* Sam?

He turned to her father. 'Mr Adamson—'

'Leo. You must call me Leo.'

Jamie swallowed. 'Leo, what does "Smulan" mean?'

Sam froze and Esther dropped her bread knife.

Leo chuckled. 'It's a Swedish pet name I've used for her ever since she was a girl.' He picked a breadcrumb from the tablecloth. 'It means "little crumb".'

Sam was staring at the table.

'Do you like it?' Jamie asked her.

Leo laughed and ruffled Sam's hair again. 'Of course she does.'

'Dad,' said Esther.

'What?'

'Maybe a successful thirty-year-old woman doesn't want to be called a "little crumb"?' Esther replied.

Leo looked at Sam in surprise. 'Smu... Samantha?'

Sam smoothed her hair back into place and looked at her father. 'I don't like it, Dad. Please, can you call me something else?'

His mouth opened and closed. 'Of course.' He paused. 'Maybe "lille troll"? Or "liten lingon?"'

'Dad,' said Esther sharply. 'I don't think "*little* troll" or "*little* lingonberry" are appropriate substitutions.'

'Why not? They're very sweet names. Perfect for our Smu... Samantha.'

'Ooh!' said Anna loudly. 'You'll never guess who came into surgery yesterday? Cecil Montgomery from the GMC!'

'That old fool,' huffed Leo. 'What did he want?'

The conversation moved along, and Jamie let it pass by in front of him. Sam was silent.

He wanted to reach below the table and touch her. To reassure her and let her know he was there. But she'd withdrawn completely, downing her glass of wine, then pouring herself another.

At the end of the meal, they took a taxi back to Sam's flat. She stared out the window. Jamie reached for her hand and gently squeezed, but she didn't squeeze it back. His heart thumped inside his chest as he plucked up the courage to talk to her.

'Sam, why are your family so much taller than you?'

She didn't turn around. 'Don't you mean why am I so much smaller than them?'

He was silent.

'I had a lot of gut issues and anxiety when I was a child. My parents thought my tummy aches were a side product of my anxiety and didn't take it—they didn't give it as much attention as they could have. They were both very busy with work and a third child can sometimes be left to bring themselves up.

'Esther and Anna were perfect, so they assumed I would be, too. My Crohn's went undiagnosed for years. A side effect in children can be growth retardation. By the time they realised something wasn't right, it was too late. I was never going to get any taller.'

She took her hand from his and crossed her arms over her stomach, still looking away. Pain filled Jamie's chest till he could hardly breathe. He didn't know what to say or do.

BACK AT THE FLAT, JAMIE WAITED FOR SAM TO FINISH IN THE bathroom. She entered the kitchen wearing the 'cute but crazy' Stitch pyjama set that had driven him wild in Kinloch.

'Do you want me to sleep on the sofa tonight?' he asked.

She shook her head. 'No, sleep in my bed. I'm sorry about today.'

When he'd cleaned his teeth, he quietly pushed open the door to her room and crept in. Sam was curled up on her side, facing away from him. He climbed into the bed and lay on his back, staring up into the darkness.

He replayed the events of the day, over and over for what seemed like hours, his body wired and on edge, sleep utterly illusive.

He felt a gentle shaking beside him and heard a soft sniff. Sam was crying. He turned towards her and put his hand on her shoulder.

'Sam.'

She shrugged him off. 'I'm fine, Jamie. Go to sleep.'

Jamie lay back, pain reaching up from his chest to scratch at his eyes. He had nothing to offer her. She didn't need him and she didn't want him.

❧ 25 ❧

The next morning Sam put on her highest heels and her bravest face. She wanted to pretend the previous day hadn't happened. Every time she thought about the coffee with Karen, she felt sick.

She didn't know what her relationship with Jamie was, but it was too precious to be shared with a journalist and millions of strangers. He was such an enigma to her. When they were intimate, she felt like his entire reason for living. But then he would withdraw. He was so quiet and shy she couldn't read him.

What had he been like with other girlfriends? She thought about asking, but knew he would completely clam up. Did she know Fiona well enough to ask? Would Zoe have any idea?

She didn't think about the meal with her family. It was just too painful dredging up memories and feelings she wished would stay dead and buried. The day after seeing them she was always so tired. She needed extra effort to remember who she was, or at least who she wanted people to think she was.

They ate breakfast in silence. Jamie seemed to be treading

on eggshells around her as if worried she might break down at any minute. This scratched at her insides, irritating her further. She'd dragged herself out of chronic ill health and had a career in a notoriously fickle and difficult industry. She didn't want to be thought of as small and weak.

Travelling into central London by car in silence, the space between them widened. Sam didn't know what new offer Sandra had for her but wanted to get the meeting over and to the one with the record label. This was what she really cared about.

She needed an excuse to tie Jamie into spending more time with her. He had his family and his life up in Scotland. He wouldn't willingly trade any of it for her without a very good reason. She was praying that money and the promise of fame and fortune in the music industry might be enough of an incentive to consider a different kind of life. A life with her in it.

When they reached the West End, Jamie said he would wander around Soho until she was done, so Sam popped a couple of paracetamol in preparation for the cloying fug of Sandra's office. Her assistant let her in and she sat down whilst Sandra finished a call.

Her agent's chair was turned around to face the window and all Sam could see over the back was a manicured hand gesticulating through a haze of vape smoke. She felt her throat tightening as it trickled in through her nostrils. She was sick with anxiety, her stomach a crawling mass of eels and spiders.

Breathe in, two, three, four, and hold, two, three, four. Breathe out, two—

'Right, love. I'm all yours.' The chair swivelled around and

Sandra put her vape down, steepling her fingers. She stared at Sam and cleared her throat.

'I'm not going to sugar-coat this for you. You're off *Elm Tree Lane*.'

'What?'

'They're not renewing your contract. You've got one week of filming left, then you're out.'

'What? Why?' This couldn't be real.

'How many grannies do you actually have?'

'Er, one?'

Sandra leaned back and propped her Louboutins on the desk.

'Well, according to you, you've had at least three. The industry is small and people talk. This is the third time you've used the dying granny excuse, and it's your last.'

Sandra fiddled with her phone, then showed Sam the screen, flicking through photos of Sam with Billy outside the balloon basket, at their concert and singing at the ceilidh.

'So, while the producers and writers worked their tits off rearranging the schedule and script for you, you're taking hot air balloon rides and singing for Brad Bauer in a pub and a bloody castle.'

Sam wanted to throw up. Just when she'd got a steady job on the UK's most popular soap, she'd blown it.

'But Bethany is a popular character. Are they just going to rest her for a bit? Send her to Manchester?'

Sandra shook her head.

Panic made Sam's vision flicker. 'What are they going to do?'

Picking up her vape, Sandra exhaled a long plume of sickly smoke. 'You're not going to like it.'

Sam gripped the edge of her chair. 'Tell me.'

'Ian's character is going to push you off the top of a multi-storey car park.'

JAMIE WAS WAITING FOR SAM AS SHE THREW OPEN THE DOOR to the street with a bang.

'What happened? Are you okay?'

Sam was vibrating with rage and too angry to cry. She was furious at herself, the producers, the world, and she wanted to kick Ian Berresford in the nuts.

'I'm off *Elm Tree Lane* as of the end of next week. They're killing Bethany off.'

'Why?'

'Because I lied to come up to Kinloch.'

'I'm sorry.'

'It's fine. It's perfect, actually.'

Everything inside her was wound so tight it was on the edge of snapping.

She forced a smile. 'It gives us more time to concentrate on the music. And anyway, who in LA has even heard of *Elm Tree Lane*? I should be celebrating. I wonder where we can get a glass of Prosecco at half ten in the morning?'

'Sam—'

'You're right, they'll have champagne ready once we sign the recording contract. We might as well go there now. Best not to be late.'

She strode briskly down the street, not bothering to check if Jamie was following. Her nervous system was vibrating at such a high frequency, it felt like there was a swarm of wasps inside her skull, their wings thrumming frantically against her eardrums.

With each step, she looked into her future, mapping new

paths, planning new routes, all of which led up the mountain of success.

Jamie walked beside her. She could see him glancing at her, his mouth opening, then shutting as if he were afraid to speak.

Don't say anything, Jamie. I've got this.

The offices for the record company were big, bold, and new. There was more glass than building. Sam stared at the façade with dread clawing its way into her throat.

As they entered the reception, she gulped in horror at the glass elevator which whizzed up inside the main column of the building. There was just so much emptiness, so much height. People on upper floors seemed suspended in thin air.

She felt Jamie's hand on hers.

'We can always ask them to take the meeting somewhere else?'

She shook him off. 'I'll be fine. This is the day for new beginnings. I can do this.'

Her heart was hammering. All she wanted to do was curl up into his chest and cry. But her body appeared to have been taken over by an ex-special forces spin class instructor who'd snorted a line of coke. She took charge, introducing them to the receptionist who escorted them to the top floor.

In the lift, Jamie stood in front of her, blocking her view. She dug her nails into her palms as her tummy left her body with the speed. She kept up a constant barrage of chat, worried if she stopped, she'd collapse. Her palms were screaming with pain, but she didn't let up the pressure.

They were shown into a corner office. Every side was glass, and her legs started to go. Jamie held her up, gripping her tightly.

'Sam, Jamie... come in, come in. I'm Pete.' A tall man in his sixties with a neatly trimmed beard, a ponytail, and an American accent extended his hand.

'Very nice to meet you,' Jamie said with more confidence than Sam had ever heard from him before.

He sat her in a chair facing away from the two walls of glass that separated the room from the clouds, then perched on the side of her chair and let his hand drop between them.

She didn't take it.

Pete introduced the other people in the room. They were the execs from the company and had listened to the recordings they'd made at Air. There was a palpable buzz of energy crackling between them. Sam kept nodding as Pete explained the deal he was proposing.

'You'll start recording the album in our studios in LA next week, and we'll also get you working on tracks for your second album. You'll do a worldwide promo tour to generate buzz, then the first album will drop with the premiere of *Braveheart 2*. After that, it's a full three-month tour and we'll also be pushing hard for an Oscar nomination.

'Depending on sales and territories, you'll cycle touring with recording, but we're also looking at promo tie-ins. We've already landed you a huge deal in Japan promoting Mopeoke on terrestrial channels. The Japanese love Scotland—and Brad —so it's a perfect match.'

Sam wasn't taking in much of what he was saying, but the part of her that was always searching for more, the part of her that had been crushed so much in the last twenty-four hours, just screamed 'yes' every time a word came out of Pete's mouth.

She was teetering on a knife edge and needed a contract in front of her and a pen in her hand to feel safe.

'So, guys,' said Pete. 'What do you think?'

'Yes, absolutely. Love it,' she replied. 'Can't wait to start. Where do we sign?'

She ignored Jamie stiffening beside her.

'That's great news.' Pete pivoted a pile of papers towards them. 'No doubt you'll want to have this looked over by your lawyers before you sign, but any questions you have now, we'll be happy to answer them.'

Sam picked up a pen from the desk. 'We're very happy to sign now, aren't we, Jamie?'

She looked at him and the knife edge started to wobble.

He gave a tiny shake of his head.

She gripped the pen tighter. 'Jamie?'

'Sam, we need to talk about this.'

She dropped the pen and stood. 'Excuse us, gentlemen.'

She dragged him into the hall and down the corridor so they couldn't be seen through the walls of glass. Her hands were shaking, so she crossed her arms.

'Jamie, we need to sign it.'

'I'm sorry, Sam. I'm not doing this.'

'Okay, okay, I'll get a lawyer to look at it. And Sandra too. Happy?'

He shook his head. 'My answer will still be no.'

'What? Why?'

'Sam, this is *your* dream. It's not mine. I can't just walk out of my life. I can't leave my job. I've already let Gregor down enough. And I can't leave Mum.'

'But they're offering us the chance of a lifetime!'

'Are they? How do you know that? It sounds like they'll own us. We'll be tied into something for years. Sure, they like us now, but what happens if *Braveheart 2* is a flop? What happens two years from now if they don't like the music we write? This is all about what *you* want. I need to think about what *I* want.'

'And what *do* you want, Jamie?' Sam could feel the rage of rejection coming up to the boil.

'I want...' He looked desperately unhappy. 'I want—'

'Your mum to wait on you hand and foot? Gymnastics twice a week? No drama? No inconvenience? Nothing that might take you out of your comfort zone?'

'That's not true—'

'You want a wee wifey. But maybe even that's too much like hard work.'

'And what do *you* want?' He pointed back up the corridor. 'Is that really it?'

'Yes, of course it is. What else?'

He shook his head. 'I'm leaving. Do you need me to stay to help you get out of the building?'

'I'm not a fucking invalid, Jamie. I don't need your help. I don't need *anyone's* help.'

He rubbed his forehead as if to remove the lines of stress. 'Are you going to stay here now?'

Everything inside her stretched apart. She nodded, her jaw so tight she could no longer speak.

He sighed. 'I'll drop the spare set of keys through your front door.'

'You're not really leaving?'

He nodded. He looked broken.

'But what about the soap awards tomorrow? Don't you want to stay for them?'

He shook his head and turned, walking away from her down the corridor. She wavered, her hands in fists by her sides, then headed back to the room of suits. She was going to sign that deal whether Jamie's name was on the contract or not.

BY THE TIME SAM GOT BACK TO THE FLAT, JAMIE HAD already left. He'd done the dishes, made the bed and left a note on the kitchen table.

I hope it worked out for you. I'm sorry to let you down.

Thank you for letting me stay and helping me get through the recording. Jamie.

Sam sat, her breath heaving in and out. She'd held it together until getting home, hoping he was still there. But he'd left. He'd rejected both her and a possible future making music together. The record label had made it clear it was a package deal. Without Jamie, she had nothing. Tears were seconds away. She needed Zoe.

The call went straight to voicemail. Could she ring her mum? Esther? Anna? *No.* In desperation, she rang Crystal.

'Hey, Sam, how did the meeting go?'

'Is Brad there? Could I speak to him?' She could hear her voice wavering, the shudders starting to move through her.

'Yes, of course.'

There was a pause.

'Babe! How's it going?'

The dam burst and wracking sobs burst out of her, so all-encompassing she could hardly breathe.

'Babe! Babe! Don't cry! Whatever's wrong, Brad'll fix it. And if I can't, then Oprah can. Hang in there, babe. We've got you.'

26

Jamie didn't bother trying to change his flight. He made his way to King's Cross and took the train north. He'd taken his bags and his guitar but left his heart with Sam.

He kept putting his hand to his chest as if trying to patch the gaping hole. The pain was unbearable. As if salt were being rubbed into his bare flesh with sandpaper.

Was this in any way comparable to what his mother had gone through when pregnant with him and his father had suddenly died? Jamie felt a new level of empathy for what she'd experienced and an awareness of the stress hormones she would have inadvertently transferred to him in the womb.

How different would he have been if his father hadn't died? Would he have stayed in Kinloch? Would he have had a family? Would he have signed the contract with Sam?

Before Sam had come into his life, he'd worried he might spend his life alone. But now, he knew with utter certainty he would. Sam was one of a kind. His diamond on an endless beach of pebbles. His perfect woman. No one could ever compare to her.

It was eleven when he finally arrived home. The house was quiet. No sounds of snoring drifted from his mother's room. She was nowhere to be seen.

He rang Fiona, who picked up sounding out of breath.

'Yes?'

'Mum with you?'

'What? No, course she's not. Why?'

'She's not at home.'

'What are you doing here? You're not due back till next week.'

'We finished recording early.'

'And you came back now rather than hang out with Sam?'

'Yeah.'

'Fuck's sake, Jamie. What's wrong with you?'

'Don't start. It didn't work out, okay? And now Mum's not here and I'm worried.'

He heard a grunt of frustration down the line. 'She's probably taking advantage of the fact you're not there to go out and have some fun.'

'But—'

'She's got a life, Jamie, and so do I. Now go to bed and let me get back to mine. I'll speak to you in the morning.'

Fiona hung up before he could reply.

Jamie sat at the kitchen table, the silence filled by the irritating buzz of the strip light above. He hated it. He'd put up with it for long enough. It was coming down.

He found a brand-new light fitting in the garage, one Fiona hadn't used when she'd moved into her house, grabbed his tool bag, and set to work. After he'd replaced it, he found an old tin of paint and painted the ceiling to hide the dirty plaster that had been hidden under the light.

He put the kettle on as he started to clear up. It was coming to boiling point when he heard voices outside. He turned to see his mother standing in the doorway, her arms braced against the sides as if trying to hide what was behind her, or stop herself from falling over.

She was red-faced and looked absolutely wasted. 'Son? What are you doing here?'

'We finished early, so I came back. Where were you? What were you doing?'

Morag lurched into the kitchen and closed the door behind her, fumbling with the key.

He got up. 'Here, let me do that.'

She pushed him away. 'Och, get away, I'm perfectly fine. Stop babying me, son.'

'Mum, you're pissed. What were you doing and who the hell were you with?'

'None of your business.'

She stared at the old strip light on the kitchen table in confusion, then at the ceiling. 'What the bloody hell have you done?'

He gritted his teeth. 'It was doing my head in.'

'There was nothing wrong with it! First thing tomorrow, it's going back up.'

She staggered towards the door and tripped on one of the chairs. Jamie rushed to hold her up. 'Let me help you to bed.'

She shook him off. 'I'm not Mrs McCreedie. I don't need any help.'

Jamie stood back as she pulled herself up the stairs. Halfway up, she turned and took her hand off the banister to waggle a finger at him.

'See, Jamie, I—'

The rest of her sentence was lost as she tumbled down the stairs with a scream.

Sam's last week on the set of *Elm Tree Lane* was surreal. Lorraine, Shelley, and all her other friends rallied around her, making her feel truly like the star of the show. Ian made a great effort to make her feel small, but his efforts were diminished by the fact that everyone acted as if he were invisible.

She'd point-blank refused to spend a day hanging off the top of a multi-storey car park for her death scene, so the storyline was changed to a hit-and-run. She went through the motions, but her mind was already on the future.

If she kept looking forward, there was no space to think about Jamie.

He hadn't rung or messaged her and wasn't on social media, so she couldn't stalk him. She didn't know if he was checking any of her accounts, so she made sure if he did, all he saw were daily updates documenting the minutiae of her fabulous new life.

Everything was filtered and spun to perfection. She'd finally made it. She was off to LA at the invitation of Brad Bauer.

What she didn't share with any of her followers was that she had no idea if any of it was going to work. Brad hadn't offered her an acting job but the chance to collaborate with big-shot musicians and producers on the score for a new film he was working on. It was so secret she didn't even know what it was about. But she didn't let that stop her focusing on everything LA had to offer.

She was escaping the greyness and small-mindedness of the UK into sunshine, networking, glitz, and glamour. She was finally going to be in the right place, at the right time, with the right people.

. . .

THE PLANE TOUCHED DOWN INTO LAX AND A RAINSTORM. After eleven hours breathing in recirculated air, Sam was desiccated. Her skin was dry, her throat raw, and her head throbbing.

She pressed her face against the cool glass of the window, but all she saw were raindrops running into each other, then squat buildings and palm trees buffeted by the lashing rain.

Brad had arranged a driver to take her to an apartment in West Hollywood, and when she exited arrivals, a small man with an enormous smile introduced himself.

'Miss Adamson! I'm Mikey. Lemme take your bags.'

'Hi, how did you know who I was?'

He presented his phone and swiped through photos of her.

'Mr Bauer also sent me a recording of your concert in the Scottish bar. Man, that was something else. Do you know the royal family?'

'Er. Personally?'

'Yeah.'

'Um, no.'

Mikey shrugged. 'Never mind.'

'Did you think I might?'

He grinned at her. 'Not really, but I ask every British person the same question. Who knows? One day I might get lucky.'

Mikey drove them to where Brad had a suite of apartments. It was mid-afternoon in LA, but Sam was ready for bed. Her apartment was small and decorated in warm chocolate browns and rich creams. Mikey opened the fridge, which was packed with groceries.

'There's food here to start you off, and an information pack on the table with everything you need to know. I'll give you my number now and you can call if you need anything. It's on twenty-four seven. You can walk to the studio from here, but

I'll drop by tomorrow at nine to take you there for your first day. Do you have any questions, Miss Adamson?'

'Please call me Sam. I don't need anything except for bed. This is so beautiful. Thank you, it's perfect.'

Mikey grinned. 'This apartment's my favourite too. Brad put you in Scandi to celebrate your roots.'

'Scandi?'

'Yes, we've got Scandi, Bali, Santorini, Miami and Nairobi in this complex.'

'Do they all have to end with an "ee" sound?'

'Mr Bauer was insistent. We did have one called Paris, but when people didn't pronounce it properly, he changed it.'

After Mikey left, Sam unpacked and took a shower. Even though noises from outside filtered in, it wasn't enough to fill the empty space inside her. She needed chatter, distractions, people. She put some upbeat music on her phone, but the sound grated, so she turned it off.

The bed in her room was huge. It was an island and she was the only inhabitant. She hugged a pillow against her aching chest and allowed herself to think of Jamie. It would be getting late in Kinloch now. Was he in bed too?

She remembered falling asleep in his arms, their limbs tangled, the gentle rise and fall of his chest, the tickling of his hair against her cheek, the sound of Morag snoring from the room next door. She wiped her eyes with the bedsheet. It all seemed so very far away.

The robotic chime of the doorbell rang with the tune of 'Auld Lang Syne' for the sixty-fourth time that day.

Jamie ground his teeth, went to the bottom of the stairs, and called up, 'I'm coming.'

Morag was not a very good patient. The downstairs toilet was too difficult to navigate with her lower leg in plaster, so she was mostly confined to upstairs for easy access to the bathroom.

When Jamie developed selective hearing to her yelling every couple of minutes with new demands, she got Fiona to buy her a doorbell and kept the ringer by her bed.

Morag hated not being at the centre of everything. She was convinced the post office would fall apart or be robbed with Linda in charge, and slept with a fire extinguisher next to her and one eye open in case Jamie burned the house down.

The concerned and the nosy in Kinloch had been popping in at all hours with food and flowers, but Jamie had sent the food away. He was determined to show his mother he could be trusted and wasn't a child anymore.

Splashing a healthy dose of rum into the mug of hot chocolate, he decorated it with freshly whipped cream and mini marshmallows, then took it upstairs.

Morag was propped up against a mountain of pillows. The room was so full of flowers it could have been a funeral parlour.

'What took you so long? What have you got there? Ooh, mini marshmallows! Is Fi here? Did she do this or did Linda pop in? You must thank her. Put it on the side, son. Now, help me plump up my pillows. Have you fixed the light yet?'

Jamie took a pillow and thumped it.

'No.'

'Why not? That's the whole reason I'm in this state.'

Jamie resisted using the pillow to smother his mother and instead tucked it carefully behind her.

'Mum, you fell because you were pissed.'

'Nonsense. And now I'm stuck here and have no idea what's going on.'

'So why are you always on the phone then?'

His mother ignored him and picked a mini marshmallow off the top of the hot chocolate.

'If it hadn't been for community spirit, I would have wasted away up here. Have you thanked everyone properly?'

He sat on the end of the bed and tidied the pile of his mother's magazines, turning over the ones with pictures of Sam on the front.

'Mum, I made the hot chocolate.'

She gazed at him dubiously and took a sip, failing to hide her delight at the taste.

'Are you sure?'

'Yes. And the cottage pie you had for dinner. And the apple turnover and custard. And the oxtail soup for lunch. I even made the bread.'

'But... but it was that fancy sourdough stuff Margaret and Donald have started baking.'

'Nope. I made my own starter. It lives in the airing cupboard and I've called it Brad.'

'Eh?'

'I've made every single meal you've eaten since you've been up here.'

His mother seemed completely confused. Like he'd just peeled off his skin to reveal he was one of the lizard people.

'But—'

Her mobile rang. She pulled on her glasses and glanced at the screen.

'Okay, son, you can go now.'

He stood. She shooed him with her free hand. 'I'll ring the doorbell if I need you later. Make sure you close the door, love.'

ON HER FIRST MORNING IN THE CITY OF DREAMS, SAM WOKE from a nightmare. She'd been standing in a huge flat desert of nothingness. All alone, except for snakes that slithered just out of her reach. Even though they looked like snakes, she knew who they were.

They were the Ians and Karens in her life—anyone who'd ever questioned or doubted her. Anyone who said she wouldn't make it and would always be on her own. The fact that the snakes didn't attack was even more terrifying. They just watched her, waiting for the inevitable.

Mikey arrived at eight thirty with a huge coffee and a smile as bright as the sunshine.

'Good morning! How did you sleep?'

'Great, thanks. You?'

'Like a baby. You ready to go?'

'Yes, I most definitely am.'

Sam was determined to make this work. She had no idea what 'this' actually was, but she'd lost her job, and any collaboration with Jamie was over. Brad was offering her a chance to start afresh in the place she'd been aiming at since childhood. She wasn't going to let him down.

A short walk from her apartment was Kode, a small recording studio known for its laid-back vibe and the innovative musicians who'd passed through its doors. Mikey passed Sam to Crystal, who was waiting in reception.

'Sam! You're here! This is so exciting! Meet Cadence. She's on reception, but if there's anything you need, she's your girl.'

Sam shook the hand of a young woman who looked like she'd stepped off a catwalk. Like Crystal, her skin was flawless and immovable, her hair shiny, and her teeth whiter than sunlight on new snow.

Standing next to them, Sam felt like she'd stepped out of a time machine from the Victorian era. She was suddenly acutely aware that her teeth weren't bleached, her lips had the plumpness of a deflated airbed, and her forehead had more lines than *Harry Potter and the Deathly Hallows*. If she were a Dickensian heroine, she'd be more Miss Havisham than Estella.

'It's so great to meet you. This is the best day of my life,' gushed Cadence like a fountain running on full-fat soda. 'And working with Th. He's soooooooooooo inspirational.' She touched her perfectly manicured nails to her perfectly pert chest. 'He touches me. Here.'

'Th?'

'Cadence! Shush!'

Her cheeks went a delicate shade of pink. 'Sorry, Crystal, it's just too exciting.'

'Er, who is... *Th?*' asked Sam.

Crystal glanced around the empty reception. 'Brad met him at an Ayahuasca retreat. He's a water musician with direct links to Atlantis.'

'And what am I meant to be doing with him?'

Crystal pulled out a document. 'I need you to sign this non-disclosure agreement.'

'Do you have a pen?'

'Don't you want to read it first?'

Sam shrugged. 'I'm sure it's just the standard stuff.'

'You need to read page seven. It has a very specific clause.'

Sam ran her eyes over the text. She blinked and re-read. 'Er, I'm not allowed to share details of this project by any form of telepathy including lucid dreaming, meditation, astral projection, or psychic possession?'

'Uh-huh. Brad had one of his best ideas stolen from him during a gong bath, so we've had to add this to our standard NDA.'

'So, if I sign this, you'll tell me what I'm doing here?'

Crystal nodded and handed her a pen.

After Sam scrawled her name, Crystal sat her down on a red pleather sofa, and Cadence went back to reception and put on a pair of noise-cancelling headphones.

'Cadence knows a lot, but she doesn't know everything,' said Crystal in a low voice. 'Brad's invited you to be part of Project S86. It's a docu-fiction film about the plight of the world's oceans and capitalist consumer culture. He wants you to work with Th on a vocal and aural soundscape.'

'Has he shot it yet?'

'No, but he's created a mood board for you to get inspiration.'

'What's it about?'

'A sacred spring in Florida is under threat from the construction of a golf course. A little girl makes friends with the manatees that live there, but her father runs the Wall Street firm behind the project and is determined nothing will stand in his way, not even his six-year-old daughter. It's very moving.'

'And does it have a title?'

'Yes.' Crystal lowered her voice further. '*Bonfire of the Manatees*.'

Sam was suddenly back in Kinloch, imagining Jamie's reaction to Brad's latest project. Even though he was thousands of miles away, Jamie felt far more real than this moment, sitting across from Barbie's younger sister on a sticky plastic sofa in LA.

'Let's go introduce you to Th.'

Sam unstuck herself and followed Crystal through a series of doors into a small studio. In the centre of the room, facing the glass wall of the control room, was a tank of water. Inside, a naked man.

He had his feet hooked under straps at the bottom and was completely submerged. He was banging on Tibetan singing bowls that were suspended in the tank and making noises into a microphone.

Sam glanced into the control room where two men sat—one twiddling knobs, the other holding a stopwatch. They were nodding in time to the beat. After a minute, the man stood up out of the tank, breathing hard. He looked at Sam and held out his hand.

'Hey, you must be Sam. I'm Th.'

27

Sam's social media life in LA was perfect. She tapped the hashtags #YOLO and #LivingMyBestLife so often she almost believed them herself.

She may not have been able to talk about what she was doing, but she could wax lyrical about trendy yoga classes, green smoothies, rollerblading along the boardwalk at Venice Beach, and attending exclusive parties every evening as she rode the coattails of Brad's patronage.

Each morning she got up before dawn to attend the most physically intensive exercise class she could find, then arrived early at the studio to come up with ideas before Th arrived.

Making music with him was like cooking a meal with helium and the letter ψ. If Brad was eccentric, then Th had grabbed the bonkers baton from him and run with it off the crazy cliff.

Sam approached each day as a ten-hour improvisational comedy performance with a stoned Yoda. She soon got used to his nakedness, although she drew the line at getting in the tank with him. During lunch she ran around the corner to attend a hot yoga class, and every evening she ate out with her new friends and went to parties to make more.

She only briefly messaged with Zoe. Any spare minute was spent online, posting pictures, and interacting with the hundreds of 'close personal friends' she'd never met in real life and undoubtedly never would.

By the time she arrived back at her apartment, she was too tired to dream. She hadn't slept in the bed since the first night. She just curled up on the sofa under a blanket, closed her eyes, and knew the next thing she'd be aware of would be the sound of her alarm the following morning.

One thing she couldn't ignore, however, was the fact that her sister was in LA presenting her paper at a conference. Esther had delayed her flight home and insisted Sam spend Saturday with her.

They met outside the Getty Museum and Esther frowned as she held Sam at arm's length.

'You look ill.'

'Nice to see you too.'

'I'm serious. You've lost too much weight and the make-up doesn't hide how tired you are.'

Esther picked up Sam's hands and inspected the white spots growing up her nails.

'You've got leukonychia. Most likely zinc and calcium deficiency.' She tilted Sam's head up, pulling her lower inner eyelid down. 'And you're already borderline anaemic. Have you stopped eating red meat?'

'I'm eating clean.'

'You're malnourished. What did you have for breakfast?'

'A green smoothie.'

Esther rolled her eyes. 'That's a toxic sludge of oxalic acid. If you keep that up, you'll have kidney stones by Christmas. You need to be eating—'

'Okay, stop!'

Esther pressed her lips together, as if fighting to keep them closed.

'Can we just go and look at some art and pretend we're normal?'

Esther sighed. 'Yes. I'm sorry. I just haven't seen you for a few weeks and you look very different. Hug?'

Sam let herself be pulled into her sister's arms, tensing as she felt Esther's fingers working their way across her back ribs. She disengaged.

'Esther! What the fuck?'

'Sorry, force of habit. But it confirms what I thought. You're underweight.'

THEY WALKED THROUGH THE GALLERIES IN SILENCE. SAM didn't like the quiet, or having her sister by her side. It felt like real life was invading her fantasy. Esther was the uninvited party guest telling everyone about the time you pooped your pants on a school trip. Sam's anxiety was building, her real feelings and emotions banging on the doors and demanding to be let in.

She focused on a Picasso painting in front of her, the person all disjointed. The woman's nose was on the side of her head, her eyes crude ovals. It was like looking at an out-of-tune piece of music. Everything was there, but it was off-key and out of place.

This was how she felt every day, a niggling sense of unease that the picture she'd put herself in wasn't right.

'Esther.'

'Yes?'

'Do you want to go to a party tonight?'

'Where?'

'Up in the hills.'

'Will it be late?'

'Only if you want it to be.'

'To be honest, I'd rather just spend the evening with you. Is it in some swanky mansion?'

She nodded.

'Okay, go on then, whose house is it?'

'Brad's.'

'Brad as in Brad Bauer? Your new BFF?'

Sam laughed. 'I didn't think you even knew what a BFF was.'

'I'm not that out of touch.'

Sam felt a sudden rush of love for her sister. She hugged her tightly. 'It's really lovely you're here.'

Esther kissed Sam on the top of her head. 'I'm glad I'm here too.'

DESPITE SAM ASSURING HER THAT BRAD'S PARTY WOULD BE catered, Esther insisted on taking her to an all-you-can-eat Brazilian steakhouse first and making her eat more than she'd done in the last few days.

Sam's stomach was grateful, and for the first time since she'd arrived in LA, she actually felt full. A glass of wine had taken the edge off her anxiety, and she smiled at her sister. Everything was going to be alright.

'So, what happened with Jamie?'

Sam flinched and dug her nails into the skin of her thighs. She shrugged nonchalantly.

'Nothing much. He didn't want to come to LA, so, er, he didn't.'

She fiddled with a pot of toothpicks, feeling the weight of her sister's gaze.

'I'm sorry. He was really nice.'

This time Sam's shrug only reached one shoulder.

'He, er.' Esther cleared her throat. 'It was clear how much you meant to him.'

Sam focused on peeling the paper wrapper away from a toothpick.

'We all hoped—'

Her eyes shot up and Esther coloured.

'I mean, ahem, *I* hoped that you felt the same way about him.'

The toothpick snapped. Years of insecurity and anger burst out. 'Have you all been talking about me behind my back?'

'No, it's not like that—'

'Then what *is* it like? Am I such a continual fuckup that you need to discuss how to manage me?'

Esther's mouth hung open.

'He didn't want this,' Sam continued. 'And he didn't want me. I don't want to talk about it.'

'Do you think you're a fuckup?' her sister asked.

Sam stabbed at the table with the broken toothpick. 'Of course I am. You know just how much of a monumental triple chocolate cluster of a fuckup I am.'

'How on earth did you come to that conclusion?'

Sam sat back and folded her arms across her chest. 'Come on, Esther, I know what you all think of me and my life choices.'

'Really?'

Her sister let the word hang in the air, then continued.

'So, tell me *exactly* what we think of you and your life choices then.'

Sam took a breath in, but her throat tightened; it didn't want her to vocalise the pain inside. She shook her head and stared at the tablecloth as it moved in and out of focus.

'Do you want to know what *I* think of you and your "life choices"?' Esther continued.

Sam was silent.

'I speak for Anna and Mum and Dad as well, as I know they think *exactly* the same as me.'

Sam didn't look up. The tablecloth was becoming liquid.

'We're in complete awe of you,' said Esther. 'You're incredible. You're the bravest person I've ever met and we're stupidly proud of you. Honestly, the things you do scare the shit out of me. I could never in a million years do what you do.'

Sam blinked hot tears onto her hands. 'You're a fucking *brain* surgeon, Esther.'

'Ugh. That's easy.'

She glanced up. 'What?'

'Did you ever consider that Anna and I took the easy option?'

Now it was Sam's mouth that hung open in shock.

'Mum and Dad were doctors. We grew up with that template. For the most part, what we do is black and white. You follow a manual, a set of instructions, rules. As long as you remember what to do, it's easy.'

Sam shook her head.

'It is. The hardest part of my job is the sideshow bullshit. The politics, misogyny, underfunding. All that nonsense. But I don't have to keep looking for work every day. I don't have my worth based on my appearance, or whether I'm flavour of the month or not. I don't have to bare my soul to the world.'

Esther shuddered.

'I know I'm good at my job,' she continued, 'and I'm used to speaking to people. But this paper I just gave, having to stand in front of a room of smug men and prove myself? Good god, Sam. I was in the toilet all morning and had to take beta blockers just to hold it together. I'd happily cut the top off someone's head twenty times a day rather than have to do that again.'

Esther sighed and reached across the table, her palm up. Sam placed her hand on hers.

'We often don't know the right thing to say because we don't know anything about your world and it's so bloody alien to us. But believe me, we love you completely and couldn't be more proud. Did you know that Dad refers to Ian as "that bastard Berresford"?'

Sam's laugh was almost a sob. 'I didn't think Dad knew who he was.'

'You're joking! We all watch *Elm Tree Lane*. Although we're having an official boycott after your last episode.' Esther squeezed her hand. 'We all felt so guilty after what happened with your health. We've never forgiven ourselves.'

Sam's chest started heaving. 'You were just a child.'

'No, I wasn't. I was at medical school. I should have listened to you. I failed you. We *all* failed you.'

A sharp pain knifed Sam in the chest, prying her ribs apart. She gulped air in, her body shaking. Esther moved to sit next to her, holding her tightly as she sobbed.

All those years thinking her family thought less of her. Had she been wrong? Esther rocked her gently, letting her cry.

Sam forgot she was in a restaurant. She forgot she was a semi-famous actress and now an even less-famous musician. She was just a little girl hurting and being comforted by her big sister.

When her tears ran out, Esther handed her a napkin and she wiped her eyes and blew her nose.

'I must look such a mess.'

Esther brushed a strand of hair off her face and tucked it behind her ear. 'You're beautiful. You're Mum and Dad's third time lucky.'

Sam's lower lip quivered, and she welled up again.

'Oh, don't cry! I'm sorry, don't cry, Sam. You need to be able to take me to meet Brad Bauer!'

AFTER A QUICK DETOUR FOR A CHANGE OF CLOTHES AND A fresh face, Sam and Esther took a taxi to Brad's home in the hills. He had several places in LA, but this was the house used most for entertaining.

Sam had already been there, so knew the layout. It was a large, modernist building, sleek and beautiful, with an infinity pool that overlooked Hollywood. Brad threw parties almost weekly. They were as much for business as pleasure and people always seemed to have conversations with one eye on the person they were talking to and the other looking for better opportunities.

Mikey greeted them at the front door and put freshly made leis over their heads.

'Welcome, Sam, and nice to meet you, Esther. Do you know the royal family?'

Esther's eyes widened. 'Do I need to know them?'

Sam laughed and put her arm through her sister's. 'He asks all British people that. Come on, I'll take you through. See you later, Mikey.'

The house was already packed. Waiting staff glided between the glitz like discreet penguins, offering food and drink and taking away used plates and glasses.

Esther clung to her. 'Don't look now,' she hissed out of the corner of her mouth. 'But have you seen who's over there?'

Sam wasn't sure who her sister was referring to as they were surrounded by famous actors, all looking smaller and slightly less attractive than they appeared on-screen.

'You get used to it. Let's go outside and see if we can find Brad.'

'Don't leave me. This is terrifying.'

'I won't. Pinkie promise.'

Sam guided her sister through the house to the landscaped gardens. Colour changing LED lights ran above their heads from the house, above the long pool and were threaded through the trees around the grounds. They both let out a collective sigh.

Brad was standing at the edge of the pool, naked except for a shimmering blue loincloth around his hips. He was wearing a gold crown and holding an enormous trident. In the water they saw the flick of an iridescent mermaid tail as a beautiful woman swam in front of him.

'Good grief. Is this really happening?'

Sam giggled. 'Brad is something else. Come on.'

She pulled her sister to where he was standing.

'Babe! Hold this, will you?' Brad thrust the trident at Sam. 'The mermaid's got the munchies.'

A server carrying a large silver platter materialised at his side and Brad expertly lifted off a piece of sashimi with a pair of chopsticks. He knelt by the side of the pool as the woman swam over with a smile. He dropped the fish into her mouth and she swallowed it, then backflipped and swam underwater to the other end. Brad stood and took back his trident.

'Isn't she *mermazing*?'

'Brad, I'd like you to meet my sister, Esther. She's—'

'No! Don't tell me.'

Brad held his palm up and braced his body as if holding back a tidal wave from breaking. He gazed at Esther then closed his eyes.

'I see a glacier, tall pines, rocks.'

He took a big breath and gritted his teeth as if straining on the toilet.

'A leather bag with silver coins. Swords in the snow. Ice, fire, scales, death.'

Sam gripped Esther's arm as she felt her sister trying to move away.

Brad opened his eyes wide. 'You're a model, second generation, and you have a Northern Inuit dog called Luna.'

'Er... I'm a neurosurgeon.'

Brad thumped the end of his trident on the poolside as if splitting the earth.

'Hot damn!' He stared at Esther, his mouth open.

'Crystal!'

His assistant materialised by his side, holding her phone to his mouth. 'It's recording.'

Brad's eyes glazed over. '*Game of Thrones* meets *Rain Man*. Possible EU grant through Irish co-pro. Speak to Birgir in Iceland re filming at Silfra. And we've gotta get mermaids in this one.'

He shivered as if waking from a trance, and Crystal moved away.

'So, you actually look inside people's heads?' he asked Esther. 'Like, literally?'

'Well, er, I operate on the central and peripheral nervous systems, not just the brain.'

'Fascinating.' Brad hooked his arm around Esther's, pulling her away from Sam. 'I'm just going to borrow her for a moment.'

'But—'

Esther looked like she was at the apex of a rollercoaster, oscillating between terror and excitement.

'It's fine,' said Sam. 'You go!'

She watched them leave with a grin, then turned to wander

through the groups of beautiful people, seeing if there was anyone she recognised. Barbara, Rory's mum—now Lady Bauer—was on the terrace, holding court as people fawned over her.

Eyes flicked over Sam, making judgements as to her importance within a millisecond before deciding she wasn't worth it. Here she was nobody special. She was just another nobody trying to be a somebody. The glitz and the glamour was fun, but only if the experience could be shared.

'Hi, wanna drink?'

A man was smiling at her. His face was tanned, his blond hair sun-bleached. He looked like a surf god.

He held out his hand. 'I'm Bryce.'

'Sam.'

'Not from around these parts either?' His Australian accent was almost hidden under a Californian drawl.

'No, I'm from the UK.'

'Whatya doing here? You a friend of Brad? I saw you talking to him.'

'I'm working on a project with him and I also wro—*co-wrote* three songs that are going to be in *Braveheart 2*.'

'No way! Awesome. What do you play?'

'I... I don't. I just sing.'

'Cool. I'm a stunt performer. You think you could introduce me to Brad?'

Sam forced a smile. 'Yeah, no worries.'

❧ 28 ❧

Jamie was at breaking point. On discovering he'd been cooking all of her meals, Morag went from baffled fear to excitement within ten minutes. Now she was ordering her food from him days in advance, circling recipes in magazines, and critiquing each dish as if she was a judge on *MasterChef*.

When the doorbell wasn't chiming 'Auld Lang Syne' to summon him upstairs, he was humming it. The tune had buried itself so deeply into his head that nothing, not even sleep, could dislodge it.

And if that wasn't stressful enough, he also didn't have a job to go back to when his mum was on her feet again. Gregor had been forced to take someone else on after Jamie told him he wouldn't return for at least another two weeks.

The doorbell rang and he walked up the stairs, his feet heavy.

His mother was sitting up in bed and...

Was she wearing *make-up*?

'Can I get you anything?'

She patted the bed. 'Sit down, son. You and I need to have a wee chat.'

'Are you okay?'

'I'm fine and dandy. I could have been up and about more last week, but I've been lazy and taking advantage of your cooking.'

'I can carry on cooking once you're downstairs, you know.'

'Aye, you could.'

She picked at the edges of her flowery nightgown.

'Son, I haven't been entirely honest with you about what I was doing that night you came home early.'

'Go on.'

'Well, I've been dipping my toes into the waters of online dating and seeing what kind of men are out there.'

Jamie's blood ran cold. He knew exactly what kind of men were out there. If there was a dating pool his mum was fishing in, it was full of sharks, with a thick layer of scum floating on the top.

'Mum—'

'And that night I went on my first date.'

Jesus Christ. Thank fuck he'd returned in time to stop whoever it was from getting in the house.

'We had a lovely time and we've been getting to know each other more over the phone. Anyway, we want to take our relationship to the next level.'

What. The. Actual. Fuck?

'Och, don't look at me like that, son. Big Jim's a sweet wee man.'

'Big Jim?'

'Aye, it's my pet name for him.'

'Is he tall?' *Please, for the love of god, say he's tall.*

Morag laughed. 'Not really.'

'Then why is he called *Big* Jim?'

His mother was suddenly fascinated by the edge of her dressing gown.

'It's just a private joke, son.'

He could see her cheeks reddening under her blusher.

'Anyway, he's coming around this afternoon and I want you to go out for a couple of hours.'

No, no, no, no, no fucking way.

'Mum, I don't know who this bloke is. I'm not leaving you alone with him.'

'Son, don't go cramping my style. You'll meet him in a bit. He's really nice.'

'Mum—'

'Just give him a chance. Promise?'

An hour later, there was a knock at the back door. Jamie drew himself up to his full height to answer it. He flung the door open, then adjusted his eyeline down. A short, slightly plump old man with grey hair, bright red cheeks, and a beaming smile stood in front of him. One hand was holding a bunch of flowers, the other was extended towards him.

'You must be Jamie. Nice to meet you, son. I'm Jim.'

Jamie didn't know whether to be relieved or horrified. His mother was dating a male version of herself.

He led Jim through the kitchen, up the stairs, and into his mother's room. The only time he'd ever seen her look this excited was when Liam was born. She was grinning like a Cheshire Cat about to get all the cream. Jim thrust the flowers towards her, trying to get past the immoveable wall that was Jamie.

'Oh, they're so lovely.' Morag sighed. 'Thank you, BJ.'

BJ?

'Jamie, can you take these downstairs and put them in some

water before you go out? Fiona's expecting you within the next ten minutes.'

Jamie opened his mouth, but realised he didn't have anything appropriate to say. So he shut it, stomped downstairs, put the flowers in a glass, and went out the back door, slamming it behind him.

BY THE TIME JAMIE REACHED FIONA'S, HE WAS RAGING. HIS mood wasn't helped by the fact his sister laughed as soon as she saw his expression.

'Did you know about this?' he demanded.

Fiona nodded. 'I think it's cute.'

'Cute? He's a fucking hobbit but she calls him "Big Jim", or BJ for short.'

Fiona snorted with laughter. 'Are you coming in, or what?'

He stormed inside. 'What am I meant to think about a name like that?'

'I dunno. That he's got a massive cock?'

'Fi! Fuck's sake! This is Mum we're talking about!'

'Oh, don't be such a prude. Let her have a bit of fun.'

He sat at the kitchen table and put his head in his hands. 'I don't know what to do.'

'Well, you can start with something to drink. Tea? Coffee?'

'Whisky.'

Fiona poured him a tumbler and he downed it.

'Where's Liam?'

'Upstairs having a nap.'

'Dunc's working on the rigs now. Why haven't you come home like you normally do? There's no one in your room.'

'Mum needed to know you could look after yourself.'

'Mission accomplished. Now you've got to come back. She's doing my head in.'

'There's a far better solution.'

'What?'

'What do you think? Finally move out, you big lump. If you can hear Mum snoring through the wall every night, how do you think you're going to cope with hearing her giving Big Jim a b—'

'Shut up! What the fuck is wrong with you? It's not funny.'

Fiona held her stomach as she cackled. 'You're right. But what *is* funny is your reaction.'

He pushed the chair back and paced up and down. 'I don't know what to do. My whole life has gone tits-up.'

'Really now? Has it?'

He stopped and stared at her. He knew he wasn't going to like what was coming next.

His sister raised her hands, counting off each point in turn.

'One, you've finally shown Mum you can look after yourself and don't need babying. Two, you've just made sixty fucking grand for playing your guitar for ten minutes. Three, you've had a taste of what life could be like away from a building site full of Neds. Four, you've written music that could take you all over the world. And five, you've fallen in love with someone totally amazing who most likely loves you right back.'

Fiona sat back and crossed her arms.

'Now, I'm going to sit here and wait for you to admit I'm right about every single point.'

Silence.

Jamie sat, his hands locked together on the table. He took a breath in, feeling all the pain bubbling up.

'She doesn't love me back.'

His sister leaned across the table and curled her small hand over his. 'Has she said that?'

He shook his head.

'Have you told her you love her?'

He shrugged. 'Kind of.'

She sighed. 'Jamie. You need to spell it out. You need to say those three words in that exact order, or she'll never know.'

'It's too late. She left.'

'From her point of view it was *you* who left.'

'But she wanted to sign that contract. She wanted us to go to LA. It was too much. I panicked.'

Fiona squeezed his hand.

'Think about it from her point of view. Her career is extremely unstable and she'd just lost her job. If you didn't know when you'd ever next find work, wouldn't you be grasping at any opportunity? And did you ever stop to think maybe she wanted the contract because it would have forced you to stay with her?'

'What?'

'You weren't exactly buying her flowers and telling her you love her, were you? She would have had no idea how you really felt. Seriously, Jamie, Big Jim's got way more skills than you in the love department.'

He hung his head. 'What the fuck am I meant to do?'

Fiona ruffled his hair. 'Think about what you'd want your life to look like if Mum and I didn't exist. Who would you be with, where would you be, and what would you be doing?'

He sighed, utterly exhausted.

'I'd be with Sam and we'd be playing music. It wouldn't matter where as long as we were together.'

His sister patted him on the head. 'There we go. That wasn't too hard, was it? Now you just need to make it happen.'

AFTER ESTHER LEFT, SAM FOUND IT MORE AND MORE difficult to convince herself that life in LA was the culmination of all her fantasies. Living her 'best life' was not bringing her any sense of happiness, peace or fulfilment.

Every morning her limbs felt a little heavier, her mind muddier, until one morning she couldn't get off the sofa at all. She could feel her heart thudding faster than normal, hear the high-pitched whine of her nervous system. She was primed for action, but her legs didn't want to work.

She tapped out a message for Mikey, saying she was too ill to go to the studio, then rang Zoe, who picked up immediately.

'Oh my god. Is this really you, or some proof-of-life call before I'm asked to pay one meeellion dollars to secure your release?'

Even smiling seemed to hurt.

'Hey, bestie.'

'Sam?'

'Yeah.'

'What's wrong?'

'Have you got time for a chat?'

'Of course. I'm just in the estate office pretending to be interested in how a quarry works beyond blowing shit up, then carrying away what's left.'

'Sounds like a Rory job.'

'Oh, totally. But he got carried away ordering explosives, so I took over. Now please tell me what's going on.'

Sam didn't know where to start.

'How's Morag?' she asked.

'Morag? Much better now. She's out of bed and back part-time in the post office.'

'Huh? Has she been ill?'

'Oh shit. Sorry. Jamie said not to tell you.'

'What the fuck happened?'

'She got drunk one night, tripped up the stairs, and broke her ankle.'

'Oh my god, is she okay?'

'Yes, she's awesome. She's got a boyfriend called Big Jim.'

'Excuse me?'

Zoe giggled. 'And she keeps calling him "BJ".'

'What the fuck is going on? Are you going to tell me now it never rains up there and you're pregnant?'

'Now you're sounding more like yourself. No, it's pissing it down right now, and I'm definitely not pregnant although I do put a lot of practice in.'

'Why didn't Jamie want me to know?'

'He didn't want you to worry. He didn't want you to be distracted from what you were doing out there. How's it going?'

'How is he?'

'Jamie?'

'Yeah.'

'Dunno really. He seems pretty miserable, to be honest. But then he's been waiting on Morag hand and foot twenty-four seven and she's been a bit of a nightmare. I know he didn't want you to know, but I thought you'd have been in touch with him.'

'Did he say anything about what happened in London?'

'No. He just said the recording went well. Sam, what's going on?'

'I slept with him.'

'Whaaaaaaaaaaaat? Jamie? *Jamie* Jamie?'

'Mmm.'

'When?'

'After the concert.'

'Oh my god, I can't *believe* you didn't tell me! Was it good? Actually, no, don't answer that. Holy shit. Did it happen again?'

'Yeah.'

'Bloody hell. I know he keeps his cards close to his chest,

but you? Do you like him? Duh, of course you like him, but you know what I mean. Fuck, I'm rambling. Why aren't you speaking to him? Did something go wrong?'

Sam puffed out her cheeks. 'We were offered a record contract, and he said no and left.'

'Why? What kind of contract?'

She suddenly felt very small. 'I don't really know. I wanted to sign without even looking at it. I'd just found out I'd lost my job, and, and...'

'Yeeeesssssss?'

'I thought tying Jamie to the contract would force him to be with me.'

There was silence, then she heard Zoe drawing in a big breath. She braced herself.

'So, let me get this straight. You tried to bully Jamie into signing his life away without reading any of the details first because you thought this was your last chance at any sort of a career, and because you didn't believe Jamie would want to be with you unless under duress?'

If Sam had been feeling bad before, this opened the festering Tupperware at the back of her mental fridge. The truth stank.

'Yes. Are you going to shout at me?'

Zoe huffed. 'I'm trying to decide whether to yell at you or burst into tears on your behalf. You're so fucking awesome. You have so many options open to you. Fuck *Elm Tree Lane*. They can stick Mopeoke up their arse. Look where you are now! You're in LA, writing music for whatever bonkers film Brad is making next. You're unstoppable.'

She made a noncommittal sound in response.

'Are you enjoying it there? Are you having fun?'

Sam thought about all the celebs she'd met, all the yoga-spin-pump-fusion classes she'd attended. All the green smoothies, all the parties, all the hours watching Th's willy wafting about underwater as he blew bubble rings.

'Not really.'

'Oh. Is that why you've been ignoring me?'

'Yes. I'm sorry.'

'Don't be daft, I just wish you'd told me. You know you can tell me anything.'

'I know. I just feel like such a dick. This has been my dream forever, but it doesn't feel right.'

'So what *does* feel right? When were you last really happy?'

'At the ceilidh.'

'And what made that so good?'

'It was the culmination of everything we'd created together. Better than the concert, because at the ceilidh we knew people liked our music so we could just belt it out. Standing on stage, seeing everyone's faces, seeing you so happy, it was perfect. And we'd also just had sex. Jesus, Zoe, it was mind-blowing. He's the fucking god of sex.'

Her best friend shrieked with laughter. 'I'll never be able to speak to him again now! It's bad enough with Morag winking at me every time she talks about *Big* Jim.'

Sam giggled, but she felt empty. She missed everyone in Kinloch, but most of all, she missed Jamie.

'Zo, I've really fucked up.'

'Then come home. Speak to him.'

'I can't. I'm still trying to write music with Th. And if I leave—'

'Th?'

'Yeah, Th. He says it's meant to evoke the sound of wind across water.'

Zoe snorted. 'This is priceless. I can't wait to tell Rory.'

'Brad's given me this opportunity and if I leave now, I'll

blow it. And anyway, I don't know if Jamie wants anything to do with me.'

'You need to ask yourself what's more important,' Zoe replied. 'Making music with Little Drip to stay in Brad's good books, or giving you and Jamie a chance?'

❧ 29 ❧

Jamie had read hundreds of his sister's romance novels, but they offered no appropriate solutions to winning Sam's heart. The only thing he knew for sure was that when they sang their songs, the universe came into alignment and everything was right with the world.

He decided he'd finish writing one of the songs they'd started but never completed, record it, then send it to wherever she was in LA. He didn't want to show up and put her under any pressure. He would simply declare his love from afar, then give her the space to decide what she wanted to do with that information.

It felt strange to be writing on his own again. He needed a sounding board, but there was no way he was going to sing the song to his sister, or even worse, his mother and Big Jim.

Clive, the owner of The King's Arms, was pestering him to perform again, so Jamie figured if he could work up the guts to play for a packed pub and they liked the new song, then there was nothing stopping him sending it to Sam.

Setting up in the pub, he felt the same anxiety and nerves

fluttering up as before, but this time he knew how to deal with them. He focused on the breathing exercise Sam had taught him, the guitar in his hands, his fingers on the strings. Clive had put him in the main bar, as there were so many people who wanted to listen.

With Duncan away working on the rigs, his sister was at home with Liam and his mum was spending the night at Big Jim's. It was odd not having one of them there, but he knew he had to get used to it. Even if his plan didn't work and Sam didn't want him, it was time to spread his wings and leave Kinloch.

He tapped on the microphone to get everyone's attention, heat spreading up his neck.

'Hello everyone, thanks for coming.'

The room broke into applause, fanning the flames that burned his cheeks.

'I'm Jamie, and I'm going to be singing you a few songs tonight. Some you might know if you've heard me play before, but one is brand new. Not even my mum has heard it.'

A few people laughed and whooped.

He strummed the guitar. 'I'm going to start at the beginning with a song I wrote a couple of years ago. This is "Call to Me".'

He closed his eyes and sang the songs he'd written on his own, the songs he'd played to Zoe, then Brad. They were so familiar, yet seemed to belong to a different version of himself. In just a few months he'd become someone he never thought he could be, and rather than feeling scared, he was excited.

When he got to the end of his first set, he took a sip of water as the applause rang around the room. He smiled, realising that he was actually enjoying himself.

'Thank you.' He cleared his throat. 'The next song is the new one. I started writing it with Sam Adamson, but it never got finished. For those of you who know me, I don't say much, and... when Sam was here, I didn't say the most important words of all. I've put them into this song and if you think it's good enough, I'm going to send it to her. It's called "My Heart". I hope you like it.'

He closed his eyes again and played the first few chords. In his mind he saw Sam smiling, laughing, pulling faces at him, holding onto him as they floated in the hot air balloon, lying in his arms as she slept.

He sang his deepest truth: the love he had for her. He finished the verse and let his voice soar as he sang the chorus, ending with the words he'd once said to her across the kitchen table: *The only thing I can offer is my heart and my life. I love you.*

Starting the second verse, his eyes shot open. There was another sound in the room, a humming that harmonised with his words. He glanced around but couldn't see anyone new. It was so soft it was hardly there. Was he imagining it? As he reached the second chorus, a voice joined his.

It can't be.

His fingers carried on playing, but the words stuck in his throat. A murmur rippled through the room as people realised what was going on.

The crowds parted and Sam was there, holding a microphone, singing his words back to him. *The only thing I can offer is my heart and my life. I love you.*

He stopped playing. Was this really happening?

The pub was silent. Everyone seemed to be holding their breath.

Jamie was so full of emotion he couldn't move.

Sam's smile faltered and she bit her bottom lip.

Was she *nervous*?

He shook himself and started the second verse, pulling a chair towards her with his foot. She sat down, their knees touching. Electricity shot through him. He struggled to get the words out, his voice cracking.

He focused on the lyrics and not their meaning as he kept playing. She harmonised with him on the third verse, then they sang together for the chorus, which they repeated as if exploring how the words felt being vocalised for the first time.

When the song finished, the room exploded with clapping, whistling, cheers, and screaming. Jamie held Sam's gaze, the one still point in the storm.

She was here. She was really here.

Out of the corner of his eye he saw Clive take Sam's microphone.

'Right then, ladies and gentlemen,' he barked. 'I think that's a good moment to have a wee break for half an hour and leave these two alone to catch up.'

Jamie looked up. The women were crying, their hands on their hearts or over their mouths. The men were either furiously blinking or yelling, 'Go on, Jamie my son.'

Clive took the guitar from him and placed it on the stand. 'Come with me, you two.'

He led them out the back of the pub and unlocked a gate in a high wall.

'This is our private garden. You'll get a bit of peace and quiet here.'

They entered a small courtyard filled with tubs of flowers. A pergola was hung with wisteria and fairy lights. Underneath was a table.

Clive put the keys down. 'When you're done, and if you're up for it, lock up and come back and do another set.' He left them to it.

Jamie sat opposite Sam. He reached his hands across the table towards her and she took them.

SAM'S STOMACH WAS JUMPING OUT OF HER THROAT. SHE thought she might feel more in control when she saw Jamie, but her body was one breath away from fainting.

He was so much more than her memories had allowed her to experience. He was bigger, his eyes darker, his hands warmer. Her heart couldn't keep up.

He took a breath in as if to speak, but she interrupted him.

'Jamie, I need to apologise.'

He shook his head and she squeezed his hands.

'I do. Right from the moment we met, I railroaded you. I took advantage of your sweet nature. I was selfish and didn't behave well most of the time.'

'No, no, that's not true.'

'It's how I feel. I couldn't read you and didn't want to lose you. I thought if I made you sign the contract, I could force you to be with me.'

'You didn't think I wanted to be with you?'

She shook her head.

He released her, running his fingers through his hair. 'Jesus, Sam. I—'

'Jamie, I need to talk to you. Please?'

He nodded and reached back across the table towards her.

'Nothing is more important to me than you,' she continued. 'I want to be with you and I'll do whatever it takes to make that happen. If you want me to move to Kinloch, I will.'

He shook his head again.

Her heart raced faster. 'I haven't been honest with myself and I haven't been honest with you. I've never loved anyone like I love you. My life no longer feels right without you in it. You're my sun, my moon, and all my stars. If you'd be willing to give me a chance, I'll move my world for you. I don't expect you to love me back—'

'Jesus Christ, Sam. I've been in love with you since we first sang together.'

'What? But you ran off.'

'Because I was so overwhelmed, I couldn't cope. I'd never felt like that before.'

'But what about the other woman?'

'What other woman?'

'The one you first sang the song lyric to. The one you took to the standing stones. The one you recited E.E. Cummings to.'

'I was talking about *you*, Sam. You're my first proper kiss, my first love, my first everything.'

'What?'

He sighed. 'Before you, the last girl I kissed was Isla Blair when I was eight.'

'But... I don't understand.' Her cheeks felt on fire. 'You're incredible at, erm, it.'

He blushed and stared at the table.

'Why didn't you say anything?' she asked.

'I tried. After my second freak-out when I brought you a cup of tea.'

Sam remembered how she'd interrupted him. How she'd assumed he was saying he'd never slept with an actress before.

She groaned and sank her head into her hands. 'I'm so sorry.'

He pulled her hands away, stroking across her palms. 'There's nothing to be sorry about.'

New fear sliced at her chest. 'But if you've never been with anyone else, don't you want to, erm, sleep around? Make sure you really want to be with me?'

His eyes widened. 'Are you cracked in the head?'

She shrugged, and he grinned.

'Sam, I didn't mean to wait until I was twenty-seven, but now I'm glad I did. You're my first and my last. You're my everything.'

Emotion rushed through her. 'I love you so much, Jamie.'

'Don't cry, sweetheart. Come here.'

He sat her on his lap and wiped her tears.

'It's all going to be fine,' he told her.

She snuggled against him, feeling his warmth, drinking in the scent of him. Finally, she felt like she was home.

'What are we going to do?' she asked.

He kissed the top of her head. 'Live happily ever after of course.'

BEING BACK WITH JAMIE WAS SO FAMILIAR, YET SO NEW. THE possibilities were limitless. Neither had any commitments except to each other.

They went back into the pub and played a second set of all the songs they'd written together, finishing with 'The Heart of Scotland', then extricated themselves from the crowds of well-wishers and went back down the dark high street to Morag's.

Jamie held her hand tightly, as if still in shock she was here and worried if he let go she might float away.

'How did you know where I would be? How did you get the second microphone?' he asked.

'Fiona and Zoe set it up for me. I arrived at your mum's just after you left for the pub.'

'She's not at home tonight.'

Sam grinned at him. 'She told me she was going to Big Jim's for an "adult sleepover", and "a bit of Netflix and chill".'

Jamie groaned. 'The sooner I'm out of there, the better. I've started sleeping in Fi's old room with earplugs in.'

She giggled. 'A few months ago you thought you'd never leave.'

'And now I can't bloody wait.'

Jamie unlocked the back door and Sam entered the kitchen and took off her shoes. She was suddenly shy and nervous. After so long yearning for him, he was finally hers.

'I like the new light.'

He smiled. 'Mum still wants the old one back, but I refused. I told her if Big Jim tried to change it, he'd electrocute himself.'

He went to the kettle. 'Do you want some tea? Coffee?' He paused. 'Me?'

Yes, yes, yes. Her body was a mob of football supporters cheering her on.

'You, please.'

He held out his hand and she was drawn into his arms. He cradled her face and rested his forehead on hers.

'I love you, Sam.'

She swallowed, trying to control her emotions. 'I love you too.'

His kisses were soft, coaxing her lips apart. Tingles spread across her skin like warm honey. She was finally back where she belonged and it was perfect. His tongue licked into her mouth and she moaned, pulling him closer.

He held the back of her head with one hand and ran the other down her spine to cup her bottom, tugging her against him. Pleasure rushed through her with every beat of her heart. She opened herself to him, needing everything.

She craved his skin against hers, his lips on her breasts, his cock buried deep inside her. He lifted her and she wrapped her legs around his back, rocking against him, threading her fingers through his hair.

He walked her to the stairs and started to climb. She held on tight, feeling his bedroom door against her back as he pushed it open. He kicked it shut, then laid her gently on the bed, his tongue dancing with hers and sending sparkles of light shivering down inside her.

She burned for him, her heart expanding with love so fierce and bright she could hardly breathe. She brought her hands between them, fighting to unfasten the button of his jeans. He broke the kiss, his eyes hazy and unfocused.

'You first.'

She shook her head. 'No, Jamie. I need you inside me now.'

He hesitated. 'But—'

'Please.'

'Do you have a condom?' he asked.

'I'm on birth control and I'm clear. If you're happy, we don't have to use them.'

His cheeks were flushed, his eyes so dark. He nodded.

She yanked the zip of his jeans down, trying to push them off. It wasn't quick enough, so she rolled out from under him. She jumped off the bed and shimmied her dress over her hips and off her head.

He stared at her, his mouth open.

'You're so beautiful.'

She stopped, feeling his eyes on her. Her wetness soaked through her underwear. Her breasts ached for his touch. She hooked one strap of her bra off her shoulder, then the other.

'Take your clothes off, Jamie.'

He yanked his T-shirt off and threw it away. She stared at his muscles as they strained with every ragged breath, then unclasped her bra and let it drop to the floor. He let out a strangled cry. She touched her breasts, tugging on the nipples. He braced his hands on his knees.

'Fuck!'

She pulled the edges of her panties away from her hips, let them fall down her legs, then stepped out.

'Clothes off,' she told him, her heart racing so fast she thought she might pass out. Her blood was fizzing, her skin prickling with desperate need for his touch.

He pulled his boxers and trousers off, then knelt on the bed. His cock was hard and swollen. She swallowed, her inner muscles clenching as if already trying to pull him inside. She could see precum slick on the thick head. She licked her lips. He gripped the shaft, rubbing his thumb over the engorged end.

She stumbled forward and he caught her, laying her down, raining urgent kisses over her face and down her neck. She spread her legs around him and he pulled her nipple into his mouth, growling as he sucked on it. She wriggled to seat the head of his cock at her entrance, feeling the glorious resistance, the pleasure as it started to push in.

He pulled back, bracing himself above her, panting, his eyes squeezed tight. She paused, breathing with him, waiting, her fingers running up and down the ridged muscles of his back.

He opened his eyes and held her gaze. He looked desperate, as if teetering on the edge of a cliff and only she could bring him back.

'I love you, Sam. God, I love you.'

She stroked down the side of his face, feeling his stubble, his burning skin.

'I love you too. You're my everything, Jamie.'

He dropped his head to her shoulder. 'Fuck!'

She soothed him, kissing his neck, trailing paths down the planes of his back as he found his control.

'Jamie?'

He nodded.

'I need you inside me. Please?'

He raised his head, his eyes boring into hers with a desperate intensity, then thrust his hips forward, filling her with a rush of fierce pleasure.

Her head thumped back on the pillow with a cry. He slowly withdrew and she tightened around him, dragging her muscles against his cock. He thrust hard again.

'Oh god, Jamie. Yes. More, more.'

He set up a slow rhythm, pulling out until only the head was inside, then pounding deep, circling his hips into her clit. He covered her body with his own, his lips by her ear. With every thrust she felt his hot breath as he exhaled his love for her.

'God, I love you. Fuck, fuck, fuck, I love you.'

Sensation spiralled and collided inside her. She met each roll of his hips with her own, bucking up, grinding against him as she gasped for air.

Nothing had ever felt this all-encompassing, this intense, this right. Love was the gasoline pouring onto the fires of her pleasure.

A rush whipped through her, like wind racing before the storm, her body tightening and bracing for a cataclysmic climax. She dug her nails into his back, holding on. There was no turning back. Her orgasm hit with unstoppable force and she surrendered to it with a scream, waves of pleasure smashing through her.

She heard him roar, his body shaking as he pumped his own release, then she lost all sense of where she ended and he began. They were blinding light, fused together in the heart of the brightest sun.

❦ 30 ❦

Jamie didn't know how he could be this happy without bursting. How did people in love get anything done? Now the stopper was out of the sex bottle, he didn't know how it was ever going to go back in.

He couldn't stop reaching for Sam and she seemed just as insatiable. They made love through the night and in the shower the next morning. He'd spent the first part of his life quiet and reserved and now his cheeks were aching from smiling so much.

Sam insisted on cooking him breakfast, but within a minute he was standing behind her, nuzzling her neck. She was frying bacon and eggs, and the smell combined with her was enough to send any man to distraction.

'What are you doing?' she gasped.

He bit on her earlobe, loving the sound of her breath catching. 'I'm helping.'

'How, exactly?'

He reached his hands to her breasts, groaning as he cupped their soft weight.

'I dunno. Give me a moment and I'll think of something.'

Her nipples were hard through her top and he scratched his nails across the fabric. She dropped her head, panting. The frying pan skidded and the spatula dropped out of her hands to the stove top. He pulled her against his erection and her head fell back against his chest.

'Oh god.'

He turned her towards him, wanting her mouth on his. There was a whump and the fat in the pan caught light.

'Fuck!'

He lifted her away towards the back door.

'Jamie! The pan!'

He ran forward and turned off the gas. She grabbed the nearest fire extinguisher, pulled the pin and aimed it at the cooker. The blast sent the pan flying across the worktop in a shower of foam, fat, bacon and eggs.

It was all over in a few seconds, but the silence that followed lasted longer.

'Jamie MacDougall,' Sam said in a perfect impersonation of Morag, 'I knew you couldn't be trusted in my kitchen.'

He was trying not to laugh. 'Fucking hell, Mum is going to kill me.'

She giggled. 'Let's clean it up and hope she never notices.'

'Yeah, then go out for breakfast, eh?'

They cleaned the kitchen and left the house. Sam grabbed his hand as soon as they were outside, and his heart swelled.

She smiled at him. 'You're mine, Jamie, and I want everyone to know.'

For once he was annoyed the high street was empty. He wanted Mrs McCreedie and her cronies, plus anyone he'd ever met in his life, to see him with Sam. Being with her was like winning the love Olympics, then being voted The World's Sexiest Man ahead of Brad Bauer.

In the café they sat opposite each other, legs entwined.

'So, Jamie. Today is the first day of the rest of our lives. What are we going to do?'

'Well, Mum and FFS Jim are due back this afternoon and I—'

'FFS? As in "for fuck's sake" Jim?'

He tried to keep a straight face. 'It actually stands for "five foot seven".'

Sam howled with laughter. 'Jamie MacDougall, you are a very naughty boy.'

He grinned back at her. 'I learned from the best.'

'So, are we cooking them dinner?'

'Yep, and Fi's coming around with Liam. Why don't you give Zoe and Rory a call and invite them over too?'

Sam took her phone outside and he watched her with a stupid grin on his face. She was jumping up and down and squealing to her friend, failing to hide that she was talking about him.

He took out his phone and rang a number. He'd finished his call by the time Sam returned.

'Zoe says they would be delighted to attend this evening's festivities.'

'Rory? Delighted?'

She grinned. 'In a gruff, manly way, of course. So, are we going shopping?'

'Yes, I thought we could pop into Inverness, although there's also someone I'd like you to meet.'

'Ye-es?'

His heart beat faster. 'You don't have to do anything. There's no expectation. Just meet him and have a chat.'

'And who is *he*?'

'Campbell King. He owns an independent record label

called Ness Records. I met him a week ago to see what our options might be for the future.'

Sam smiled, but her eyes were liquid.

He grabbed her hand. 'You don't have to. It was just an idea.'

She shook her head and brushed her tears away.

'No, I do. I want to. Thank you, Jamie. Thank you for not giving up on me.'

CAMPBELL KING LIVED IN A LARGE DETACHED HOUSE outside Inverness. It was a dark grey stone building, but inside it was light and airy with high ceilings and bright colours. Campbell was in his sixties, tall and heavy-set, with a shock of curly red hair that was gradually retreating from his forehead.

He was full of energy and greeted Sam and Jamie like long-lost friends, pulling them inside a large room which served as his office. The walls were lined with framed gold discs and posters of the artists who were signed to his label.

Jamie tried to work out what Sam was thinking as she gazed at them.

'Sam, it's a real pleasure to meet you,' said Campbell. 'The music you and Jamie have written is right up my Strasse, so to speak. Let me tell you a little bit about myself and what I think we can do for you.'

Jamie sat back as Campbell talked, intertwining his fingers with Sam's when she reached for him. He'd heard it all before, but a repeat performance only solidified his opinion. Sam asked the same questions he had, then more of her own. Within half an hour, she was leaning forward in her chair, being as animated as she could whilst refusing to relinquish her hold on his hand.

. . .

THEY LEFT CAMPBELL'S HOUSE AFTER A COUPLE OF HOURS and despite the lack of sleep the night before, Sam's excitement levels were through the roof.

Jamie loved her energy. He loved listening to her. He just loved everything about her. He'd been sleepwalking through life, and she'd dragged him kicking and screaming into a technicolour world of possibilities.

After food shopping, they headed home and started dinner. His mum had specified rib of beef with Yorkshire pudding, veg and gravy, and a chocolate roulade. He'd already made the flourless sponge and it was wrapped around greaseproof paper to retain the shape. Making food with Sam was like making music—an effortless creative dance of harmony.

As people started to arrive, his nerves reared their head. Would they treat him differently? Would they take the piss? Did he have to stop touching Sam in front of them?

He needn't have worried. Everyone seemed to take it in their stride that they were now together, and he even sensed his mum was relieved.

They all crammed around the dining table and Morag held her hands up as the cue for them to take the hand of the person next to them. Everyone closed their eyes.

'Dear You Upstairs. Bless this family and bless this meal. Thank you for all your divine interventioning this year. If I may be so bold, you've surpassed yourself. You've taught our Jamie how to cook without burning the house down, and persuaded Sam to take him off my hands...'

Jamie opened his eyes to see Zoe and Fiona grinning at him. He shook his head.

'You saved the castle and made sure Liam's first word was most definitely "Nana".'

'*No, it wasn't*,' Fiona mouthed.

'But above all that, you over-delivered blessings by sending me my Scottish stallion, Jim...'

Jamie and Fiona rolled their eyes as Zoe and Sam bit back laughter.

'For he truly is the full package with the big package—'

Rory opened his eyes and looked askance at Jim, who, save for Morag, was the only person with their eyes still closed.

'So, as we're clearly in your good books, if you've got any more gifts to share, the winning numbers for the lotto would be lovely.'

Everyone closed their eyes again as Morag finished.

'Thanking you in advance and keep safe in your love those who are no longer with us. Amen.'

A squeeze rippled through everyone's hands and they opened their eyes. Morag handed Jim the carving knife.

'Would you do the honours, love?'

THE MEAL WAS FAMILIAR TO JAMIE—LAUGHTER, BICKERING and conversation. But with the addition of Zoe, Sam, and Jim, the volume was cranked up to Liam-tantrum levels. If Zoe was loud, Sam was louder, and if Sam was louder, Jim rivalled his mother after eight Dubonnet and full-fat Cokes.

Jamie caught Rory flinching a couple of times as Jim laughed so hard the picture frames rattled.

'Is this like being in Afghanistan?' he shouted across the table at him.

'Worse,' replied Rory, setting off another round of hoots and cackles.

Zoe turned to Sam. 'So, have you any idea what you're going to do next, then?'

The table went quiet as everyone turned to look at them.

Sam squeezed his hand under the table as she told them about meeting Campbell King.

'He was straight down the line and I really liked him. We'll record the first album up here and prepare for release. We'll divide our time between here and London, then I'll rent my flat out and we'll take a van on tour.'

'A van? You?' Zoe didn't sound convinced.

'Yes, it's going to be amazing. I'm embracing minimalism.'

'Remind me how many suitcases you brought the last time you were up here?'

'Ah, but now I know what's important to pack.'

'A sense of humour to put up with him?' asked Fiona, pointing at Jamie.

Sam gazed at him, her cheeks pink and her smile soft. 'Jamie is all I need.'

There was silence as he stared at her, his chest so full of love it was difficult to breathe. Morag frantically fanned her face, her jaw clenched as if desperately trying to hold her emotion at bay. Zoe's lower jaw was wobbling, and Rory pulled her into him and kissed the top of her head.

Fiona gagged. 'Honestly, you're nearly as vomit-inducing as Mum and Jim.'

AFTER THE MEAL THEY CRAMMED INTO THE LIVING ROOM and Sam and Jamie played for everyone. There was no need to close his eyes anymore. If Sam was there, he wanted to see her. Their impromptu concert felt like an ending and a beginning. An expression of how far he'd come, the love they had for each other, and all the places they still had to go.

It was late by the time they called it a night. Now that Rory's mum was with Brad, the castle was empty, so Rory had offered them the chance to stay there. Jamie was grateful. He wanted to let his mum and Jim have their privacy and felt like he'd finally outgrown his childhood home. He was ready to move on.

They packed overnight bags, said their goodbyes, and went up to the castle.

'Zoe said we could have any room or just stay in the flat. What do you fancy?' Sam asked him.

'You.'

She grinned. 'And where do you fancy me, Jamie MacDougall?'

'Anywhere. That old storeroom was pretty mind-blowing.'

'Well, maybe we could try out a few options?'

'Sounds like a plan, Sam.'

He stopped and pulled her to him. Her face was shining in the darkness. He brushed a kiss across her lips.

'I love you to the end of the universe.'

She dropped her bag and wrapped her arms around the back of his neck. 'And I love you to the end of the universe and back.'

EPILOGUE

Sam interlocked her fingers with Jamie's, resting their hands on the skirt of her green silk gown. It complemented his kilt. They were in the middle of a sea of stars and she was sick with nerves.

This moment had crept up on them. What was once a tiny sail glimpsed on the horizon was now a tall ship bearing down on them with gale-force Brad behind it.

Braveheart 2 had opened to mixed reviews. The higher-end film critics had dismissed it as historically inaccurate nonsense. Audiences, however, had loved it.

Their album sales had been good, but after the film was released, they went higher even than sales of spiced shortbread. Sam and Jamie found themselves headlining gigs rather than being the support act, and nobody was surprised when they were nominated for an Oscar.

Now they were here, in the enormous theatre, awaiting their fate. Sam had made it to LA, but not quite as she'd imagined. Her life with Jamie was beyond anything she could have predicted and she couldn't have been happier.

Jamie was still shy and preferred not to speak in interviews, but he wasn't the same man she'd first met in Kinloch, and she wasn't the same woman who'd railroaded him. He'd handled the pressure of performing 'The Heart of Scotland' half an hour before in front of an audience of millions, but now seemed even more anxious.

She leaned over to whisper in his ear. 'The hard part's over. We can relax now. It's not like we're going to win.'

He nodded, but she could see a muscle twitching in his jaw, his body tense. Their category was coming soon and the pressure was rising.

Breathe in, two, three, four, and hold, two, three, four…

'And the Oscar for best original song goes to…'

She gripped Jamie's hand tighter.

'Sam Adamson and Jamie MacDougall for "The Heart of Scotland"!'

Their song filled the theatre, rising above the cheers and claps. They were both too stunned to move and were urged to their feet by those around them. They stood, making their way to the end of the row. Jamie looked grey.

She grabbed his hand. 'Don't worry, I've got this.'

They stepped onto the stage. It seemed vast, the lights blinding. They were given their statuettes and Jamie stepped back, letting her make the speech. They'd worked on it together, but he'd wanted her to deliver it.

This was something she'd trained for. This was something she could do. She knew they didn't have long, so kept it short and funny, making the audience laugh, especially when Brad yelled 'Yeah baby!' from the front row.

When she finished, she turned to Jamie.

'Do you want to say anything?' she whispered.

He nodded and stepped forward. Her eyes widened with

surprise as he came to her side and leaned down towards the microphones.

'Hello, everyone.'

'Hello, Jamie,' the crowd replied, followed by a ripple of laughter.

He cleared his throat. 'I'm not a great talker, so I won't take too much of your time. I just wanted you to bear witness for me on the most important day of my life.'

Sam's heart was as big as her smile. She had no idea winning an Oscar meant so much to him. He looked at her. What was he doing?

'Sam, you are my sun, my moon and all my stars. You are my first, my last, and my life. You are my everything. Chonay DaneH'a'? Will you marry me?'

Time stopped in a perfect moment of shock, confusion, incredulity and joy. He looked so nervous, staring at her with his dark eyes, his breath held.

She woke from her trance, nodded, and the spell broke.

He started breathing again and his eyes lit up as the theatre rang with whistles, cheers and the stamping of feet. She threw her arms around him and he lifted her off the floor.

'Is that a yes?'

'God, yes.'

She yelled towards the microphones, 'Lu'! Yes!'

Their song swelled around them as the cue to leave the stage, and Jamie scooped her up in his arms. They were assaulted from all sides by lights, noise, and people, but all Sam saw was him.

He was the stuff of which her dreams were truly made.

THE END

❧

THANK YOU SO MUCH FOR READING MUSICAL GAMES! I hope you enjoyed reading it as much as I loved writing it. If you have a moment, please write me a review!

❧

LOVE SAM AND JAMIE? YOU CAN CATCH UP WITH THEM AND all the stars of the Kinloch series in Wedding Games. Here's what it's all about!

Say 'I do' to Scotland's wedding of the year!

Wedding bells are finally ringing for Rory and Zoe! But setting a date and saying yes to the dress is a lot more complicated when their mothers are mortal enemies and Rory's stepfather is a Hollywood star with a death wish.

And if their families weren't complicated enough, their friends are determined to make the bachelor and bachelorette parties ones they will remember forever – or desperately try to forget...

A castle, a cast of thousands, a superstar who's lost the plot, and an unlikely stripper. Can Rory and Zoe unravel the tangles in time to tie the knot, or is eloping the only answer?

Get your glad rags on and hold onto your hats as it's time to unleash matrimonial madness!

Wedding Games *is a steamy, laugh-out-loud romantic comedy, with a guaranteed happy ever after and all your favourite characters from the Kinloch series.*

Get your copy of Wedding Games now by going to www.eviealexanderbooks.com

NEWSLETTER SIGN-UP

Newsletter freebies are waiting, just for you...

In my newsletter you get Evie news before anyone else, as well as exclusive content and goodies.

Newsletter subscribers are my extra special friends, and get everything from bonus epilogues, 19,000 words of deleted sex scenes, free stories, free audiobooks, extracts from my current work-in-progress, and exclusive offers and giveaways.

Sign up now!

http://www.eviealexanderauthor.com/subscribe/

REVIEW MUSICAL GAMES
WRITE A REVIEW & MAKE MY DAY!

Thank you so much for reading Musical Games! I hope you enjoyed reading it as much as I enjoyed writing it!

Even if just a couple of lines (or star rating), writing a review is the most amazing thing you can do! It helps people find my books, and lets them know what you loved about them.

You can review Musical Games at:
Apple
Amazon
Kobo
Barnes & Noble
Google Play
Goodreads
Bookbub
And any other storefront or platform you use!

And, if you want to share more about Musical Games on social media or your blog, please **help yourself to our library of graphics, elements and more by going to -**

www.eviealexanderauthor.com/musical-games/

Thank you!

Evie

Enjoyed Musical Games? Here's what you can read next in print, audio, or eBook format!

WEDDING GAMES
Rory and Zoe want to get married.
Not easy when their mothers are mortal enemies and Rory's step-father is a Hollywood star with a death wish. Can they pull off their wedding without a hitch, or is it doomed before they even set the date?

LOVE AD LIB
(Foxbrooke series book 1)
Uptight Lord Henry Foxbrooke needs a fake girlfriend.
Austen-obsessed actress Libby Fletcher needs a job. But when they arrive in Somerset for Henry's birthday celebrations, neither are prepared for their reception.
As friendship blurs and faking it starts to feel a little too real,

disaster strikes. Can Libby and Henry be true to themselves and each other, or has their entire act just bombed?

Tropes
Fake Dating, Grumpy/Sunshine, One Bed, Small Town, Opposites Attract, Different Worlds, Fish-out-of-Water, Jane Austen obsessed, London, Somerset, Steamy

www.eviealexanderbooks.com

SEX INDEX
(AKA THE GOOD BITS)

There have been many great contributions to the world of literature. Gutenberg invented the printing press, Shakespeare invented romantic comedy, and J K Rowling invented Harry Potter. However, all of these achievements pale into insignificance compared to my contribution – the sex index.

Here you can re-read some of the steamier moments from Musical Games. Enjoy...

And if that wasn't enough, don't forget I've got nineteen thousand words of super-hot deleted sex scenes from Highland

and Hollywood Games available exclusively for newsletter subscribers.

If you want some extra action, get yourself signed up today at

www.eviealexanderauthor.com/subscribe/

ACKNOWLEDGMENTS

Musical Games is dedicated to two amazing women - Erica Connors and Sarah Lin Turner. Sarah Lin's blog - Top Ten Romance Tropes That Need to Die Already and Erica's amazing virgin trope rants on Instagram were responsible for me changing the direction of this story for the better.

In Musical Games, I've touched on Crohn's disease and Helminth therapy. I have very close family members as well as friends who have had their lives severely impacted by Crohn's. Each of them manage their condition in different ways, and there is no 'one fits all' approach. I wanted Sam to be someone who had found her own way to deal with it so it no longer impacted on her day-to-day life.

I use Helminth therapy to help control my auto-immune disease and it has been incredibly beneficial for me. If you're interested in learning more then I recommend this Facebook group https://www.facebook.com/groups/316009255121703 and this website https://helminthictherapywik-i.org/wiki/Helminthic_Therapy_Wiki as a great place to start.

Keeping with the medical theme, I want to thank my lovely cousin, Aimee Farrell. She is a doctor and supplied all the correct medical terminology for Sam's disastrous conversation with Jamie's boss. Researching this part was hysterical, especially when Aimee told me about real-life situations she has come across during her medical career...

For the musical expertise, thank you to Seton Daunt, a songwriter, producer, and general rock star of a human for all the info about writing, recording and selling music. Your assistance was invaluable and helped give Sam and Jamie's story more depth.

Thank you to my editing team: Aimee Walker, Chris Wheary, Margaret Amatt and Mike AF, all of whom helped get this book to where it needed to be. Thank you to Bailey McGinn for designing another wonderful cover and Mark Karasick for taking such fabulous photos of me.

My team at Emlin Press: Victoria, Mandy, and Liezl. Thank you for doing everything I can't, won't, or don't have time for. Thank you for tolerating my foul mouth, laughing at my unfunny jokes and sticking around.

Thank you to my outstandingly supportive friends, in particular my alpha reader, Pash, who has been my biggest cheerleader right from before the very beginning and Margaret, who indulges my rants on a daily basis. Huge hugs and thanks also go to Julia, Kelly, Linden and Lyndsey for their understanding of me as well as the creative process. Thank you for always believing in me, even when I didn't believe in myself.

My family of course gets a special mention, in particular the two people who suffer the Evie Experience on a daily basis. Husband, you are the best decision I have ever made. Elway, you are the best luck I have ever had. I love you to the end of the universe and back.

And last, but by no means least, I want to thank my fabulous ARC team, the incredible online community of book lovers and YOU, the reader! Thank you for your continued support and for reading Sam and Jamie's story. Each time you read my books, write me a review and recommend me in countless different ways, my heart gets a little fuller. Thank you!

Evie ♡

Ps - I love love LOVE hearing from my readers so please get in touch via email or social media to ask me anything or just tell me about your day!

ALSO BY EVIE ALEXANDER

Get all of Evie's books in print, audio, or eBook format, as well as special offers, early releases, and exclusive deals at www.eviealexanderbooks.com

THE KINLOCH SERIES

HIGHLAND GAMES

Zoe's given up everything for a ramshackle cabin in Scotland. She wants a new life, but her scorching hot neighbour wants her out. As their worlds collide, will Rory succeed in destroying her dream? Or has he finally met his match? Let the games begin...

Tropes

Small Town, Enemies-to-Lovers, Grumpy/Sunshine, Fish-out-of-Water, Opposites Attract, Forced Proximity

HOLLYWOOD GAMES

In a last-ditch attempt to save Kinloch castle, new lovers Rory and Zoe throw open the doors to a Hollywood superstar. But when it all goes south, it's up to them to rewrite the script, save the castle's future, and find their own happy ending.

Tropes

Small Town, Soulmates, Grumpy/Sunshine, Fish-out-of-Water

KISSING GAMES

Bodyguard Charlie has a new mission: teach workaholic Hollywood actress Valentina how to play, one wild adventure at a time. But when no-strings fun turns into something more, they have to face some hard truths. Can they find a future together, or will their love remain a Highland fling?

Tropes

Small Town, Dark Secrets, Bodyguard/Actress, Forced Proximity, Alpha-roll hero, Dating Game

MUSICAL GAMES

After lying to a Hollywood megastar, Sam needs Jamie to write an album with her in just ten days He's got the voice of an angel and the body of a god, but fame is the last thing on his mind. Will he help make her dreams come true?

Tropes

Small Town, Grumpy/Sunshine, Male Virgin, Cinnamon Roll Hero, Opposites Attract, Fish-out-of-Water, Forced Proximity

WEDDING GAMES

Rory and Zoe want to get married. Not easy when their mothers are mortal enemies and Rory's step-father is a Hollywood star with a death wish. Can they unravel the tangles in time to tie the knot, or is eloping the only answer? Get ready for Scotland's wedding of the year!

Tropes

Small Town, Grumpy/Sunshine, Opposites Attract, Soulmates, Fish-out-of-Water

CHRISTMAS GAMES

Having a baby's easy, right? Until wayward in-laws, an out-of-control cow and mad Santa get in the way. All Rory and Zoe want is a relaxing Christmas before their baby arrives, but straightforward is not their style...

Tropes

Small Town, Grumpy/Sunshine, Opposites Attract, Soulmates, Fish-

❧

THE FOXBROOKE SERIES

ONE NIGHT IN FOXBROOKE

When chef Ben 'Kenobi' Walker gets the call to help save a VIP dinner at Foxbrooke Manor, he doesn't expect to run into old flame Leia Perry. She's all grown up and even more attractive than when they were teenagers – but she hasn't forgotten what happened ten years ago, and she *definitely* hasn't forgiven him. Will one night give Ben the second chance he needs to prove himself and win back Leia's heart?

Tropes

Small Town, Second Chance, Return to Hometown, Enemies-to-Lovers, Bet, Brother's Best Friend, Work Colleagues, Forced Proximity, First Love, Reverse Grumpy-Sunshine, Opposites Attract

LOVE AD LIB

Shy and reserved Lord Henry Foxbrooke needs a fake girlfriend. Free-spirited actress Libby Fletcher needs a job. But when they arrive in Somerset for Henry's birthday celebrations, neither are prepared for their reception. As friendship blurs and faking it starts to feel a little too real, disaster strikes. Can Libby and Henry stick to the script, or has their entire act just bombed?

Tropes

Small Town, Fake Dating, Grumpy/Sunshine, Opposites Attract, One Bed, Different Worlds, Fish-out-of-Water

AN UNHOLY AFFAIR

Gorgeous Jack Newton has fallen in love with Eveline Shaw. But she's a female vicar dreaming of marriage and kids, and he's a male escort heading out of town. Can Jack show Eveline heaven and keep his secret safe, or are they both headed straight for hell?

Tropes

Small Town, Forbidden Love, Love at First Sight, Sworn off a Relationship, Priest, Different Worlds, Opposites Attract, Dark Secret

THE UPPER CRUSH

James Hunter-Savage is a cocky city boy who isn't used to anyone else taking the reins. Lady Estelle Foxbrooke is a fiery country girl who's about to show him who's boss. Can they learn to fight for love rather than with each other, or will their love hate relationship destroy everything they're working for?

Tropes

Small Town, Enemies-to-Lovers, Alpha Hero, Love/Hate, Playboy in Love, Different Worlds, Workplace Romance, Fake Dating

THE LOVE POSITION

Beautiful academic, Sophia Hunter-Savage, has run away to an ashram to reinvent herself. Hot yoga teacher, Isaac Hayward, has left town to avoid the only woman able to tempt him off the spiritual path.

But karma sucks.

Now Isaac's teaching Sophia and they're finding themselves in all kinds of unexpected positions. Will their forbidden love bring inner peace and happiness, or end in a tangled mess?

Tropes

Forbidden Love, Opposites Attract, Teacher/Student, Sworn off a Relationship, Forced Proximity, Love at First Sight, Different Worlds, Fish-out-of-Water

CHRISTMAS OFF SCRIPT

Best friends, Leo Foxbrooke and Ella Chamberlain, have never been single at the same time. Until now... Playing Cinderella and Prince Charming in the Christmas pantomime, their on-stage chemistry kindles an unexpected spark behind the scenes. Can they rewrite their friendship this festive season and finally unwrap true love?

Tropes

Small Town, Friends-to-Lovers, Best Friend's Ex, Oblivious to Love, Unrequited Love, Fake Relationship

ONE NIGHT ONLY

Pop star Avery Taylor craves a break from her public life, and a one-night stand with a stranger feels like the perfect escape. A year later, while recovering from an injury, she's stunned to find her nurse is Connor Foxbrooke, the man who touched her soul that night. Avery is ready to break the rules for love, but Connor, who values his quiet life, fears heartbreak. With Avery set to return to the spotlight as soon as she's recovered, can they bridge their worlds and turn their one night into forever?

Tropes

Second-Chance, Mistaken Identity, One Night Stand, Different Worlds, Opposites Attract, Injury, Forced Proximity, Fish-out-of-Water, Celebrity, Pop Star, Small Town

RIGHTING MR WRONG

Mooning a party of nuns is bad for anyone, but for TV star Aiden Wilder, it's catastrophic. Enter Willow Foxbrooke, a quiet PR worker who's tasked with saving his reputation through a fake relationship. As Willow teaches him how to recover his image, they start to fall for each other. But how can true love grow from something that was never real to begin with?

Tropes

Emotional scars, Male Virgin, Protector, Opposites Attract, Forced Proximity, Boss/Employee, Different Worlds, Dark Secret, Small Town

UNDER THE INFLUENCER

Sunny Summer Foxbrooke's career as an Influencer is over. Now she's forced to work with grumpy Finn Oakley, the man who's avoided her for years. Will Finn finally return her love, or will she always just be his best friend's little sister?

Tropes

Brother's best friend, Grumpy/Sunshine, Beauty and the Beast, Age Gap, Unrequited Love, Rivals, Different Worlds, All Grown Up, Small Town

Get Evie's books in all formats as well as special offers, early releases, and exclusive deals direct from her website:
www.eviealexanderbooks.com

ABOUT THE AUTHOR

Evie Alexander is a multi-award-winning author of sexy romantic comedies, blending snort-laugh humour and panty-melting chemistry into unputdownable stories that will steal your heart.

When she's not dreaming up swoony heroes and relatable heroines, Evie can be found in the beautiful West Country of the UK, where she lives with her ridiculously patient husband, miracle daughter, and two dogs who think they run the show.

eviealexanderbooks.com

www.eviealexanderauthor.com

instagram.com/eviealexanderauthor

facebook.com/eviealexanderauthor

x.com/Evie_author

bookbub.com/authors/evie-alexander

amazon.com/Evie-Alexander/e/B08ZJGLP29?ref=sr_ntt_s-rch_lnk_1&qid=1630667484&sr=8-1

pinterest.com/eviealexanderauthor